DIAGNOSIS:
Married

To George,
Best wishes for an
uncommon relationship!

Kathy Dawson

Most Perigee Books are available at special quantity discounts for bulk purchases for sales promotions, premiums, fund-raising, or educational use. Special books, or book excerpts, can also be created to fit specific needs.

For details, write: Special Markets, The Berkley Publishing Group, 375 Hudson Street, New York, New York 10014.

DIAGNOSIS:
Married

How to Deal with Marital Conflict,
Heal Your Relationship, and Create a
Rewarding and Fulfilling Marriage

KATHY DAWSON

Foreword by
Ellen Kreidman

A PERIGEE BOOK

A Perigee Book
Published by The Berkley Publishing Group
A division of Penguin Putnam Inc.
375 Hudson Street
New York, New York 10014

Copyright © 2000 by Kathy Gould Dawson
Cover design by Jill Boltin
Cover art by Ruth Sofair Ketler
Author photo copyright © 1999 Clifford Norton Studios.

All rights reserved. This book, or parts thereof,
may not be reproduced in any form without permission.

First edition: December 2000

Published simultaneously in Canada.

The Penguin Putnam Inc. World Wide Web site address is
http://www.penguinputnam.com

Library of Congress Cataloging-in-Publication Data

Dawson, Kathy.
    Diagnosis—married : how to deal with marital conflict, heal your relationship, and
create a rewarding and fulfilling marriage / Kathy Dawson.—1st ed.
        p. cm.
    Includes bibliographical references and index.
    ISBN 0-399-52640-4
    1. Marriage. 2. Interpersonal relations. 3. Interpersonal conflict. I. Title.

HQ536 .D335 2000
306.81—dc21   00-044112

Printed in the United States of America

10 9 8 7 6 5 4 3 2 1

I dedicate this book to my husband, Dick Dawson. From the instant our eyes met, I knew he was nothing less than a gift from God. The fact that I have always liked the person I am when I am in his company says more about him than the string of accolades I could most certainly list. To share my life with his is a privilege and blessing beyond my understanding.

Contents

Acknowledgments

FRANKLY speaking, if it weren't for Dr. Ellen Kreidman, I would never have had the opportunity to teach, coach, or write about relationships. Because of her support and encouragement, I am doing what I love most. I value the gift of her knowledge, her wisdom, and more than anything, her friendship.

Living with my son, David, and daughter, Katie, feels like living in a football stadium filled with eighty thousand cheering fans. The love and support I've received from them during the writing of this book is enough to keep me writing for decades. You're the best.

My love and appreciation go to my stepson, Michael, for his enthusiasm about this book. A writer himself, his interest meant a lot to me.

I owe much of this book's creation to the insight and expertise of my literary agent, Janis Donnaud. Because of her belief in its message, the book found its perfect publishing home.

So much of my gratitude goes to my editor, Sheila Curry Oakes, who acknowledged the promise of this book enough to want to publish it. As a natural communicator of the written word, her influence has made this book the very best it could be.

Heartfelt appreciation goes to Sharon Krnc for her advice on a professional level and her enthusiasm on a personal level.

To everyone at *The Morning Exchange* and WEWS–Channel 5, I thank you for the years of support you've given me. Working with you in broadcasting relationship information has been an experience I will always treasure.

To the producers and reporters at Channel 3 News–WKYC, I thank you for all of the relationship features you have filmed from my home over the years. It has been a privilege.

I thank the editors of the Cleveland *Plain Dealer*, who believed in the value of marriage enough to allow me to write a weekly relationship column. You have made a difference.

To the women of Amity Circle at The Federated Church in Chagrin Falls, Ohio—thank you for inviting me to speak on relationships, thereby igniting a passion that has been aglow ever since.

To all of the men and women who have participated in The Marriage Movement workshops over the years—thank you for sharing your lives with me. You've made me a better teacher for those who have followed you.

Words cannot express how much the support and contagious enthusiasm of my dear friend Mary Lynn Fuqua has meant to me. Her excitement has brought me so much joy.

Sandy Vetrovsky's friendship has always been an irreplaceable brick in the foundation of my life. She has been no less than that during the making of this book.

I am, as always, grateful for the steadfast support of Joy Resor. Her belief in what I do keeps me doing it.

To Rose Bucklan, I thank you for being you. You've taught me the meaning of eternal youth. I won't grow up.

Knowing Dr. Dean Ornish has been one of my life's precious gifts. The care and friendship he has shown me and my family over the years will always be remembered.

To my cousin Susan Small, you are a shining light in my life. Your humor and belief in me is one of life's biggest blessings.

To my cousin Janet Sternberg, you are the meaning of perseverance. With you as a role model, I will never quit.

To my cousin Marianne Roberts, thank you for making me see that lead was not a place in South Dakota. You changed my life.

An eternal fountain of gratitude lives in my soul for Rose Dickson. Thank you for being my angel.

My love for what I do, helping others create healthy, long-term relationships, comes directly from being raised by my parents, Corrine and Dave Gould. These two people taught me more than they would have believed possible about the relationship between a husband and wife married forty-five years. Thank you for being incredible teachers.

Finally, and most importantly, thank you, God, for all of the above and more.

Foreword

IF I wanted to earn a great deal of money, I wouldn't go to someone who was struggling to make ends meet and ask for advice. I'd ask for advice from someone who was already wealthy.

If I wanted advice on how to raise a child, I wouldn't go to someone who had no children or whose children were delinquents. I would go to someone who has raised happy, loving, well-adjusted children.

If you want advice on how to have a rewarding and fulfilling marriage, one that is filled with romance, excitement, communication, and intimacy, you have to listen to someone who is happily married and is already living that life. I've always felt that a true expert should have the initials K.G.F.E. after their name, signifying *Knowledge Gained From Experience*. Kathy Dawson is the "First Lady of Motivation" and a true expert in the field of love and life. She is a living example of everything she teaches. I've seen firsthand her role as a wife and the loving relationship she has with her husband. The love, respect, and devotion that they have for each other can be duplicated in everyone's life if they follow the principles set forth in this book.

I'm not sure of the exact moment when our relationship changed from me being her teacher to her being my peer and a wonderful friend. I do know that when Kathy first contacted me, I thought she would be a great detective.

In 1991 I was traveling throughout the United States promoting my second book, *Light Her Fire: How to Ignite Passion, Joy, and Excitement in the*

Woman You Love. I was in Cleveland and had just finished doing a local television show when the producer gave me a note saying that a woman had just called and said she had to talk to me before I left the city. Not having enough time to get from the TV station to the next radio show, I put the note in my pocket. By the end of the day I had a note waiting at each radio and TV station and in case I hadn't gotten those messages, there was one waiting for me at my hotel.

I couldn't imagine what this persistent woman wanted to talk about. I discovered that her perseverance came from a personal mission to teach my relationship workshops in Cleveland. According to Kathy, my books and audio cassette programs had made such a difference in her own marriage, she felt compelled to teach everything she had learned to other people.

In February 1992, Kathy traveled from Cleveland to California to be trained by me. It was then that I met her husband and saw how supportive he was of her new career. After her training, we kept in contact by phone. She began teaching her first class in March of that same year.

Kathy quickly took what I taught her, added her own experiences, and delivered the message with her own unique twists and personality. Each time she taught a class, she became more effective. She became a role model for thousands of men and women and began taking Cleveland by storm. What started out as my message took on a life of its own.

When Kathy called me in the fall of 1994 and asked if she could incorporate my teachings with her own and change the name of the workshops from "Light His Fire" and "Light Her Fire" to "The Marriage Movement," she received my blessing. I felt as if I had planted a seed that had grown and blossomed into the most beautiful flower. Knowing that I had given birth to an idea that had grown, matured, and continued to transform lives, gave me an incredible sense of satisfaction.

Over the years Kathy has provided a safe environment for people to share with her their innermost feelings as they learn about love, life, and happiness. For those who cannot attend her lectures, seminars, or couples retreats, this book will be a constant reminder that getting married is the easy part. Staying married and feeling close, connected, and passionate takes a daily commitment. A marriage, unlike a painting, poetry, a novel, or architecture, is never done. It is an ongoing process that can always be improved upon, but never completed. We are all a work in progress.

You have in your hands a book that will provide you with the information you need so that you can love more deeply, relate more intimately, communicate more effectively, and enjoy yourself more fully.

There is nothing routine about human interaction. There is nothing routine about Kathy Dawson. She has always listened a little more closely, cared a little more deeply, and above all, led by example.

You'll find as she and I have, that changing your life for the better is one of the most rewarding and fulfilling experiences you'll ever have. As you strive for a better marriage, your life will have more clarity, depth, and meaning. I know this is the beginning of an incredible journey and I wish you all the happiness you deserve.

—Ellen Kreidman, Ph.D
Author of *Light His Fire* and *Light Her Fire*

Introduction

CONTRARY to popular belief, the most common disease in our society today is not cancer or heart disease. The affliction that runs rampant in men and women throughout our world is loneliness. Ironically, nowhere is isolation more prevalent than in the institution of marriage.

Picture the average married couple, Mr. and Mrs. Jones, sitting in a doctor's examining room, worried, anxious, waiting; knowing something is definitely wrong with their relationship, but not sure what. Finally, after what feels like forever, the doctor steps into the room, takes a deep breath and in a somber voice says, "Mr. and Mrs. Jones, your test results are in. You're . . . married."

This simple diagnosis explains everything: the feeling of loneliness and isolation, the decrease in sex drive, feelings of boredom, depression, low self-esteem, and finally, the feeling of wanting to look outside of marriage for love and support.

How could this have happened? Mr. and Mrs. Jones were head-over-heels in love with each other the day they got married. But now their relationship feels like every chronic ailment rolled into one. Chances are that Mr. and Mrs. Jones, along with millions of other couples, began their lifelong relationship with less skills, less information, and less professional support needed to achieve a tolerable marriage let alone a fulfilling one. It's as if they decided to fly a plane without ever having taken a flying lesson.

A relationship is no less fraught with potential difficulties than an airplane that has instruments that can fail, a crew that can make errors, or can find itself in an unpredictable weather pattern.

Marriages inevitably will encounter their own forms of turbulence. Although many partners think they are going to spend a lifetime together and not have conflict, I can guarantee there will be problems over finances, in-laws, job loss, illness, parenting styles, communication differences, or an array of other minor to major situations. No marriage is safe from disagreements or discord.

However, being told marriage brings with it a lion's share of stress and anxiety is no reason to commit yourself to the single life. In fact, the problems you encounter with your mate are not only surmountable, they are a blessing. The difficulties that are inherent in any marriage are precisely what give your relationship the glue, the guts, and the stamina to withstand the test of time. A marriage isn't a chronic condition to endure, it's a blessed vehicle for sharing your life with your mate. The bumps and potholes you encounter on your journey together don't have to be viewed as aches and pains, but rather as opportunities for growth.

Diagnosis: Married is designed as a preventive guide to help you deal with, and in many cases, head off marital strife. It addresses a wide array of relationship topics—from dealing with in-laws, to grappling with money matters, to igniting your love life.

Each of these topics can be read in a few minutes and provides inspiration, information, and a specific "Just Do It" or "Think About It" idea for you to use in your relationship. This book is not about theory. The information in it is not meant to be intellectualized. The purpose of *Diagnosis: Married* is to propel you into a "marriage improvement movement." Change can only occur when you act upon new information. If you do what the "Just Do It" tells you to do, your relationship will move in a positive direction, even if making that move feels awkward or painful at first.

Whether you read one essay a day or one a week, I hope that you will use the information in *Diagnosis: Married* to take a proactive role in your marriage.

CHAPTER ONE

A Vital Connection

IF men and women make one mistake in their relationship, it's that they underestimate the importance of maintaining a solid connection between one another. Many think that living together under the same roof with a marriage license and a joint bank account ensures them of a blissful, lifelong relationship. It doesn't matter if you're a billionaire and your marriage license is signed by the Pope himself, if you and your mate don't have a functional system for communicating with each other, your relationship hasn't a chance of lasting a lifetime.

Communication, whether it be verbal or nonverbal, is what I consider to be the most important element in any relationship, especially between a husband and wife. Words, gestures, facial expressions, tone of voice, and touch are the connective tissue between you and your partner.

As "far out" as this may sound, think of your relationship as a NASA space project. On any given day, you and your mate switch roles as mission control and the astronaut in space. In an actual space mission, there must be open communication between the space craft and the people running the control center in Houston. Without it, the lives of the astronauts are at major risk.

1

This intergalactic situation is no different than marriage. If you and your partner don't maintain an open line of communication, your relationship will drift aimlessly just as sure as any space capsule left unattended in outer space.

Keeping your channel of communication open is not easy when there are so many ways it can be shut down. There isn't a couple walking the earth who hasn't sabotaged their relationship by screaming at each other, interrupting one another's conversations, or blaming each other. Throw in jibes of sarcasm and periods of silent treatment and you've got a surefire recipe for communication failure.

Miscommunication in any relationship is normal and is going to happen. You and your mate aren't mind readers and never will be. When signals get crossed or lost in the translation, your relationship won't be any worse for the wear and tear as long as your basic line of communication remains wide open and you can talk about what went wrong and how it can be avoided in the future. Any situation, whether it be about life's minutiae or life's catastrophes, can be dealt with when two people know they have each other to talk to.

Don't worry if you don't consider yourselves conversationalists. It's not how much you talk that matters, but how open your mind and heart are when you do talk.

Imperfect Timing

Tact is after all a kind of mind reading.

SARAH ORNE JEWETT

THERE are good times to talk to your mate. There are bad times to talk to your mate. Knowing which is which can make the difference between having conversations graced with ease or fraught with tension.

Unfortunately Blanche had a habit of picking the worst times to engage her husband in a conversation. Because she was a morning person, Blanche often tried to discuss important issues with Hal when they first woke up. Because her energy level was high and her mind was sharp, it made perfect sense to her to approach Hal at dawn.

What Blanche failed to realize, however, was that when her husband awoke he was focused on getting dressed, fed, and out of the house in time to catch the 7:45 A.M. train to work.

Whenever Blanche followed him into his walk-in closet to express her worries about their son's grades or her father's health, Hal concentrated more on which color tie to wear for the day than Blanche's anxiety. Frustrated with what she perceived to be her husband's lack of attention, Blanche usually became aggravated, making the start of their day stressful. Although she and Hal often talked later in the day about Blanche's concerns, her habit of bad timing took a toll on their relationship.

Whether or not an authentic, meaningful conversation occurs between you and your mate has as much to do with the timing as it does with the words. If you time it right, you can talk to your partner about anything from your opinion on politics and religion to your feelings on finances and raising children. If you time it wrong, discussing whether or not to change brands of toilet paper can escalate into a controversy.

If you are the least bit unsure about whether or not it's the right time to talk to your mate, be courteous enough to ask him or her first. Many people practice this technique as part of telephone etiquette. As soon as greetings are exchanged, the caller asks the person being called whether or not it's a good time to talk. "Hi, Bob. I need to talk with you about tonight's meeting. Is this a convenient time for you?" Without interrupting a conversation, Bob is given the opportunity to say if he can talk. It's a simple gesture, but it speaks volumes.

The same courtesy that is extended to friends and even strangers should be extended to your mate. If your mate tells you that it's not a good time to talk, it's fair for you to ask him or her when would be a better time and to agree on exactly when you will talk.

We all know that it's difficult to have a coherent and significant conversation when feeling rushed, distracted, or fatigued. You can save your relationship from unnecessary stress and tension if you pay attention to your timing, and ask your mate if the time is right.

Think About It:

Think about the last few times you asked your mate to talk about something. What was he or she doing at the time? What you may have labeled as your mate's inability to listen may have had more to do with your timing.

Yackety-Yack

There is no such thing as conversation. It is an illusion.
There are intersecting monologues, that is all.

REBECCA WEST

JUST as the silence between notes turns music into a song, silence between words or sentences makes for meaningful conversation. Think about what talking with your mate would be like if your partner never stopped conversing long enough to take a breath. You might stay in the same room with him or her out of courtesy, but your mind would check out after five minutes of his or her talkfest.

I am guilty of such talkathons. Usually when I feel strongly about something my attempts at conversation turn into a monologue. At times like these I want so much for my husband to see my point of view that I tend to beat my point into the ground.

Whenever you engage in a nonstop discourse, you not only throw your mate into information overload, you make it nearly impossible for him or her to interact with you. Say what you have to say and let silence carry your message. Your silence does two things. First it gives your mate an opportunity to participate in the conversation. Secondly, it gives your partner the time he or she needs to absorb what you've said.

Inviting silence into your conversations takes faith. You must believe that you can relinquish the steering wheel long enough to let your partner drive

5

for a while. The weight of your message can only truly be felt in the silence. If you talk your message into the ground, your mate will tune you out and not hear what you have to say.

If one of your complaints about your mate is that he or she never listens to you, then it's time you listen to yourself talk. If you are what I call a "go-oner," someone who goes on and on and on . . . you may not realize it, but you're teaching your mate how not to listen to you.

One of the keys to healthy communication in any relationship is learning how to use silence. More happens in the few seconds or minutes that we keep our mouths shut than in all the hours we spend chattering and pontificating. Give silence a chance, and the sound of your voice will become music to your mate's ears.

Just Do It:

Pay attention to how you sound and what you say when you talk to your partner. If you tend to soliloquize, practice using silence when you speak. If you've become so immune to the sound of your own voice, you might want to try tape recording yourself to help you realize what you sound like.

A Closet Tirade

The test of a man or woman's breeding is how they behave in a quarrel.

GEORGE BERNARD SHAW

WHETHER it came from a parent, a teacher, a neighbor, or a sibling, the sound of someone yelling at you when you were a child evoked a terrible, unforgettable feeling.

In many instances, the words alone were not half as harsh as the intensity, tone, and volume with which they were said. Take for instance, the sentence, "I said, sit down." If said in a calm, yet firm manner, these words would compel you to take a seat. On the other hand, if these words were bellowed at you like a military order, the impact on you would be extremely different.

When you and your mate disagree, you both have complete control over how you react to what each other says. If you feel yourself raising your voice, you have the power to avoid a highly charged conversation and maintain a low voltage discussion. If you hear your tone becoming accusatory, stop yourself in mid-sentence if you have to, take a deep breath, and change your tone. Practice listening to how you sound when you're angry. Observe yourself.

Developing an awareness of how you sound when you are angry is the first step to defusing your tirades. As hard as it is to be an objective observer of your own voice when you're on the edge of lashing out with your tongue, it *is* possible. When you feel an argument coming on, do two things. First, take a few deep breaths, inhaling through your nose and exhaling from your mouth. Second, practice silent self-talk. When you feel yourself heating up to the point where you begin to raise your voice, gently remind yourself that screaming will only make the situation worse. Tell yourself to remain calm and to keep your voice at a firm, but even level.

If you think you absolutely cannot control your temper, do what I do to avoid a shouting match. Excuse yourself from the situation, let your partner know you will be back momentarily, and head for the nearest closet. Although you can vent your anger by writing down your feelings or punching a pillow, a closet provides a private space to air your frustrations at the moment you feel them.

My walk-in bedroom closet has been my best friend at times of uncontrollable anger. I can close my closet door, rant and rave to my heart's content, and know that whatever I say won't be directed toward anyone. The value of letting off steam at my double-breasted blazers and high-heeled shoes is priceless. Once my rage is sufficiently vented, I can return to the conversation with my husband with a clearer mind and calmer voice.

Screaming is something that must be left out of your conversations with your mate. Shouting at your partner only ensures that he or she will not hear a word of what you're saying. Your verbal blastings will do nothing but make your mate feel berated and you will feel rotten for doing the berating.

Just Do It:

In preparation for the next time you might raise your voice to your mate, have a closet or other receptacle ready and waiting to house you when your emotions run rampant.

Time Larceny

A burglar who respects his art always takes his time before taking anything else.

O. HENRY

W HILE it may sound strange, in order to communicate in a relationship you have to learn to act like a thief, a burglar, or a robber.

You and your mate are given the exact same amount of time as every other couple walking this earth. You don't get twenty-one hours in a day while the couple down the street gets twenty-six hours. Regardless of how much time you have together, the time will eventually run out.

Between working, sleeping, parenting, and all of the other zillion things you find yourself doing, it doesn't take long for your allotment of hours to be devoured. In order for you and your mate to talk about anything, whether it be your grief over a lost parent, your frustration with your city's school system, or the baseball score, you have to become an expert at time larceny in order to communicate with each other.

If you own the luxury of having dispensable time on your hands to have a lusciously long conversation with your mate, take advantage of it. But if you're like the rest of us who can't seem to find time to go to the bathroom, let alone converse with our mate, then you need to join the ranks of "time snatchers."

To become a proficient time snatcher you have to make yourself aware of abundant conversation opportunities. Waiting in line at a grocery store, in a doctor's office, or at a car dealership affords you the chance to talk to your mate at a time when you might otherwise zone out. Although this probably isn't the time for intimate sharing, you can certainly talk, or even whisper about something that will make you feel connected.

You are each other's captive audience while driving in a car together, and you wouldn't think you'd have to steal time with your mate, but you do. How often have you and your partner driven somewhere and between the time you leave and the time you arrive, you haven't said two words to each other? My guess is that in situations like these, the sound of the radio, cassette tape, or CD creates more noise than either of your voices. If you're not careful, your mobile entertainment center will rob you of precious moments with each other. Turn off the outside world and reclaim what is rightfully yours—uncluttered time.

You have more "down time" in your life than you may realize; time when you're with your mate and not doing anything in particular. Pay attention to these unscheduled, unobligated moments. Snatch them for your relationship before they disappear.

Think About It:

Think about your schedule this week. When will you and your mate be in the car together? Will you be anywhere that you'll have to wait? If so, snatch that time to connect with each other rather than letting it slip away.

Put It In Writing

Sir, more than kisses, letters mingle souls.
For, thus friends absent speak.

JOHN DONNE

IT was when her husband, Charlie, wrote Maggie letters while stationed in the army that she felt the closest to him. Now, almost forty years later, she was beginning to feel the same warm, fluttery feeling in her stomach that she had felt then.

Charlie began writing Maggie letters again. Sometimes they would come through the mail. Sometimes she'd find them leaning against a vase or a pencil holder. After she realized her husband's letter-writing wasn't going to be just a passing fancy, she decided to respond in kind. "This is silly," she thought. "Here we are living under the same roof and corresponding with each other as if we were oceans apart."

Without realizing it, Maggie and Charlie shifted the energy in their relationship by simply choosing to communicate differently with one another. It didn't matter what they expressed in their letters. What mattered was that they changed their pattern of communication.

We would all do ourselves a favor if we took the sage advice of Julia Cameron, the author of *The Right to Write*. " 'Put it in writing,' we say when we are talking about contracts. Our human contracts are contracts, too, but we seldom put them in writing anymore, and when we do, the shift it creates can be astonishing," says Cameron.

Some people are intimidated by writing. They think they can't spell, punctuate, or make a complete sentence, and would flunk penmanship. Don't let these kinds of excuses hold you back from changing how you communicate with your partner.

If you're used to talking with your mate at the same time of day, in the same place, and in the same way, you've talked yourself into a rut. Take something as mundane as telling your mate how your workout went at the gym, put it in writing, and you've got a whole new twist on what could be a very dull conversation.

Everyone likes getting mail. Whether it's a letter from the postman, from the Internet, or from someone who has slipped an envelope under a pillow, being on the receiving end of a correspondence makes you feel special. Start a new way of communication and, if you would like a response, let your mate know.

The key to making letter-writing a part of your relationship is persistence. If you write to your mate, but don't get an answer immediately, don't give up. Although it might take some time to get a letter-writing rhythm going, you'll know you're successful when all of a sudden, you've got mail!

Just Do It:

Stock up on a few different kinds of stationery and blank greeting cards, colored markers, felt-tipped pens, and stickers. Relax. Enjoy communicating with your mate differently. Enjoy the responses you receive.

Reality Check

God offers to every mind its choice between truth and
repose. Take which you please. You can never have both.

RALPH WALDO EMERSON

WHEN it's 5:00 P.M. and you haven't heard from your mate since he
or she kissed you good-bye at 7:00 A.M., even after you've left three
messages on his or her voice mail, you probably won't dial up your local psy-
chic to find out why your mate has been incommunicado. Instead you'll give
into the irresistible temptation to tap into your own telepathic talents and
exercise what I call "marital mind reading."

Men and women in relationships so often try their hand at this presump-
tive power because they're afraid to hear the truth. It's easier and feels safer to
rationalize a mate's behavior by imagining his or her thoughts. Husbands and
wives, boyfriends and girlfriends, would rather think that they automatically
know what's going on in their mate's head than to face reality by finding out
what it is their partner is really thinking.

For Andrea and Jason, Andrea's "time of the month" became a predictable
mind reading disaster. Whenever Andrea became irritable, Jason went into
his telepathic mode and *assumed* she wanted to be left alone. Because he pre-
sumed she didn't want to be touched, asked any questions, or even looked at,
he stayed clear of her until she was back to "normal."

Each time Jason retreated from Andrea, she *assumed* he was repulsed by

13

her once a month blemish, distended abdomen, and erratic behavior. Her premenstrual predicament was hard enough to get through with emotional support. Without it, it was seemingly insurmountable.

In the beginning of their relationship, Andrea and Jason rebounded fairly quickly from their monthly jousts at ESP, but as time went on, their mind reading habit drove them further and further apart.

No matter how intuitive or instinctive you think you are, you *cannot* read your mate's mind. As soon as you feel yourself making an assumption about how your mate thinks or feels, stop yourself. Ask your partner to tell you the truth about what's going on for him or her. Unlock the shackles you have on your mate's mind and let the truth set your relationship free.

Just Do It:

Get in the habit of asking what's on your mate's mind rather than reading it. Remember that there's nothing more disaster-provoking in a relationship than assuming you know what your mate is thinking.

Use It . . . Don't Abuse It

Transport of the mails, transport of the human voice, transport of flickering pictures—in this century as in others our highest accomplishments still have the single aim of bringing men together.

ANTOINE DE SAINT-EXUPERY

ODDLY enough, some things that can be distractions and keep you and your mate apart can actually be instrumental in bringing you together—if you use them to your relationship's benefit.

The telephone, a major distraction when it rings at inopportune times or becomes a semi-permanent fixture attached to your ear, can be one of the best lines of communication between you and your partner. In addition to using the phone to exchange information having to do with the logistics of living: household, financial, or child-related updates, it can be your chance to tell your mate how much he or she matters to you.

When Stewart paid the phone bill, he didn't care how much he owed at the end of the month. He looked at Ma Bell as an investment in romance, one that paid huge dividends in his relationship. Stewart called his wife, Kendra, every day to tell her how much he loved her. Because he traveled a lot, he sometimes called her from places as far away as Europe or South America. The telephone was their lifeline to a vibrant, spirited marriage.

When face-to-face communication isn't feasible, technology can be your relationship's cupid. If you have a fax machine in your home, it can be a great way for you and your mate to send other messages. Nadine owned a home-based business, which included a fax machine. Being an avid comic strip reader, she loved to fax her husband funny cartoons from the newspaper. It was a great way to let her husband know she was thinking of him.

The Internet, although more often a distraction than an attraction in a relationship, brings with it a marvelous method of communication: e-mail. Since the invention of this technological mail carrier, I've heard couples rave about its advantages to their relationship.

For Ashley and Brandon, the sound of "You've got mail" did more for their relationship than eight months of marriage counseling. The privacy and efficiency of electronic mail made it easier for them to tell each other things that they might not have been able to say face-to-face. Many times a particularly meaningful e-mail message prompted a phone call, making an even more powerful connection between them.

In today's technological world, there is absolutely no excuse for you to say you can't find the time to communicate with your mate. It takes less than two minutes to make a phone call, send a fax, or use e-mail. The means to connect with your partner are available.

Just Do It:

Once this week, fax, e-mail, or phone your spouse. Don't worry about being high-tech. The simple act of a phone call can work wonders at making a connection and opening the lines of communication.

The Power of the Unspoken Word

Everything can change, but not the language that we carry inside us, like a world more exclusive and final than one's mother's womb.

ITALO CALVINO

IF anyone has ever said to you, "Shut up," "You're stupid," "I love you," or "You're the greatest," you know the potency of spoken language. Believe it or not, the power of the unspoken word is as strong, if not stronger, than verbal communication.

In fact, ninety-three percent of communication is nonverbal so it is evident that the unspoken word wields a huge amount of influence. A sharply raised eyebrow or arms folded across a chest can relay a poignant message.

With this much power of expression at our fingertips, it's unfortunate that so many people are unaware of it. If a man and woman pay attention, nonverbal communication can become the connective tissue between them, especially if they don't communicate as clearly and effectively with words.

Alyssa was always more verbal than her husband, Sean. She was well-read, expressive, and was often eloquent whenever she spoke. She never had a problem expressing what was on her mind or in her heart. Sean, on the other hand, often felt as if he had a shut-off valve attached to his larynx. For Sean, knowing his thoughts and feelings was no guarantee he'd express them verbally.

Although Alyssa sometimes felt she should have applied for a mind-reading license the day she applied for a marriage license, she had a sense that Sean was speaking to her in other ways, but she wasn't paying enough attention to get his messages.

Many an argument ensued in Sean and Alyssa's relationship because nonverbal messages were never heeded. On the days when Sean felt frustrated or hopeless about something at work, he'd come home at the end of the day with a body posture that screamed, "I feel defeated and war-torn." When all he really wanted was a big hug from Alyssa and a few caring words, he was often greeted with questions about how to fix the computer or how to install batteries for the garage door opener.

It wouldn't be until later in the evening that they would have "words" that had nothing to do with what they were really arguing about. To an outsider it might have appeared that Alyssa and Sean were fighting about finances or household chores; what was beneath their spat was the fact that Alyssa hadn't "heard" the message in Sean's body when he came home that evening.

Between posture, facial expressions, and gestures, you have a plethora of opportunities to communicate with your mate. Even though his or her mouth may not be moving, your partner is talking to you. Pay attention—the message may never be delivered the same way again.

Just Do It:

For the next week, keep track of how many nonverbal messages you get from your mate. Keep a notebook close by and record each time he or she says something to you without ever opening his or her mouth. Review your list at the end of the week. How many messages would you have missed if you hadn't been paying attention?

Sharing the Floor

Technique is communication: The two words are synonymous in conductors.

LEONARD BERNSTEIN

No one likes being interrupted. It's an invasion to have someone cut you off in mid-sentence. Not only do you lose your train of thought, you're suddenly gripped by the emotions of disbelief, indignation, and frustration that come along with not being able to complete a thought or sentence.

If you, your mate, or both of you are interrupting, you can't possibly be listening to what the other is saying. You are formulating your next expression of your agenda and expressing it, not being open to their position. For genuine, open communication to happen between you, you have to get down from your soapbox long enough to let each other say what you'd like to say.

If you've been an interrupter most of your life, it will be a difficult but not impossible habit to break. Howard Markman, Scott Stanley, and Susan L. Blumberg, authors of *Fighting for Your Marriage*, suggest a tangible way to break this habit of intrusion. They say, "Use a real object to designate the 'floor.' You can use anything: the TV remote control, a piece of paper, a paperback book—anything at all. If you don't have the floor, you're the Listener."

Markman, Stanley, and Blumberg encourage couples to share the floor

19

over the course of their conversation, passing the object back and forth as the floor changes hands. As contrived as this might feel at first, it is a simple solution to the interruption problem so many couples face. If a man or woman is prone to pontificating, it is suggested that a time limit for "having the floor" is set before the conversation begins.

You won't have to take your TV remote control with you to a restaurant or wedding reception. Passing an object back and forth is only meant to be used in the privacy of your own home to break a bad habit; just as nicotine gum would be used to break the smoking habit, or nail polish would be used to break a nail-biting habit. Before long, you and your partner will be so good at sharing the floor the only thing passed back and forth between you will be the feeling of respect you have for each other.

Just Do It:

The next time you and your mate interrupt each other, reach for anything handy to represent the "floor." Use this technique to help you both listen instead of interrupt.

Finger-Pointing

If we had no faults of our own, we should not take so much pleasure noticing those in others.

FRANCOIS, DUC DE LA ROCHEFOUCAULD

BLAMING is probably the easiest thing to do in your relationship, but it does the most damage. As a child, you tried your hand at this all too easy method of taking the monkey off your back and putting it onto someone else's. With statements like, "He did it," "It's her fault," and "It wasn't me," you used blame as a quick and easy way to remain unaccountable.

As a youngster, this technique may have worked in shifting attention from yourself to someone else, but it won't work in your relationship with your mate. As soon as you point a finger at your partner, an invisible but no less impermeable barricade immediately rises between you. Even if your partner is guilty of your accusation, blaming will do nothing but put your mate on the defensive in preparation for an assured argument.

Most of Pamela and Abe's disputes were a direct result of Abe's habit of blaming Pamela whenever he felt angry or frustrated. If they spent more money than was in their monthly budget, it was because Pamela went shopping too often. If they were late to a party, it was because Pamela took too long getting ready. If Abe banged his head on a cupboard door, it was because Pamela never closed the cupboard doors.

Instead of owning up to his own feelings about a situation and being willing to discuss the possible reasons for something happening, Abe automatically turned his anger into blame. An easy way for him to vent his frustration, blame kept him from having to look at what part he played in any situation.

When you get angry or frustrated about something you think your mate is responsible for, you can't control what has already happened, but you can control how you react to it. By pointing your finger at your partner, whether it be literally or figuratively, you're not going to solve anything. After you say to your partner, "You didn't . . . ," "You never . . . ," or "You always . . . ," he or she isn't going to say, "You're absolutely right. I'm so glad you brought my mistake to my attention."

Even if you're sure your mate is to blame, hold your judgment. Talk about your feelings around the situation, instead of why you think it happened. It's harder to argue about feelings than it is to discuss them.

Think About It:

Think about how you feel when you get blamed for something. Your mate feels the same way when you blame him or her. Keep finger-pointing out of discussions with your partner and you'll reduce your chance of arguing.

Silence Is Not
Always Golden

Loneliness is never more cruel than when it is felt in close propinquity with someone who has ceased to communicate.

GERMAINE GREER

SILENCE is golden when peace is the ultimate goal. However, when you are so angry at your mate that you decide to become mute indefinitely, your wordlessness becomes the silent killer of your relationship.

If your excuse for not talking to your partner for days on end is your fear of saying something you'll regret, be careful. Holding your tongue for a few hours is one thing, but clamming up for too long could do serious damage to your relationship.

Zipping your lips shut may feel peaceful at the time of anger, but sweeping your problems under the proverbial rug only adds another layer of resentment to your already growing heap of relationship complaints.

Every time Beth asked her husband, Larry, whether or not he submitted his business expenses, they would start a cold war that would last no less than three days. The topic of business expenses caused Beth and Larry to retreat to their separate camps until their next skirmish, usually a week later.

They were successful at avoiding an uncomfortable subject at the expense of their relationship. The silent treatment they gave each other became the breeding ground for new resentments as little things started to bother them. Larry became annoyed at the way Beth parked the car in the garage. Beth became peeved about Larry's gum-chewing habit. What was behind their vexations was the fact they had never talked about the root problem—the business expenses.

If you're so angry at your mate that you feel like putting your fist through a wall, silence is your best strategy. Short-term silence buys you time to cool down and regroup. When your ears turn red and your pulse speeds up, it's time to take a break. Just don't let your time-out last so long that you ignore why you withdrew in the first place.

Just Do It:

The next time you get angry and want to give your mate the silent treatment, take a deep breath. Tell your partner you don't want to talk now, but that you will talk later. Agree on a specific time to pick up the conversation, after the blood drains from your ears.

Dripping with Sarcasm

One often contradicts an opinion when what is uncongenial is really the tone in which it was conveyed.

FRIEDRICH NIETZSCHE

WHEN speaking, the tone of your voice becomes the whole shooting match. If you're not careful how you use it, you and your mate just might get into one. Ask a simple question like, "Is the front door locked?" and if your words are dripping with sarcasm, prepare to draw your pistol.

Simply put, sarcasm will destroy your relationship. The Greek meaning of the word sarcasm is "to tear flesh." Whether your serving of it is subtle or glaring, sarcasm will rip apart your partner and undermine any goods intentions. Attached to the end of a sarcastic statement are the unspoken words, "You idiot," and I don't know anyone who has a healthy, loving relationship with someone who they think is an idiot.

If you've been raised in a family where sarcasm was dished out regularly, trying not to use it yourself will feel like breaking an addictive habit. It's going to be grueling, but not impossible.

Before you can change how you talk to your mate, you first have to be aware of how you sound. Instead of concentrating on the specific words you choose, focus on the tone of voice you employ. Unfortunately, your sarcasm may be so ingrained into your thinking that your caustic tone is involuntary. To make the change, carefully listen to your inflection.

Practice taking the sarcasm out of what you say. When you hear yourself using it, apologize and start over. Your willingness to change your tone, will take the sting out of your words.

Sarcasm's negative cousin is "kidding." Don't fall into the trap of trying to pass off your sarcastic quips as humor. They're not. Sarcasm disguised as humor is only your way of rationalizing the use of it. Justifying its use won't reduce or eradicate its harmful effect.

Be prepared for the fact that while you work to change your inner and outer tone, the outside world continues to operate with sarcasm. Self-discipline and self-encouragement are your most powerful tools in this admirable project. If you slip and go back to your old sarcastic tone, and you probably will, give yourself a break. Mistakes are meant to precede change. Stay with it. Be relentless. Anything that's worth doing, is worth doing wrong until you get it right. What is at stake is more important than any momentary pleasure you might get from a sarcastic dig.

Just Do It:

Pay attention to your tone. If you have trouble hearing it, tape record a conversation with your mate. Commit to ridding yourself of sarcasm.

Agree to Disagree

A philosopher who is not taking part in a discussion is like a boxer who never goes into the ring.

LUDWIG WITTGENSTEIN

IMAGINE for a moment being in a relationship with a person exactly like you. You and your mate would both have corresponding interests, opinions, and ideas. No more compromising, sacrificing, or negotiating. Decision making would be a snap and arguments would be nil. Unfortunately, so would stimulation.

Although there are times when there is nothing more aggravating than having a partner with a different opinion, the alternative is an intellectual death sentence. As much as you think life would run smoother if your mate would see it your way one hundred percent of the time, nothing could be further from the truth.

If you have a mate who always says, "I agree with you totally," you could stand it for a few weeks maybe, but after awhile, you'd want to get in his or her face and say, "Don't you have your own opinion on anything?"

Differing opinions aren't bad. What is bad is not accepting the fact that your mate is allowed to have them. Accepting someone's different opinion doesn't mean you give up your own. It just means you accept the fact that the two of you don't agree. In other words, you agree to disagree.

There is only one time when having a different opinion from your mate is a problem. If your opposing opinions are attached to basic values having to do with things like child-rearing, religion, or money, then you need to ask yourself if it's a value you're willing to compromise.

Tiffany and Jason dated for six months before the topic of marriage and family arose. The more they discussed their future together, the clearer it became that they weren't going to have one. Tiffany had a promising career in advertising and planned to work while raising her family. Jason had been raised by a stay-at-home mom and was adamant about wanting the mother of his children to postpone her career until after the children were raised. Once Tiffany and Jason realized they had different opinions attached to different values, they agreed to stop seeing each other. Neither was willing to compromise their values.

Many times, however, couples argue over different ideas rather than different values. When you and your mate blame one another for having different opinions, you do nothing but suck the life force out of your relationship. If, instead, you honor your mate's thoughts, you breathe energy into your partnership.

Don't be afraid to disagree with your partner. At the same time, let him or her disagree with you. Accepting the fact that you each have different opinions strengthens your relationship. Remember, you *want* to be with someone who thinks differently. Living with a clone of yourself doesn't make for much of a relationship.

Just Do It:

The next time you and your partner disagree, remind yourself that it is a good thing rather than a bad thing. End your conversation by acknowledging that you both agree to disagree.

Get a Life

Deep down, I'm pretty superficial.

AVA GARDNER

THERE'S no escaping it. You have to spend time doing the nuts and bolts of everyday life or the laundry won't get done, the car won't get washed, and the kids won't get to piano lessons or soccer practice. As much as your household, financial, and family's needs can become the driving force in your life, you can't let them become the driving force in your relationship.

If most of your conversations with your mate revolve around topics like repainting the garage door, subscribing to the local newspaper, or enrolling your children in summer camp, you're bogged down in what I call the "logistics of living."

Yes, getting to the grocery store is important. So is getting your son or daughter to the barber or hairdresser. Be careful though. Life with your partner is more than cross-checking each other's daily planners.

If, while you and your mate are discussing whether or not to subscribe to the newspaper, you don't discuss what you think or how you feel about what's on the front page, your relationship will be reduced to nothing but the who, what, when, and where of life. You'll miss out on "why" the two of you got together in the first place!

My husband and I have two active children, three cats, a home, and two careers. When we allow it to happen, our conversations revolve around one thing and one thing only: the mundane act of exchanging information. Like programmed computers, we trade household and child-related data. "I took back the library books." "Did you pay the paperboy?" "I picked up the dry cleaning." "Would you call the baby-sitter?"

There's no doubt that these are questions that need to be asked and answered in order to live from day to day. If, however, you let the logistics of life become your whole life, you'll have no life.

At least once every day, talk to your mate about something that matters to you; something you feel strongly about. Life with your partner is meant to have meaning and substance. You are a living, breathing individual who has feelings and passions. Share them with your mate, even if it means doing it between loads of laundry or while standing in the frozen food section of the grocery store.

As easy as it is to live logistically in your relationship, push yourself to go deeper with your mate. Share your excitement, your anger, your fear, or your lust. In other words, get a life—before a lack of one gets you!

Just Do It:

Check your "feel-o-meter" to see if you've talked to your mate lately about your feelings on anything. If it's been more than one day since you've shared any feelings with your partner, do so today!

CHAPTER TWO

Practical Life

WHEN you and your mate first decided upon a life together, your minds were filled with the magic of romance, dreams, and possibilities. You fantasized about the family you would someday have, the home you would build, and the memories you would create. You focused on the big picture and knew that the details would somehow fall into place.

What you may not have known was that those details, the practical side of life as a couple, would soon play a huge role in your lifestyle. Practical life in a marriage is the logistics of living with another person under the same roof. Beginning with the first day you live together, you develop a rhythm of how you move throughout a twenty-four-hour period. From running a household to maintaining your car, you and your partner are faced with numerous everyday, practical life situations.

Chances are you and your mate approach the logistics of living differently. For you, being an organized vacation planner may be number-one on your list of practical life skills; your mate may feel more strongly about the importance of doing household chores in a timely manner. Whatever your differences are in handling the upkeep of everyday life, you and your partner have to learn the art of brainstorming, delegation, and implementation.

Facing a dirty house, pet maintenance, or entertaining a house full of guests don't have to be insurmountable problems. If you have a practical life strategy, like brainstorming, you can tackle any situation. Sitting down with your mate with a pen and pad of paper and listing whatever it is that needs to get done is a wonderful way to plan for the inescapable—the practical side of life.

Once you've both put your thoughts on paper, you can begin delegating who does what. The main reason why couples argue over household duties and daily maintenance issues is because they're confused as to whose chore is supposed to be whose. Making delegation a joint effort compels you and your mate to own your part in the day-to-day business of living.

If you let it, practical life can bog you down. Armed with a strategy for the business of living, you and your partner can refocus on the magic and endless possibilities of your relationship.

Chore War

The labor of keeping house is labor in its most naked state, for labor is toil that never finishes, toil that has to be bigger again the moment it is completed, toil that is destroyed and consumed by the life process.

MARY MCCARTHY

DOING the laundry. Mowing the lawn. Washing the dishes. The world of practical living consists of the mundane but necessary tasks of everyday life. In today's society of material upkeep, you and your mate may find yourselves doing battle in what's commonly known as the "chore war."

As we enter the new millennium, with dual income families becoming the norm, household duties are up for grabs. Kitchen and maidlike tasks are no longer arbitrarily assigned to women, and lawn care and handyman jobs aren't reserved for just men anymore.

Which gender does what job is usually not the cause of battle. Resentment traditionally builds around the fact that one mate feels he or she does more than his or her share of the dirty work.

In Tyler and Rachel's case, it was Rachel who felt the domestic duties were out of balance. She couldn't remember when, but somewhere in between saying "I do" and taking maternity leave she acquired the majority of the household chores. In the beginning, it felt natural for her to be the one to make the bed, cook the dinner, and water the plants. It was when she realized her domestic ventures had expanded to cleaning the garage and weeding the vegetable garden that her simmering resentment turned into boiling anger.

Because Rachel was home full-time raising their son, Tyler assumed she would handle most of the chores except for the seasonal heavy work of shoveling snow or mowing the lawn. During one of their chore skirmishes, Tyler threw up his hands and said, "How was I to know you needed help with the house?" Exasperated, Rachel was dumbfounded that her husband hadn't noticed how difficult it had been for her to juggle cleaning, cooking, organizing, and mothering.

As with ninety percent of the other couples in their neighborhood, not much attention was being paid to who was doing what chore simply because life was so hectic couples had no time to talk about chores let alone notice who was or was not doing them.

In the area of chore distribution, marriage is no different than running a business. There isn't a profitable company in existence that doesn't have an operating strategy. In most well-run enterprises, a job description is often a standard addition to an employee's contract, and is commonly negotiable.

Although not written into your marriage license, how to divide day-to-day household duties has to be discussed before you and your mate live together under the same roof. Playing it loosey-goosey by assuming the domestic chips will fall where they may is courting nothing but disaster.

Just Do It:

Even if you have a chore distribution strategy, revisit it every three months to make adjustments. If you don't have one, make one. Draw a line down the middle of a piece of paper with your name on the top of one column and your mate's on the top of the other column. Between the two of you, decide which chores you each like doing first. Divide whatever is left over, by pulling the names of the chores out of a hat if necessary. Hang your chore distribution list in a visible spot. Carry out your responsibilities for the next three months.

Too Close for Comfort

Your damned nonsense can I stand twice or once, but sometimes always, by God, never.

HANS RICHTER

BATHROOM botherations. They're little things, really. On a good day, neither my husband nor I let them annoy us. On a bad day, they're the fuel for an emotional rampage.

Must he douse himself with so much talcum powder each morning that I feel like I need rubbers to walk across five feet of ceramic tile? And why is it he needs to line up every brand of cologne across an already crowded bathroom counter? Going through his mind, I'm sure, are the questions, "Can't she remember to throw away her feminine hygiene wrappers?" or "Why can't she use her own razor to shave her legs?"

What happens in your bathroom, more than any other room in your house, can negatively impact your relationship. Your bathroom habits are an intimate matter. If you and your mate are lucky enough to have separate bathrooms, how you maneuver the "land of the lav" won't be an issue in your relationship. If, however, you and your partner share the same sink, shower, and toilet, you'll need strategies for bathroom protocol.

The romantic idea of "what's mine is yours and what's yours is mine" won't work in the bathroom. There are some things you just can't share with your mate without feeling encroached upon. When you and your partner start using the same toothbrush, deodorant, razors, and bath towels, it's time to set boundaries. An occasional swipe of your mate's razor or deodorant stick is okay, but done regularly and you'll not only pass germs back and forth, you'll feel like nothing is sacred.

In order to create the least amount of irritation around practical living in the bathroom, you and your mate need to keep your toiletries separate and be mindful of your own personal peccadilloes. If you're one to leave hair in the sink, the toilet seat up, or the toothpaste tube top off, pay attention to which bathroom quirks may be annoying to your mate.

It's the little things you and your partner do that will aggravate each other. Even though a towel left on the bathroom floor for the sixth day in a row isn't going to be grounds for divorce, it may be just the annoyance to set you off into a full-blown argument.

Airing your personal pet peeves can go a long way in preventing bathroom botherations. If something your mate does starts to annoy you, nip it in the bud by discussing it right away. Don't let too much time pass before a minor irritation turns into a gross injustice.

Just Do It:

A bathroom can easily become a breeding ground for conflict between you and your mate. To prevent that from happening, you both have to mark your territory. Talk to each other and agree on designated personal space. Air your annoyances with each other before they become major grievances. Be sensitive to your partner's bathroom botherations.

That's Entertainment

At every party there are two kinds of people—those who want to go home and those who don't. The trouble is, they are usually married to each other.

ANN LANDERS

AS Winona offered her dinner guests another cup of coffee, she cleared her throat loudly one more time in order to wake her husband, Gil. Gil's head snapped back for the fifth time at the same moment his wife's patience snapped. Gil groggily followed Winona into the kitchen to get his own cupful of coffee, but got an earful instead. What started out as a pleasant evening with friends, ended as a screaming match between Winona and Gil. While they argued about another party gone bad, their guests quietly sneaked out the front door.

Entertaining can be a wonderfully gratifying and successful endeavor that enriches your relationship or it can be a havoc-filled experience that stresses your coupleness to the max. Because opposites usually attract, it's likely that you or your mate fall at one end of the entertainment spectrum of loving the social scene and reveling in playing host or hostess while the other falls somewhere toward the opposite end of being completely content to skip the whole shebang.

To whatever degree you and your mate enjoy planning and executing parties, you have to face the fact that the two of you must work as a team. In order to successfully host a social gathering in your home or at an outside facility, you must learn the art of delegation. Knowing what each of you is responsible for doing is a prerequisite to planning a party.

As with running a household, the trusty legal pad and pen will be your strategizing tool. Before you decide which of you will plan and execute what, you and your mate have to brainstorm and list every possible responsibility that needs to be fulfilled in order to have the optimum entertainment experience. In other words, get organized so you can have a blast.

Some of the duties on your brainstorming list might be: shopping for food and supplies, preparing food, cleaning the house beforehand, greeting guests, hanging up coats, serving drinks, refilling drinks and serving dishes, and cleaning up after the party.

The most important decision to make has to do with when you and your mate want your party to end. It is much better to agree on what time to shoo your guests out the door before the party begins rather than waiting until you're both tired, irritable, and saturated with socializing.

It's best to inform your guests in your invitation of what time the party will be over, but for those people who like to linger, you may need an alternate strategy. Whether your plan is to bluntly tell them it's time to go home, or subtly suggest that you have to get up early the next morning, you and your partner have to decide exactly how and when to clear your home of visitors.

The practical life of entertaining as a couple is no different than the practical life of running a household or planning a vacation. It takes forethought, organization, and implementation. Work as a team and entertaining will be a joy for all seasons.

Just Do It:

The next time you and your mate want to entertain, don't just talk about it. Write it down. Brainstorm and delegate duties on paper. Discuss everything that needs to get done, from food shopping and preparation to dismantling decorations. Be so organized that the last thing on your list is to simply enjoy yourselves.

The Discomforts of Home

Give us the luxuries of life, and we will dispense with its necessities.

J. L. MOTLEY

YOU may think you live one life; in reality you live multiple lives. Your bathroom life is separate from the life you lead in the kitchen and the life you lead in the kitchen is separate from the life you lead in the family room. Your bedroom life is separate from all of them.

How you live in your bedroom affects your relationship more than how you live in any other room of your house. When you neglect your bedroom, you neglect your relationship.

After spending six months remodeling and redecorating their home, Amber and Joel were proud of the fact they had worked within the parameters of their decorating budget. Unfortunately, their budget hadn't included a penny for their bedroom. After spending four thousand dollars, they still shared the same clothes closet, couldn't open a bedroom window that had been painted shut years ago, and could only read from one side of the bed because of a nonfunctioning electrical outlet. On a good day, they became cranky with each other if they had to spend more than one waking hour together in their bedroom. Instead of turning their bedroom into a haven of comfort and convenience, they had put all of their energy and financial resources into their kitchen.

39

In her book *Is There Sex after Kids?* Ellen Kreidman says, "I used to ask the women in my class which room in their home had cost the most to decorate. Invariably, the answers would range from the living room to the dining room to the children's rooms, but never was it the master bedroom. Most people attach far more importance to the rooms where they entertain other people than to the room where they entertain each other."

Your bedroom can be your sanctuary from the outside world. It's a place in which you and your mate should be able to dress and undress with ease, relax in comfort, and make love in complete privacy. None of this is possible, however, if what is supposed to be your private palace is instead a place to pile laundry, a space used to do office or school work, or a playground for your children.

If you haven't done it already, it's time to transform your bedroom from a rat's nest into a love nest. Life in your bedroom is meant to be enjoyed not endured.

Just Do It:

Within the next week, take the bedroom comfort and convenience test. Ask yourselves how couple- and lover-friendly this room is. Is the furniture placed in a way that makes moving throughout the room effortless? Does the decorating put you in a mood for intimacy? Is everything from windows to electrical fixtures in good working order so as to simplify life and make it as stress-free as possible? If not, do whatever it takes to make it so.

Good Move

It's interesting to leave a place, interesting even to think about it. Leaving reminds me of what we can part with and what we can't, then offers us something new to look forward to, to dream about.

RICHARD FORD

I T was horrendous. Every time Beatrice and Marcus moved, they questioned whether or not their marriage would survive. Married for seven years and having been transferred four times with Marcus's company hadn't made moving any easier. With each van line that was hired and each box that was unpacked, resentment grew.

Beatrice knew from the beginning that Marcus's position as regional sales director of a large consulting firm would mean multiple moves in their lifetime. She didn't have a problem with that. What bothered her more than anything was the grueling procedure of transporting their belongings from one point to another.

She was tired of feeling like the president and CEO of her own transportation company. If she was going to have to talk to one more dispatcher or rent one more dolly while contending with whining, screaming children on moving day, she was going to explode.

Moving is stressful. It involves change, and change brings tension and anxiety with it. Even if you've married your high school sweetheart and have decided to settle down in your hometown, chances are you're still going to experience the inevitable at least once. You're going to have to move.

Moving is one of the most daunting projects you and your mate will ever undertake. It's the mother lode of all chores. To do it successfully takes communication, compromise, and cooperation.

In our fifteen years of marriage, my husband and I have moved six times. By the fourth move, we felt like transportation entrepreneurs. Admittedly, our first move was done by the seat of our pants and caused enormous conflict between us. By the third time we packed our wares, we had figured out that planning and delegating responsibilities was the answer to our problem.

We hope to stay in our present home for at least twenty years, but when we do move, we now have an operating strategy for the big event. With legal pad and pen in hand, I'm confident our relationship would survive even space travel to Mars or Venus!

Just Do It:

As soon as you and your mate decide to move, begin your strategy. Brainstorm with your partner by writing down every possible responsibility that goes along with leaving one place and moving to another. Once you've done that, draw a line down the middle of a piece of paper and begin dividing up the duties. Next to each duty put a completion date. Pace yourselves so that neither of you feels rushed or overwhelmed. Relax and enjoy the fruits of communication, compromise, and cooperation.

Clutter Control

Chaos often breeds life, when order breeds habit.

HENRY B. ADAMS

W E all have Oscar Madison, the sloppy, disorganized bachelor from *The Odd Couple*, living inside of us to some degree or another. Unless you are akin to his neataholic roommate, Felix Unger, you are probably somewhat prone to clutter and disarray yourself.

Both Maria and Preston were experts at accumulating clutter. The more time they spent in a room, the more debris piled up. On Sunday mornings Preston would begin his day with a freshly delivered, organized newspaper and a cup of coffee. By noon, sections of the paper were strewn across the floor. To Maria, crossing the room felt like maneuvering her way through a land mine.

Her clutter disorder manifested itself not on the floor, but on most other flat surfaces. Whether it was the kitchen counter, her nightstand, or the dining room table, she had a chronic habit of piling up mounds of stuff throughout the house. Deposits of pens, car keys, purses, and books seemed to appear and multiply in every room.

Neither Preston nor Maria could honestly blame each other for neither was particularly neater than the other. The stress and tension they created by letting clutter overtake their environment put a strain on their relationship that was easily avoidable.

Elaine St. James, author of *Simplify Your Life*, suggests, "Of course, it's much easier to keep your life free of clutter if you make it a habit not to hoard in the first place. You can stop things from accumulating by getting in the habit of throwing them out now, rather than later. Every time you start to store something in the back of your closet or in a dark attic, ask yourself, "Do I *really* want to save this, or will it end up adding to the clutter? Then discipline yourself to throw it out now."

If throwing out your cherished debris is too hard for you at first, the next best thing to prevent "stuff" from taking over your home is to strategically place clutter baskets throughout your house. Each basket, which can be decorated to fit the decor of the room its in, serves as a catchall for clutter that pops up on any given day. At the end of each week, you and your mate can collect your baskets, put the contents away, and start all over again for the next week.

Our family owns a large stair-basket designed in such a way as to sit on our staircase. Anything and everything that doesn't look like it's where it's supposed to be ends up in this basket. Once the basket is full to the brim, my husband, my children, and I empty it and return our belongings to their respective places just in time to start the clutter catchall process again.

Just Do It:

Set time aside with your mate to do an inventory of clutter in your home. As you walk from room to room, own your own "stuff" by acknowledging what clutter belongs to you. Once you've designated whose debris is whose, place your clutter in a strategically placed collection basket. Once every week, on an agreed upon day, clean out your clutter.

Unhappy Holidays

A perpetual holiday is a good working definition of Hell.

GEORGE BERNARD SHAW

ONCE Vince turned his calendar to the first day of December each year, he resigned himself to being a married-single adult for the next six weeks. Every year for thirteen years he watched his wife, Danita, disappear into the land of shopping malls, mail order catalogues, and wrapping paper. Between baking five hundred cookies and mailing two hundred Christmas cards, Danita had little if any time for her relationship with her husband.

"From the moment the first Christmas decoration appears in the stores to the day we drag the Christmas tree out of the house for garbage collection, my wife is a whirling dervish," said Vince. "I've always wanted to help her prepare for the festivities and share some of my family traditions, but I don't dare get in her way."

Jo Robinson and Jean Coppock Staeheli, authors of *Unplug the Christmas Machine: A Complete Guide to Putting Love and Joy Back into the Season*, tell us, "Men, as well as women, yearn for the spiritual dimension of the holiday, but the traditional male role has limited their ability to shape it. The typical husband is expected to provide financial support, help out with the errands, make a handful of suggestions, and be responsible for a few well-defined parts of the celebration. If women are the Christmas magicians, then men are the stagehands tugging a few ropes."

To avoid Danita and Vince's situation, I suggest you and your partner plan your holiday in September. As crazy as it sounds, your look-ahead mentality will make you feel connected to each other and more in control of your holiday season.

Start by talking to one another about one meaningful holiday tradition that you would like to incorporate into your family's celebration. Decide who will be in charge of what holiday preparation. Share with your mate what you like doing and what you detest doing. If you can't stand decorating cookies but love to string lights, tell your mate. He or she may be happy to take over your job.

Whether you celebrate Christmas, Hanukkah, Kwanza, or Winter Solstice, you and your mate need to hunker down and strategize in order for your relationship to survive the holidays. Because the winter holiday is so long, with preparations often beginning before Thanksgiving and lasting until the first of the year, the stress accompanying your six-week celebration can take a huge toll on your relationship.

One of the best ways to make your coupleness center stage during such a distracting time is to commit to spending some holiday time alone together. Every year before our children's school lets out for vacation, my husband takes a day off of work and we do something festive together. One year we went Christmas shopping in the Amish country, away from the commercial hustle and bustle. Another year we went for high tea at a downtown hotel and walked around our city to enjoy the decorations.

When you make your relationship a priority during the holiday season by spending time together and honoring each other's need to be involved, you can't help but enjoy the true meaning of such a special time of year. You have the power to make your holidays happy.

Just Do It:

Devise your holiday strategy with your mate three months before the season is in full swing. If you want to make changes in your game plan along the way, you'll have plenty of time to do it. Tell each other what part you want to play in the preparations and what family tradition is important to you. Mark a date on the calendar for you and your mate to celebrate the holiday season alone together, doing something that has meaning for you both.

A Mobile Home

*No other man-made device since the shields and lances of
the ancient knights fulfills a man's ego like an automobile.*

SIR WILLIAM ROOTES

D EPENDING on how far you live from where you work, shop, go to
school, or visit family and friends, much of your waking hours could
be spent in your car. In today's on-the-go world, claiming your automobile as
a second residence is not that far-fetched.

Out of all the hours you spend driving, my guess is that at least a third of
that time is spent accompanied by your mate. Even if you don't spend much
time in the same car as your partner, you may share the same car. The time
you spend in your vehicle is a part of your practical life as a couple.

Cars don't excite me. I look at them as a mode of transportation to simply
get me from point A to point B. If I never own a car with a recognizable hood
ornament, I won't suffer in the least.

My husband, on the other hand, adopts cars. He doesn't merely own a
vehicle, he parents it. He feeds it only the best fluids, hand bathes it, and buys
it accessories so it won't get lonely at night.

The one and only time I've seen my husband become so angry that I was
afraid of what he might do was the night I ran into his Nissan Maxima not
once, but twice in a rush to pull out of the driveway. Since that night, I've
learned to respect my husband's relationship to cars.

My daily habit of collecting trash between the front seats until it's elbow high will not be tolerated when my husband is at the wheel. If I accumulate garbage or clutter during a drive, I've learned to keep it close to my bosom.

As I've come to respect my mate's relationship to cars, he has learned to respect mine as well. Because I drive the "family vehicle," my car gets traffic from our children as well as their friends. Nowadays when my husband slides into the driver's seat of my car and smells the residue from the latest teenage gastrointestinal episode or hears the bumping and clumping of five baseballs, he takes a deep breath and remembers the word *respect*.

The state of your car reflects the state of your individual lifestyle. When you spend time with your mate in his or her car, be flexible and deferential. Otherwise, you'll "drive" yourself and your relationship crazy.

Think About It:

If you walked into a friend's house, a place that reflects his or her lifestyle, be it neat and organized or in complete disarray, you wouldn't comment on the environment. You would respect the fact that your friend's house is his or her domain to do with what he or she pleases. Your mate is your friend and the car is his or her house on wheels.

On the Level

Sleep is when all the unsorted stuff comes flying out as from a dustbin upset in a high wind.

WILLIAM GOLDING

EVERY twenty-four hours you and your mate lead a life within a life. Your horizontal existence under your bedcovers is an entirely separate world from your vertical life. Your life of slumber with your mate can enhance your waking hours together or it can grate on and tax your relationship.

Sleeping with your mate plays a major role in your practical life together. How you share mattress space, whether you like the windows open or closed while you sleep, or how long you read with the light on can create a considerable amount of tension between you.

At one time, life with my husband between the hours of midnight and 7:00 A.M. was tumultuous, as we engaged in "undercover" conflict. No matter how many blankets I'd burrow myself under, I'd eventually awake shivering next to a mound of bedding, under which was my husband.

While he was busy hogging the covers, however, I was hogging the bed. Not long after our wedding night, my nickname became "creeper." Each night I would drift off to sleep on my side of the queen-sized bed and each night I would creep my way across the mattress until I'd slowly but methodically nudged my husband to within a quarter-inch of the edge of the bed. It wasn't until he kissed the floor a few times that we finally faced the issue. Considering he always made a soft landing, cushioned by my half of the blankets, I never felt too remorseful.

My habit of creeping and his habit of hogging finally forced us to purchase a king-sized water bed, making a remarkable difference in our horizontal life together. It is much harder to creep across a full-wave mattress and the water bed heater keeps me warm whenever my covers disappear.

Unless one of you snores, and you absolutely have to sleep in separate bedrooms, you'll probably be waking up together in the same bed for a long time. During that time, your horizontal life as a couple deserves as much attention as your vertical life.

Just Do It:

Within the next week, talk with your mate about your life between the sheets, practically speaking. If life is running smoothly under the covers, great. If either of you is uncomfortable, decide on what to do to change the situation. Otherwise, your unresolved horizontal life will eventually affect your vertical life.

On the Mend

I want a house that has got over all its troubles; I don't want to spend the rest of my life bringing up a young and inexperienced house.

JEROME K. JEROME

YOUR home is the center of practical living. You and your mate have to learn to move through your environment in a conflict-free manner in order to go with the flow of logistical living. When your home is in need of repair, however, the logistics of living can seem anything but logical.

You would think that by moving into a newly purchased and inspected home, we would have had little or no reason to be concerned with home repairs. That was our mindset when my husband and I bought our second home ten years ago. We were so busy dealing with the everyday issues of practical living like cleaning, decorating, and organizing that repairing a roof and replacing a floor was the last thing on our minds; until the day so much rain came through our family room recessed lighting that it filled eight buckets.

Having just mortgaged our lives to the hilt with a "new" home, my husband felt it would be wiser to become Bob Vila from *This Old House* and tackle the job of patching the roof and replacing the floor himself, rather than hiring someone to do it. Having had no prior home repair experience, I couldn't help but wonder how he was going to pull the whole thing off. But pull it off he did—the roof and the floor—leaving a gaping hole big enough to swallow several children. The only problem was that my husband had no clue how to fill the hole he had created. After his ego was soothed and our home improvement loan was approved, we hired a home repair company to finish the job.

Even if you build a brand-new house, you will eventually be faced with some type of home repair. Chances are the renovation to your home, whether large or small, will put a certain amount of stress on your relationship. Frustrations, bruised egos, and emptied bank accounts or pocket books can add to the tension between you and your mate.

Your relationship can't help but be impacted by whether or not you've prepared for the possibility of a home repair. Ever since our family room rain shower, we protect the sanity of our relationship with the motto "Prepare to Repair!"

Just Do It:

No matter how you look at it, home repair is stressful. To ease the strain, open a bank account and deposit money into it exclusively for fixing your house. When a roof unexpectedly leaks, a pipe breaks, or a furnace quits, you'll at least have some money in your account to cushion the blow. If you or your mate do not absolutely enjoy the home improvement and repair scene, do your relationship a favor and hire someone to handle the repairs for you.

Practical Living with Pets

I've always thought a hotel ought to offer optional small animals . . . I mean a cat to sleep on your bed at night or a dog of some kind to act pleased when you come in. You ever notice how a hotel room feels so lifeless?

ANNE TYLER

THE logistics of living become challenging enough when life consists of you and your mate or you and your mate and your children. Toss one or more pets into the equation and you add a whole new dimension to practical living.

Getting our cat Squeak was a family decision. We all wanted a pet. Because our children were too small to help with the cat's daily care, my husband and I shared the duties of feeding the cat and cleaning her litter box. I fed. He cleaned.

Once Harry, our second cat, came along, practical life became a little more complicated. We adopted Harry a few years before we lost our home to a fire. In moving from our house to a neighbor's house to a rental home and then back to our house, Harry became depressed and began urinating throughout our newly restored home. After several trips to the veterinarian, Harry was put on antidepressants and was soon back to his normal litter box behavior.

Our third cat—yes, I know, we're crazy—was completely my choice. While accompanying a friend to the animal hospital to watch her select a kit-

54

ten, I went home with one of my own. Sammy was immediately embraced by the family and my husband, but as soon as our kitten contracted diarrhea, he was *my* cat. I was the one who took him into the emergency room at the animal hospital at 2:00 in the morning when his fever spiked to 106 degrees and I was the one who held him down while the veterinarian hydrated him intravenously.

In my opinion, pet care falls under the domain of a family's or couple's obligation. Unless a pet is brought into the home without the consent or blessing of your mate, such as our Sammy was, both of you need to share in the responsibility of taking care of it.

If you know your mate will be ecstatic about owning a pet, go ahead and surprise him or her. If you have the slightest doubt that he or she will be thrilled with an addition to the family, always consult your mate first.

With a pet, whether it's a guinea pig, a dog, a bird, or fish, comes a new breed of chores. If you or your mate are not willing to share every caretaking duty connected to your pet, then you have to approach its maintenance the same way you'd approach the upkeep of your home—divide the duties and conquer them!

Just Do It:

Before you integrate another living being into your family and household, you and your mate need to communicate clearly with each other about who is doing what in order to care for your pet. Make a list of every possible pet care responsibility. Both of you choose what you like doing first, then divide up the less desirable duties.

A Real Trip

I have found out that there ain't no surer way to find out whether you like people or hate them than to travel with them.

MARK TWAIN

VACATIONS with your mate don't begin as you step off the plane or slip your magnetic key card into the hotel room door. Your traveling experience begins with the words, "Where do you want to go on vacation?" The moment you begin brainstorming travel spots is the moment you embark on your journey.

Although taking trips with your partner is often viewed as one of life's benefits, it's filled with a plethora of practical life situations—situations that if not handled with care, can turn your treasured R and R time into a frazzled fiasco. There is hope, however.

Communication and compromise are the keys to creating a delightful trip with your partner. You and your mate must be able to tell each other what you want from your vacation while at the same time accepting that you may not get all that you want.

Expressing your desires is not just about telling your mate you don't want to ride on a mule down into the Grand Canyon because you're terrified of heights. It's about telling your partner you want help in packing for the trip or that you don't want to be the designated bellboy in charge of carrying luggage the entire time.

If you and your mate are driving to your destination, talk about the distribution of driving time and who will be the navigator in charge of map reading. Spare yourselves the aggravation of not knowing how to get where you're going.

Talk to each other about your expectations for dining. Whether or not a vacation is enjoyable has a lot to do with the food you plan to eat. If you're planning a trip to Boston and one of you is allergic to shellfish, discuss the issue and the alternative dining options.

Never leave for a vacation assuming your mate knows what you want. Unless you share your expectations with your partner, bet on the fact that he or she won't have a clue.

I have a vivid childhood memory of a dining nightmare while on vacation with my family on Montauk, Long Island, in New York that illustrates my point. I remember my father taking us to a formal restaurant that had a floor-to-ceiling stone fireplace. Wigs being in style during the 1960s, my mother wore her favorite dress and Zsa Zsa Gabor wig, expecting to participate in nothing short of a first-class dining experience. What she didn't expect was to be seated by a roaring fire for two hours.

By the time her main entree had been served, lines of sweat dripped down what had once been freshly applied makeup. Deciding that eating an expensive meal in between menopausal hot flashes and mounting heat from a blazing hearth was not her idea of a fun night out, my mother slammed her napkin down on the table and stormed out of the restaurant like a fire-breathing dragon. The evening was a disaster.

To have the optimum vacation experience, you and your mate have to play out as many practical life situations as possible before you leave your house—from whether or not you want to do laundry while traveling to how much money you want to take in traveler's checks, you have to be clear and thorough about your expectations.

Just Do It:

Before you and your mate travel, pick each other's brain about everything and anything imaginable. Make a travel checklist on which is listed everything from who makes hotel reservations to who packs the car, from expectations about dining to expectations about sightseeing, and from who reads the map to who carries the traveler's checks. Based on how much you communicate and compromise, you'll be taking a trip to heaven or hell.

A Full Plate

There can't be a crisis next week. My schedule is already full.

HENRY KISSINGER

IN a world where people's Daytimers are attached to their hip and digital watch alarms sound as reminders, it's no wonder the art of scheduling has become as important as daily exercise and meditation.

Regardless of whether you're a couple with or without children, you are probably like the rest of society and have a lot on your plate. If you're not employed outside of the home full-time or part-time, you're at home raising children, volunteering, busy with your avocation, involved with a home project, or caretaking family members.

Living with and jockeying your own schedule of events is hard enough. Include your desire to have an authentic, healthy relationship with your mate and you have the potential for complete chaos.

You'd be amazed at how many husbands and wives try to carry on a functional relationship with each other without a social, business, and personal calendar to aid them. I knew of a couple who lived in mass confusion. Between hit-and-miss phone calls about client dinners, and half-scribbled notes explaining each other's whereabouts, they were clueless about each other's (and their own) comings and goings.

My husband and I have a central calendar that hangs on a bulletin board in our kitchen to keep track of business, social, and personal appointments. What we've learned is that whatever calendar we use has to have big enough squares for each day so as to allow us to write at least three appointments or events per day. Next to the description of the activity we write a "P" for personal, a "B" for business, or an "S" for social.

As parents who are involved in their children's activities and who make time for a social life as a couple, I can't imagine the state of our relationship without a calendar. Scheduling is an anchor, without which any relationship would be like a boat adrift at sea.

Just Do It:

Make sure you display at least one calendar in your home to record your appointments, activities, and special events. The calendar needs to be big enough to be easily written on and read. Put your schedule where it is visible. Remember to look at the calendar every day.

The Giving Story

The only gift is a portion of thyself.

RALPH WALDO EMERSON

NO matter what excuse you come up with to avoid it, whether it be for financial reasons, time, or discomfort, you're going to have to face the practical life issue of gift giving in your relationship. Somewhere in a year's time, you will have to present your partner with a material present. Good luck sneaking by his or her birthday without showing your mate your thoughtfulness in some physical form.

Every year Evan started feeling nervous eight weeks before his wife's birthday. Having grown up watching his mother reject most of his father's birthday and Christmas presents had made him gun-shy about gift giving for any occasion. His most vivid memory was of a Christmas morning when his father gave his mother a gold-and-silver braided necklace that was fit for a queen. He could still hear his mother's loud and hurtful complaint of how heavy the necklace felt around her neck. It seemed to Evan that with each rejection, his father tried harder to please his mother. But with each expensive and elaborate gift, came a more piercing rejection.

Evan's wife had never given him a reason to feel hesitant or unsure about gift giving. Whatever he gave her, whether it was handmade or store purchased, she always received it with enthusiasm and appreciation. She understood that the true value of a gift was not the gift at all.

61

Gary Chapman, author of *The Five Love Languages*, tells his readers the real meaning of giving. He says, "A gift is something you can hold in your hand and say, 'Look, he was thinking of me,' or, 'She remembered me.' You must be thinking of someone to give him a gift. The gift itself is a symbol of that thought. It doesn't matter whether it costs money. What is important is that you thought of him. And it is not the thought implanted only in the mind that counts, but the thought expressed in actually securing the gift and giving it as the expression of love."

Evan's wife understood the concept of giving, but because Evan had witnessed his mother's misunderstanding of giving for so long, he was still insecure about his ability to give.

Giving presents is a part of your practical life with your mate. Knowing that the material gift you give is, in essence, inconsequential allows you to give more freely and without anxiety. Think of your partner, give with your heart, and gift giving will become joyous regardless of the size, cost, or shape of your offering.

Just Do It:

Give into the joy of gift giving and receiving by relating more to the thoughtfulness behind the gift rather than the material item. The next time you give your partner a present, give him or her the story of why and how you chose it. The next time you receive something from your mate, ask for the "giving story" that goes along with your trinket or bauble. The story is the real gift behind the present.

End Your Day Together

Come, cuddle your head on my shoulder, dear,
Your head like the golden-rod,
And we will go sailing away from here
To the beautiful land of Nod.

ELLA WHEELER WILCOX

TIMING is everything. A pivotal moment in your relationship is that moment when you and your mate pull down the bedspread and prepare to fall asleep together. Even if you didn't see much of each other during the day, getting under the covers at the same time reminds you that you're a pair, a duo, a couple.

It doesn't matter whether you make mad passionate love before you fall asleep or drift off into dreamland with your little toes touching. What counts is that you get into the habit of ending your day together.

Inevitably there will be nights when one of you has to burn the midnight oil to meet a deadline for work or finish a household project. But avoid a routine where one of you goes to bed earlier than the other every night. Getting into bed alone night after night or falling asleep next to someone who's been asleep for two hours is not the way to create a close relationship.

One of Sylvia's biggest gripes about her relationship with her husband, Tom, was that for the five years they had been married, they had fallen asleep together only a handful of times.

Tom had gotten into the habit of watching late-night television and would go to bed at 1:30 A.M. every night. By the time he crawled under the covers next to his wife, she had already been asleep for three hours.

They weren't unhappy in their marriage, but Sylvia complained of a sense of emptiness in their relationship. Without Tom next to her, she fell asleep feeling not only tired, but lonely. Although she woke up with him by her side, his presence didn't fill the void from the night before.

Granted, you and your mate may have opposite internal clocks. You're a morning person and he or she is a night person, or vice versa. That's fine, but don't buy into the notion that because of this difference you can't go to bed at the same time with at least some regularity.

Whether or not you're in different personal time zones, you and your mate have to allow yourselves the luxury of ending your day together. It's a frill no relationship can afford to be without.

Just Do It:

If you and your mate are in the habit of getting into bed at different times, pick three days this week when you'll end your day together. Gradually work your way up to crawling under the covers simultaneously at least five out of seven nights.

CHAPTER THREE

A World of Distractions

WHEN you and your mate first met and fell in love, nothing short of a sonic boom distracted you from your relationship. As a couple you were encased in your own invisible bubble that protected you from the outside world. Your one-track minds were free of diversions, allowing you to focus on only one thing—each other.

It didn't matter if you were at a baseball stadium surrounded by forty thousand screaming fans or in a crowded smoke-filled bar with a blaring, seven-piece band. Nothing—not the weather, the economy, nor the state of the union—could interfere with your fascination for your mate.

Gene Kelly's preoccupation with Debbie Reynolds in the movie *Singin' in the Rain* is a perfect example of how outside influences can't phase a person who is head-over-heels in love. Not even a torrential downpour kept Gene Kelly from dancing, singing, and dreaming about the one he loved. I suspect if a tornado had touched down he would have kept hoofing his way through the puddles, without missing a beat.

At what point the dulling, dark intruder called "familiarity" invades a relationship is different for every couple. When two people in love start to get used to each other, the magic of their oneness gives way to the interruptions of the real world. For some, it happens within the first few months of dating. For others, it takes years. Once familiarity sinks its teeth into your relationship, it becomes harder and harder to stave off distractions.

With each added diversion, the invisible bubble that was once your protection from the outside world develops a series of pinhole leaks. Little by little the outside world seeps into your private relationship and your protective bubble collapses. Once that happens, your relationship is fair game for any distractions, from one as seemingly harmless as the telephone to one as destructive as an affair.

The first step to fending off distractions is to be aware of them. To create a balance between your relationship with your mate and everything else in your life, you have to be aware of when you are out of balance. When your interactions with your children, family of origin, friends, or the television begin to take precedence over the time and energy you spend on your relationship with your mate, you will know your priorities are out of whack.

Obviously, you can't spend every waking moment paying attention to only your mate, nor would you want to. It is important, however, to be selective about how you spend your time. There are hundreds of distractions out there, and they all want a piece of you. Once you fall prey to too many of them, your life will be reduced to a juggling act, with your relationship being one of the many things up for grabs.

It's a fact of life—distractions are not going to disappear. If you don't learn to deal with them, however, your relationship *will* disappear. Couples who arm themselves with strategies to handle distractions are the ones whose relationships survive and last a lifetime. They cherish the time they have together and celebrate their relationship. In the topics that follow, you will learn techniques that will enable you to handle your responsibilities and obligations, yet maintain your relationship as your top priority.

The TV "IV"

Already we viewers, when not viewing, have begun to whisper to one another that the more we elaborate our means of communication, the less we communicate.

J. B. PRIESTLEY

SITTING in the privacy of your own home, you would think that nothing from the outside world could possibly invade your relationship with your mate. Yet you brought the threat into your living room and probably placed it at center stage. It promises to relax you, to take your mind off your worries, and to entertain you. It does all that, for sure. But if you're not careful, it will seduce you and rob you of precious time with your mate.

The power of the television is insidious. You start out simply flipping through the channels until an image catches your attention. Before long, you are drawn into a show in progress. Your eyes glaze over, your jaw drops slightly, and the electronic intravenous feeding tube is hooked up for another night.

You fully intend to spend an evening with your partner, but by the time you turn off the power button on the remote control, it's late and your day is done.

What would have happened between you and your mate if the television hadn't been on? What story would you have told? What feeling would you have expressed? What dream would you have shared? What memory would you have made? For one more night, you'll never know.

You might tell yourself it's all right to watch television when you're watching it with your mate. But even under the best of circumstances, with you and your partner cuddled up together on the couch, ninety percent of your senses are being dulled by electronically transmitted stimuli. You may find yourself unable to start a conversation with your mate because you can't concentrate long enough to gather your thoughts before another image grabs your attention and you get hooked again.

At the end of a long day, the temptation to "veg out" is strong. It's okay to give into it now and then. More often than not, fight it. You have a small window of opportunity in the evening to spend time with your mate. The more often you shut it, the more you won't bother to open it.

Just Do It:

Pick two evenings this week when you would normally view television and turn off the TV to spend time with your mate. Whether you play cards, take a walk around the block, or talk to each other about your day, do something as a couple rather than watch something as a couple.

A Crisis in Disguise

When written in Chinese the word crisis is composed of two characters. One represents danger and the other represents opportunity.

JOHN F. KENNEDY

JUST when you think life is humming along and you've got everything under control, the universe drops a bomb on your bliss. Whether your trauma is financial, physical, or emotional, it will affect the dynamics of your relationship and test your fortitude. Personal crises are unpredictable and inescapable, but they don't have to be insurmountable.

As hokey as it sounds, a crisis can be a blessing. It's a time during which your relationship will be pushed to the limit—and you'll see what it's made of. Once you and your mate survive a crisis, side by side, you'll always have that experience to remind you of what you are capable of overcoming as a couple.

How your relationship fairs through a major problem depends on the severity of the situation, along with how you and your mate handle stress. When I look back on the day my husband and I lost our home to a fire, I am still amazed at how differently we each reacted to the situation.

When our neighbor called to tell us she saw flames shooting out of our gutters, I became hysterical. Working to get our children and pets safely out of the house, I cried, screamed, and hyperventilated all at once. My husband, on the other hand, moved through the process of evacuation with immense calm. His levelheadedness is what helped him think of grabbing our two car phones before running out of the house, a wise decision considering cellular phones were to be our only means of communication until we found somewhere else to live.

We used those car phones for the next two weeks as we worked together to put our lives back in order. Every morning, my husband and I set up a makeshift office at a nearby coffee shop from where we called insurance agents, contractors, and realtors. Living like nomads for several weeks while trying to maintain a sense of normalcy in our two children's lives, put an enormous amount of stress on our relationship.

After weeks in a crowded motel room, and nine months in a rental house, we moved back into our original home. We made it. It was a distinct triumph that added guts to our coupleness. Would we want to go through it again? Of course not. Was it good for our relationship? Absolutely.

Think About It:

The next time a crisis occurs in your life, take a deep breath and tell yourself it is a golden relationship opportunity. When the trauma is over, know that you have added another brick to the foundation of your couplehood.

Making a Bad Call

Our inventions are wont to be pretty toys, which distract our attention from serious things.

HENRY DAVID THOREAU

THE telephone. It's a double-edged sword. As an amenity of the twenty-first century, it is your link to the outside world. Without it, you would feel isolated, stranded, disconnected, and out of touch with almost everyone.

However, if you depend upon it too much, this electronic device will own you. Can you deny ever jumping up from the dinner table to rush to answer the phone? Have you ever been in the middle of a conversation with someone and said, "Oh, excuse me. That's my phone." More than a few people will admit, when pressed, that they have halted their lovemaking at least once to reach for the receiver.

The phone that connects you to people thousands of miles away can also disconnect you from your mate. If you're in the habit of talking on the phone when your partner is around, the telephone is having more of a negative impact than you realize. You're kidding yourself if you think that because your mate can see or hear you talking to a third party it counts as time together.

I learned the hard way how distracting the telephone can be. My husband came home one evening upset about something that had happened at work. As we stood by the kitchen sink, he poured out his heart to me while I listened intently. He was almost done venting his anger and frustration when the phone rang. I still can't believe what I did, but my knee-jerk reaction kicked in and I heard myself tell him, "Just a second. Let me get the phone." *Let me get the phone!!?* What could I possibly have been thinking? As I reached for the receiver, I knew I had made the wrong decision, but it was too late. I looked at my husband as I put the phone to my ear and saw the hurt in his eyes before he turned and walked away.

Be aware of how you use the phone. Do you talk on it with people around you? Are you on the phone for hours on end? When you hear the phone ring, do you drop whatever you are doing so that your answering machine or voice mail doesn't get to your caller before you do? If you answered *yes* to these questions, it's time to answer the mating call instead of the phone call.

Just Do It:

Think twice before you answer your next phone call. If you're talking with your mate when the phone rings, take that opportunity to let the answering machine or voice mail pick up the message. Show your partner that whoever is calling can wait.

Career Coronary

You take my life
When you do take the means whereby I live.
WILLIAM SHAKESPEARE

Y OU can call it what you want: "canned," "fired," "let go," or "down-sized." The result is the same—you're out of a job. To say that losing a job is a distraction from your relationship is an understatement. If you "get the ax," chances are you'll have trouble concentrating on brushing your teeth let alone concentrating on your mate.

Losing a job ranks high on the list of the most stressful life experiences. Right below the death of a spouse or loved one, it is a trauma that is known to throw you for a monumental loop. If you ever get fired, you may react differently from someone else in the same position, but chances are you'll go into a state of shock, even if you've suspected your job was at risk.

My husband, Dick, who is a psychologist and has been an outplacement consultant for twenty years, works every day with people who lose their jobs. He is expected to be at a company the day an employee or several employees are being fired, counsels the men and women immediately after their positions have been terminated, and helps them leave the building with some sense of dignity. Unfortunately, Dick has become known in our city as "Dr. Death," for when he walks through the front door, employees know there will be a reduction in staff.

Although most people's first and foremost fear right after losing a job is

73

about how to get another one, my husband assures them that starting a new career is the least of their worries. He knows from experience that people who get downsized usually get a better position at another company in a relatively short amount of time, and often make more money.

His major concern is not about a person's future employment, but rather the relationship the man or woman has with his or her mate. From years of experience, he knows that if couples fail to nurture their relationship during unemployment, their job won't be the only thing they'll lose.

Whether your tendency is to want to talk about your feelings after a job loss or hide in your bedroom for months, it is vitally important that you eventually invite your mate into your experience of transitioning from one career to another. If allowed, your partner can be a tremendous support to you—a shelter from the storm. If, on the other hand, you push your mate away from you and try toughing it out on your own, you'll do nothing but erect a cement wall between you and the one you love.

In addition to being a source of love and encouragement for you, your partner can be a wonderful resource for networking. You never know—their contact's contacts might lead you to a job opportunity.

Remember, if you are unexpectedly unemployed, your mate desperately wants to help in some way. Invite him or her to assist you with the nuts and bolts of a job search. If envelopes have to be stuffed with resumés, let your partner help. If you feel overwhelmed by the number of want ads in the newspaper or on the Internet, let your mate do some of the research.

As devastating as it is to lose a job, it is an opportunity for you and your mate to work together as a team for your future. Surviving in the working world is important, but not nearly as important as surviving in your relationship.

Think About It:

If you're ever out of a job, remind yourself that it's better than being out of a mate. Don't be afraid to ask for or accept your partner's help. You'll get through the experience as long as you don't try to get through it alone.

Married Singles

In a bad marriage, friends are the invisible glue.

ERICA JONG

I F all you and your mate did was spend time alone together, without any social interactions with anyone else, you'd get tired of each other, your conversations would get stale, and you'd crave outside friendships and distractions.

When you and your partner met, you each had your own circle of friends. Once you and your mate decided to commit to each other, some of your friends stayed in your social circle and some of them dropped away.

Women, in general, have more intimate friendships than men. Women surround themselves with people who talk about feelings. Men may have lots of friends, but they usually surround themselves with activity buddies: people with whom they can do things like play golf or ride motorcycles.

Whether the friends outside of your relationship like to talk or play poker, it's important to have them in your life. Your outside friendships give variety and spice to your relationship and add vibrancy to your conversations with your mate.

There is, however, a fine line between having outside friendships and becoming what is called "married singles." When you spend more time with your friends than you do with your partner, you walk that fine line.

Corrine and Ted had been married for three years when they realized they were drifting apart. When Corrine met Ted, he was a tennis pro and played in tournaments three or four times a week. His circle of friends included many people he had taught over the years.

When their courtship was in full swing, Ted played in only one tournament a week and gave plenty of his time to Corrine. It wasn't until their second year of marriage that Ted began increasing his playing time to two to three times a week. Before long, he was back to competing in matches four nights a week.

As Ted gradually played more and more tennis, Corrine started to widen her circle of friends in order to fill time during the lonely nights when Ted was out. Before they knew it, they were each out every night with separate groups of friends and were falling into the "married singles" rut.

Fortunately, Ted recognized the destructive pattern that had occurred in their relationship. He and Corrine talked about their lack of time together and stopped the "married singles" momentum before they drifted too far apart. They began spending more time together as a couple and less time with their separate friends.

Because outside friendships are so vital to the health and balance of your relationship, you may not detect the "married singles" syndrome until your relationship has been off course for a while. If spotted early enough, this relationship disorder can be easily fixed and balance restored to your coupleness.

Think About It:

Be aware of the warning signs of the "married singles" syndrome. Are you and your mate socializing more with friends than you are with each other? If so, talk with your mate about how to create a healthy balance between time with your friends and time alone together.

An Affair to Forget

The first breath of adultery is the freest, after it, constraints aping marriage develop.

JOHN UPDIKE

O F all the outside influences that can distract you from your relationship, the most destructive and hardest to disengage from is an affair. Unlike the daily distractions of the television, the telephone, or the needs of your children, an affair swallows a piece of your soul and rarely, if ever, coughs it up without a fight.

Having an affair while pretending to be loyal to your mate is like commuting between heaven and hell. Your extracurricular activities may feel blissful while you're engaged in them, but coming back home is torture. One side of you has to act as if life is on its normal course while the other side of you is distracted—thinking of nothing else but the person with whom you're having an affair.

Sylvia had no intention of engaging in an extramarital activity when she hired a contractor to renovate her kitchen. Her husband, Bill, had been immersed in his job for months, so she thought a household project would assuage her increasing loneliness. Sylvia became involved, however, with more than the refurbishment of her galley. She became involved with the contractor.

* * *

What began as a business relationship in which she shared her dreams of a new kitchen, slowly evolved into an acquaintanceship, then friendship in which she shared her sorrow and intimate details of her troubled marriage. Once the emotional connection had been made between them, the physical connection was quick to follow. Sylvia and her employee began to see each other outside of her home. The more she met with him, the more preoccupied she became with how wonderful she felt when she was with him.

Her days were filled with the usual activity of running a household and parenting three school-age children, but her body simply went through the motions. Her heart and mind became prisoners of her new relationship.

As time passed, living in her own home became more and more uncomfortable. Sylvia found herself lying to her husband and her children about where she had been during the day, and where she was going whenever she left the house. A part of her wanted to tell her husband the truth, but the exhilaration of the affair was something she didn't want to relinquish.

Eventually, Sylvia became so distracted by the affair she was having that she had difficulty concentrating enough to finish her own sentences. Her bizarre behavior finally compelled her husband to question her. It didn't take long for her to break down and tell him the truth. Their relationship took years to heal, and Sylvia realized that the short-lived satisfaction she gained from her affair was not worth the torment that accompanied it.

Think About It:

Think long and hard before you consider having an affair. The heavenly sensation you first experience is only transitory. Before you know it, it will be replaced by its opposite—hell.

Work Around It

Perpetual devotion to what a man calls his business is only to be sustained by perpetual neglect of many other things.
ROBERT LOUIS STEVENSON

Y OUR career is important. Whether you work outside of the home or run a home-based business, your job is what puts food on the table and cash in your pocket. If you're one of the fortunate ones, your profession also provides self-satisfaction and makes you *want* to go to work every day.

Unfortunately, many men and women spend an inordinate amount of time working. For some, what is supposed to be an eight- to ten-hour workday can easily turn into a twelve- to sixteen-hour workday, every day.

People work excessively for a variety of reasons. Some push themselves to earn more money so that they can spend more money. Some drive themselves to reach a higher level of prestige in their profession. Others are just plain driven.

Our society is the master programmer for what has become an obsessive work ethic. Attaining and achieving at all costs has become the mantra for the American family.

In his book *Awakening from the Deep Sleep: A Powerful Guide for Courageous Men,* Robert Pasick, Ph.D., reasons why men make work their number-one priority. "The primary characteristic of the deep sleep is an unbalanced life. After years of developing the qualities that prepare us for success in the workplace, men often become preoccupied with work and the mindset it requires. The workplace becomes more comfortable and rewarding than home. We may spend excessive hours at work and even find ourselves toiling when we're home, by working on the computer, making business phone calls, reading work-related material, or by establishing a home office. Even when not overtly engaged in work-related tasks, men are often preoccupied with thoughts of work."

Men are no longer alone in this cultural phenomenon called "workaholism." Women have staked their claim on imbalance, making power and success the weights that tip the scale. More and more women are working in high-powered corporate positions as vice presidents, presidents, and chief executive officers. They are successful entrepreneurs who own restaurants, retail stores, and service companies. Women business organizations abound throughout the country.

As exciting as the climb up the corporate ladder or the building of a new business is, the fallout on a couple's relationship can be devastating. The price of "success" is heavy and often not worth its weight in gold.

The climb for Clark was steady. Promotions came once a year and with each one came a healthy raise and a prestigious title. As a newly appointed partner at the law firm, he had reached the salary of his dreams. But along with the monetary reward came the company's demands on Clark's time.

A father of four children, Clark rarely saw any of them before bedtime. Because he arrived home from work no earlier than 9:30 P.M., he usually found them already bathed and tucked into bed, fast asleep.

The novelty of their $700,000 home had begun to wear off for Clark's wife, Julianna. She had enjoyed decorating it and furnishing it, but was tired of spending most of her time in it without him.

The money she had deposited into their vacation bank account had grown large enough for them to take three trips around the world, but Clark could never seem to pull himself away from the demands of his job to take a vacation. It wasn't until Julianna threatened him with divorce that Clark was forced to reprioritize his life.

Facing his addiction to work forced Clark to make some hard but worthwhile lifestyle changes. Although he no longer works at the same law firm and has moved to a smaller home, he now eats dinner with his family every night and feels reconnected to his wife. Balance has been restored.

Think About It:

If you spend more than sixty percent of your waking hours at work or doing work-related activities, you may be a workaholic. Do the math, then step back from your situation and pay attention to how your work habits are affecting your relationship with your mate. Talk to your partner about how he or she feels about how you manage your time. You may have a reason to make some lifestyle changes and restore balance.

Stay Out of the Doghouse

There is something in the unselfish and self-sacrificing love of a brute, which goes directly to the heart of him who has had frequent occasion to test the paltry friendship and gossamer of mere Man.

EDGAR ALLAN POE

WOULD you savor whatever your mate served you for dinner, even if it was out of a can? Would you never get mad at your partner even when he or she was yanking your chain? Would you yelp for joy at the sound of your mate's footsteps? If you answered yes to all of these questions, then you have the privilege of being ranked in the same esteemed category as dogs.

Beth Fowler, author of *Could You Love Me Like My Dog?* tells us, "Anyone who has ever had a dog knows dogs give unconditional love. It occurred to me that maybe they're here to show us how."

The fact that your dog or other house pets give so freely of themselves is why you naturally pay a lot of attention to them. Your pets never hold a grudge, they always think you look good no matter what you have on, and they don't mind when you tell them they have bad breath. What's not to love?

The problem is not that you return your pet's love, it's that you may not pay as much attention to your mate as you do to your cat, dog, or iguana. I realize it's hard not to show interest to a creature who the minute you walk through the door, wags its tail, pants, and looks at you with big adoring eyes that say "Love me, love me, love me."

As much as household pets are an endearing addition to the family, they can get in the way of your relationship. Instead of telling her husband, Aaron, how she felt about his obvious affection for their pet, Dena harbored resentment against him for years. Day after day, she watched him come through the door after work and gush over their dog. In response to their dog's glee at his nightly return, Aaron would get on his knees and hug, kiss, and spout loving expletives in its ear. What made it worse for Dena was that Aaron would then get up off his knees, offhandedly say, "Hi, Dena," and go straight for the mail.

Finally Dena decided she was tired of watching her husband have a love affair with a canine. She figured she was due some attention. The next time Aaron walked through the front door, he found his wife center stage on all fours. She panted, wagged, and even threw in a few barks for good measure.

As crazy as Dena felt imitating a dog, it's exactly what it took to get her husband's attention. It wasn't until she took such drastic measures that Aaron understood that their pet was getting all the love and devotion his wife deserved.

Beth Fowler reminds us that pets are masters at unconditional love. Take her advice. Love your mate like your pet loves you and you'll stay out of the doghouse.

Just Do It:

The next time you have an opportunity to greet your pet or your mate, greet your mate first. Make sure you put the same energy into your mate's salutation as you would into your pet's.

The Calling to Be a Couple

There is no duty we so much underrate as the duty of being happy.

ROBERT LOUIS STEVENSON

REGARDLESS of your spiritual or religious orientation, your place of worship is intended to be an environment conducive to love, closeness, and connection. For you and your mate, spending time in your church, temple, or mosque is meant to strengthen your relationship with God and each other.

Religious and spiritual institutions offer us a place to pray and belong to a spiritual community, as well as the opportunity to serve by volunteering. Giving back to the place you call your spiritual home is a basic spiritual principle, and one in which I believe strongly.

If, however, you offer so much of your time and talent that your relationship with your mate suffers, your gift of service becomes a dreaded duty. Rather than feeling peaceful and content, you'll walk away each week feeling drained and resentful. Ironically, your place of worship—possibly the place you and your mate exchanged vows—can become a major distraction in your relationship . . . if you let it.

When my husband and I finally found the spiritual home that felt right for us and our children, we were euphoric. For years, we shopped for a church that provided the balance of religion and spiritually we were looking for.

When we finally found it, volunteering to help the church in any way possible felt like a natural reaction to our immense gratitude.

At the time we joined the congregation, the church needed a youth director as well as another board member. My husband and I jumped at the opportunity to help. We believed so strongly in promoting the growth of the church that we viewed our new positions as a serious responsibility and an investment in our family's spiritual growth. Unfortunately, the church's gain soon became our relationship's loss.

Not long after we began work as youth director and board member we realized that our volunteer efforts were compromising our coupleness while at church. When we first began attending services, we sat as a couple, hand in hand. Our time together after the service was spent getting to know other couples and families in the congregation.

It wasn't until we were completely overextended by volunteering that we realized how little time we spent together at church. We began to realize that our original feelings of peace and serenity were being replaced by those of deprivation and an overwhelming sense of obligation.

Volunteer burnout can occur regardless of where you donate your talent. Any big organization, from a Parent Teacher Association to a charity, can solicit your time and energy. Unless you know your own limits and learn to say *no* when you don't want to volunteer, you risk your peace of mind as well as your coupleness.

Just Do It:

You and your mate are a couple first, volunteers second. If your coupleness feels compromised, back off from serving your church, school, or charity until you feel reconnected to your mate.

Technological Temptations

To err is human, but to really foul things up requires a computer.

ANONYMOUS

I T allows us to communicate instantly with people around the globe. If we need an obscure piece of information, we don't have to go to the library to find it. The Internet is a phenomenon.

As astounding as this technological resource is, it can be a real threat to your relationship. Just as the telephone and television can lure you away from your partner, so can the information superhighway. Having access to the Internet is like having the biggest public library imaginable in your own home. If you have an inquiring mind, it will beckon you to sit in front of it for hours and research endless topics.

If you are the least bit lonely in your relationship with your mate, the Internet promises to cure your feeling of isolation, for it is your gateway to millions of other people. You can easily use it under the guise of research, but for the real reason of escape.

Of the three years Mike and Sandy had been married, the last several months put a strain on their relationship. Since Mike's promotion, he had been working fourteen to sixteen hours a day. Many nights he wouldn't come through the front door until midnight.

Most of Sandy's friends were busy on weeknights, so she spent the majority of her evenings surfing the Net. On one of her worldwide explorations, she ended up in a chat room with a man from another state. Her conversations with him were initially friendly and full of small talk, but it became evident over a matter of a few weeks that their online friendship was deepening.

The more evenings Mike spent working, the more Sandy looked forward to using the Internet to fill the void in their relationship. Eventually, Sandy and her new computer friend made arrangements to meet one another. The beginning of their face-to-face relationship was the end of the one she had with Mike.

If the Internet didn't exist, and you missed being with your mate, would you go out to parties and bars every night to escape the feeling of loneliness? You'd be tempted, but most likely wouldn't. The party is now at your fingertips and it's up to you to know the hazards. The Internet is a marvelous wonder. If used for the wrong reasons, its wonder isn't so wonderful anymore.

Just Do It:

Before using the Internet, question your motives. If you're trying to escape a feeling of loneliness, turn off the computer and face your mate.

Toxic Couples

We cannot always assure the future of our friends; we have a better chance of assuring our future if we remember who our friends are.

HENRY KISSINGER

I N today's society, being happy in a relationship can be a lonely place to be. For those of you who enjoy the fact that your relationship with your mate is a fulfilling one, there is an outside world just waiting to convince you otherwise. Being content as a couple can sometimes make you feel like you're swimming against the current of hundreds of unhappy, dissatisfied couples.

These disgruntled men and women wear a shroud of negativity around them concerning their own relationship plight and seem eager to share their unfortunate situation with anyone who is willing to listen. Beware of situations where you're in the company of people who you like individually, but as a couple are toxic for your relationship.

It doesn't take long to discern which couples you want to avoid. They're the ones who pick each other apart little by little. With icy stares or subtle sarcasm, they wear away at whatever healthy relationship they have left. Spending an evening with them drains you and your partner of energy.

I remember going to dinner with a couple who, as individuals, my husband and I enjoyed, but who we dreaded spending time with as a couple. Before we'd get together with them, we'd give each other a pep talk before getting out of the car. Our ritual was to take three deep breaths, turn to each other and say, "Okay, are you ready? Let's go."

An evening with them was like watching a heated tennis match, as they'd volley insults, sarcasm, and put-downs back and forth. The morning after being with this husband and wife team felt more like we'd been through a war than a sociable evening. We found ourselves attending to emotional wounds we'd suffered in the cross fire.

For the sake of your relationship, be selective who you decide to spend an evening, a weekend, and especially a long vacation with. Having friendships with other couples is valuable, unless the couple with whom you choose to spend time has an unhealthy, negative relationship. If you've worked hard to make your relationship a good one, surround yourselves with couples who view theirs in the same positive way.

If you're one of those people who tear your partner down and vice versa, pay attention to how happy couples treat each other. Watch for their gestures of courtesy such as not interrupting one another or their signs of mutual respect: the pride in their eyes and the warmth in their voices. Try duplicating what you see and hear. It's never too late to re-create your relationship.

Just Do It:

Make a list of couples you know are happy together. Set a date to spend time with one of them in the next two weeks. When you're with this couple, pay attention to how the man and woman treat each other.

The Road More Traveled

Commuter—one who spends his life
In riding to and from his wife;
A man who shaves and takes a train,
And then rides back to shave again.

E. B. WHITE

ONE of the most common outside influences to affect your relationship with your mate is the distance or physical space between you and your partner. Distance created by plane, train, or car travel can separate you emotionally as well as physically.

Nowadays, women "hit the road" as much as men. Regardless of who travels, you or your spouse, one of you has to "hold down the fort" while the other is out of town.

Travel is stressful. Whether you or your mate take short jaunts or week-long trips, the time you spend away from each other puts a strain on your relationship. When you or your mate pack your bags in preparation for travel, you pack a suitcase of feelings as well. The feelings in your piece of emotional luggage range from loneliness to excitement, with resentment, frustration, and fatigue sandwiched in between.

Being in a relationship with a partner who travels is as exhausting for the person at home as it is for the mate who is "out there," especially if the couple has children.

When Cathy married Ray, she knew he would eventually have to travel for his company. Ray was a transportation consultant and was required to visit client companies all over the world.

During the first few years of their marriage, Cathy missed her husband terribly each time he traveled, but managed to keep busy with her own career and friends while he was gone. Once they had children, Cathy's feelings changed dramatically. She still missed Ray when he was gone, but along with her feelings of loneliness came its sidekick—resentment.

From the day their first child was born, Cathy felt like a single parent. Although Ray came home on the weekends, Cathy bared the brunt of five days' worth of childcare responsibilities, stress, and headaches. She looked forward to her weekends with Ray, but was often too fatigued to enjoy them.

William Hendricks and Jim Cote, authors of *On the Road Again: Travel, Love, and Marriage*, give advice to partners of "veteran road warriors," such as "Allow family, friends, and others to meet your relational needs. Develop a valuable network of people you can turn to for help and encouragement while your husband or wife is away."

Developing a support system will relieve feelings of resentment for a while, but if you and your mate are without a game plan to stay connected over the miles, the feeling of bitterness will revisit you.

Authors Hendricks and Cote suggest strategies for staying connected, the most important one being phoning each other. According to them, phone calls need to be made on a regular basis—whatever fits the rhythm of your relationship. They suggest your calls include four things: feelings, support, information, and if necessary, decision making.

If you or your mate travel, your stress-o-meter automatically rises. Take heart. A grab bag full of strategies to stay connected is available to you even if your communication is intercontinental. With the use of e-mail, the phone, the fax, Federal Express, and the old-fashioned method of hiding notes in luggage, you and your mate can overcome an habitual long distance relationship.

Just Do It:

If you or your mate travel, create a strategy for staying connected. Carry a photo of your partner with you, make frequent phone calls, swap e-mail messages, and make it a habit to reach out and touch each other.

In-Law Invasion

Marry the mountain girl and you marry the whole mountain.

IRISH PROVERB

THEY are your mate's parents. You are forever grateful to them for conceiving the person with whom you've chosen to spend the rest of your days. You want them to be a part of your life, but you want control over how *much* they are in your life.

You want them to share in the joys of your relationship, your personal success, and even your frustrations and sorrow. If loving boundaries are not established from the get go, however, you open yourself and your relationship to the stress of the "in-law invasion."

Loving honesty is the key to preventing encroachment from your mate's parents. Brutal honesty is brash and hurtful, but sharing your feelings openly will build a bridge of authenticity for the future.

The healthiest way to set boundaries with your in-laws is to share your feelings and game plan with your mate first. Doing this spares him or her from any surprises, and makes it more likely that your partner will give his or her full support to your needs and requests.

Warren's parents came to visit him, his wife, Jessica, and their daughter every three months. Although they lived six hours away, they were active grandparents and planned their trips to see their son and his family well in advance.

Five times out of the last ten that Warren's parents visited, Jessica developed a migraine the day before they arrived. Each time she was sick, she would take her medication, put on a pretend "happy face," and act as if everything was dandy. Jessica somehow survived her in-laws' visits, but paid dearly for them by being bedridden for a day or two afterward.

The day before her in-laws' next visit, Jessica developed another migraine. After her last in-law invasion, she vowed to herself to never spend another weekend pretending to feel good when she felt lousy.

This time she sat down with her husband and explained how important it was for her to take care of herself instead of entertaining his parents. She suggested that if his mom and dad could be a little flexible, she'd be happy to invite them for the following weekend instead.

Warren understood completely and volunteered to call his parents. Instead of taking the easy way out and letting Warren make the call, Jessica decided she would be the one to break the news. As uncomfortable as it was for her, she knew this was her chance to start a new pattern with her in-laws. After Jessica spoke honestly from her heart about her decision to take care of herself, Warren's parents received the news with understanding, empathy, and a willingness to be flexible. From that moment on, Jessica knew that she could speak honestly about her health and no longer have to pretend to be the happy hostess if she weren't feeling good. What had once felt like the "in-law invasion" soon felt like the "in-law invitation."

Just Do It:

If you want boundaries between you and your in-laws, you are the only one who can set them. Before you lay down new ground rules, talk about it with your mate. With your partner's support, put them in place with loving honesty.

Downshift to Enjoyment

Enjoyment—the first half of it consists of the capacity to enjoy without the chance. The last half consists of the chance without the capacity.

MARK TWAIN

S O that you don't become a slave to external influences, pay attention to how you spend your time. Although it may seem otherwise, you, and you alone, control the use of it. You have the power to either fill it up or free it up.

Recently, my husband and I decided to step off what we call the "airport walkway of life." You've seen these moving walkways at airports. Once you step on them you are compelled to move in one direction as part of the crowd. When my husband and I feel like our time is dictated by everyone and everything but ourselves, we take action and get out of the fast lane.

Realizing we had been moving in one direction for too long, on the road to "burnout city," my husband took the initiative and made a drastic move. He took a day off from work.

Our day of freedom began at the breakfast table with our two children. As I offhandedly mentioned to our son and daughter that their father was staying home from work, they looked at me in surprise and said, "Why is he doing that?" With a peaceful sigh I announced that the day belonged to us and that we were going to spend it enjoying each other's company.

Our thirteen-year-old son rolled his eyes and mimicked my proclamation saying, "Ohhh, they're going to spend the day together." Although he wouldn't admit it, I could sense his approval.

For the next six hours, keeping distractions at bay, my husband and I treated our time together as sacred. With no planned agenda, we began our time alone with a walk around a nearby lake and ended it with lunch at our favorite restaurant, which was completely empty except for the two of us. There was no doubt about it, we had protected our time together and the universe had supported us.

Just Do It:

If you're stuck on the "airport walkway of life," step off of it for a while. Remove yourself from the demands of the outside world to enjoy spending time alone with your mate.

The Consummate Caregiver

There are only the pursued, the pursuing, the busy, and the tired.

F. SCOTT FITZGERALD

I T'S called the "sandwich generation," and it's not about reubens, clubs, or submarines. It's about a phase of life in which you feel tired and torn— pulled between the needs of the generations before and after you. Trying to juggle the demands of your active children and your elderly or ailing parents is difficult enough. If wedged between the force of generations is your desire to foster intimacy with your mate, you have a recipe for a nervous breakdown.

Paul and Cindy were married for seventeen years and had two teenagers when Cindy's father was diagnosed with Alzheimer's disease. Because Cindy was an only child and her mother had passed away a few years before, she was completely responsible for her father. Within a week of his diagnosis, Cindy moved her dad into her home.

Even if other areas of your life are running smoothly, having an ill parent stresses you out enough to make it almost impossible for you to focus on your relationship with your partner. Depending on how strong the bond is between you and your mate, your coupleness will only withstand the pressures of the sandwich generation for a limited amount of time.

It didn't take her long to realize the affects the new living arrangement was going to have on her relationship with Paul. Cindy's father required constant attention. He suffered from dementia and would often awake in the middle of the night completely disoriented. One morning Cindy awoke to find her father missing. After searching for hours, Paul found him wandering around a neighborhood on the other side of town.

Between the stress of raising two teenage daughters and caring for Cindy's father, Paul and Cindy had virtually no time alone together. Their date nights, which used to be every Friday evening, became a faint memory. Transporting their daughters to assorted activities and keeping a watchful eye on Cindy's dad made them feel like bunkmates rather than lovers.

Paul and Cindy knew they had to take measures into their own hands or their relationship would suffer irreparable damage, so they sat down and brainstormed on ways to reclaim their coupleness. Having attended a few support group meetings for caregivers of Alzheimer patients, they learned that certain hospitals and nursing homes offered adult day care centers for patients who lived at home with their families.

They immediately started taking advantage of a local program and it made a huge difference for them. A few hours each week, they left Cindy's father at an adult day care center and spent time alone together. They promised one another that during this time, they would not talk about her father's illness.

When dealing with an ill parent, you have to fight to keep your relationship with your partner a bigger priority than your role as caregiver to your parent. In fact, the energy you spend keeping a close relationship with your mate will give you the strength you need to care for your sick parent. Otherwise, resentment over lost time with your partner will suck you dry of empathy and compassion for your mother or father.

Just Do It:

If you are caring for an ill parent, work to make your relationship with your mate more important than your relationship with your parent. Brainstorm with your partner and make a list of resources available to relieve you of some of the caretaking duties. Use some of your newfound time and spend it with your mate.

A Guest in Your Own Home

Makin' a long stay short is a great aid t' popularity.

KIN HUBBARD

LIKE *The Man Who Came to Dinner* and didn't leave for days, house guests can distract you from your relationship. Even invited guests can wear on your nerves and end up making you and your mate feel like strangers to each other.

Entertaining for an evening is draining, but when family or friends sleep in your home, eat your food, and take showers in your bathroom, you're forced to be more accommodating than normal. In your efforts to maintain your guests' comfort, your attention is often riveted on them and them alone.

I remember the family reunion my husband and I hosted a few years ago. Although my side of the family is relatively small, we housed twelve people in our home for five days. It had been twenty-three years since everyone had been in the same room at the same time. It was a joyous occasion.

As delightful as it was to have my family stay with us, by the third day, my husband and I began to feel like roommates. My sensitivity to our guests' toiletry needs, as well as my husband's responsiveness to the level of coffee in their coffee cups, made us feel more like bed-and-breakfast proprietors than a married couple in our own home.

I know of a couple whose family comes to stay with them for a week at a time, five times a year. The wife tells me she and her husband have been so used to lodging their families over the years that they've developed tactics to stay close as a couple.

They take advantage of the abundance of adult supervision available and go out alone together for an afternoon or evening. Their children get to spend time alone with their grandparents, aunts, uncles, and cousins, and they get to take off their host and hostess hats for several hours.

Their frequent family reunions have forced them to get inventive with sleeping arrangements. Because their parents are elderly, they offer their bedroom to them when they visit. Instead of sleeping on the Hide-A-Bed in the guest room, this couple camps out in the walk-in closet off the hallway. Before anyone arrives, the closet is transformed into a lover's hideaway. Inside is a sleeping bag, candles, a tape player, cassette tapes of romantic music, and a bag full of snacks.

With a little bit of planning and effort, you can turn what could easily be a distraction from your relationship, into a chance for you and your mate to sneak away and be lovers.

Just Do It:

The next time you have overnight house guests, plan ways to stay emotionally and physically close to your mate. When you invite family and friends into your home don't let them come between you.

CHAPTER FOUR

Cultivate Your Coupleness

Y OUR relationship is a living, breathing thing. Although it feeds off the energy of the two people in it, it must be nurtured and cared for in and of itself. Just as a plant needs water and sunshine to grow, your relationship needs attention for it to flourish.

Although they are both vital life forces, there is a marked difference between a plant and your relationship. In the winter, a plant sleeps under the guise of death, with the assurance of returning to life in the spring. If you and your mate slip into a marital coma, without a game plan for nourishment, there is no guarantee your coupleness will survive, let alone reawaken.

Nourishment can come in the form of a therapist, a relationship workshop, a new perception of yourself, a fresh outlook on your partner, time away with your partner, or time away from your partner. Before you can "till the soil" of your coupleness, however, you have to accept the fact that for your relationship to grow it has to change.

If Bob Dylan hadn't seen change as his ticket to growth, his music wouldn't be as popular as it is today. My husband will always remember the Dylan concert he attended in 1975. As one of the thousands of fans in a packed stadium, he was confused and shocked when the stage lights came up and illuminated Bob Dylan and a twelve-piece orchestra. Having rearranged his old favorites to fit the sound of a small symphony, Dylan's new image was rejected by a booing, dissatisfied audience. After five minutes, Dylan silenced the crowd by slowly approaching the microphone and saying, "Did you think I'd never change?" My husband recalls the hush of the crowd as everyone realized how unfair it was to expect such a gifted musician to remain rootbound with no chance to change or grow. Dylan played the rest of his concert to an enthusiastic crowd.

Your relationship is going to change. It's a given. It can change for the better by growing or it can change for the worse by not growing. Accepting that fact will make the difference between your relationship's life or death. Cultivate your coupleness and live!

The Improvement Movement

There's only one corner of the universe you can be certain of improving, and that's your own self.

ALDOUS HUXLEY

THE decade of the nineties could easily be named the decade of self-improvement. From the invention of step aerobics to the creation of the juicer, the last ten years have called men and women to take stock of themselves and adjust, amend, and enhance who they are.

Whether yearning to make spiritual, physical, or emotional adjustments, people are running, not walking, to the nearest motivational speaker to learn the seven most effective ways to be a better person. Infomercials are broadcast, tape programs are sold, and seminars are given to sold out crowds telling them the best way to reach enlightenment, lose twenty-five pounds, or become prosperous with no money down.

This improvement movement has infiltrated the corporate world as well. Many companies and businesses expect their employees to update their skills by attending workshops designed to keep them abreast of the latest information in their field. People don't hesitate to take a sales training seminar or a management course so that they can perform to their best in their career. If they don't embrace the improvement movement mindset in their profession, they risk losing their job.

Just as you can get fired from a job for not staying on the cutting edge of your field, you can get fired from a relationship for not knowing how to take care of it. Unfortunately, people are much less inclined to take workshops or courses to improve their marriage or relationship than they are to improve their skills in their profession.

Marriage and relationship workshops are less prevalent than financial seminars or courses on how to manage your own business, but they are available. Churches and temples often offer workshops or retreats for couples. Your community may have a center for marriage and family counseling that provides continuing education for relationships.

The resources for relationship improvement are there, but many people don't take advantage of them. The problem lies in the mindset of society. We spend more time improving our homes and our careers than we do improving our relationship with our mate.

For your relationship to grow, you and your mate have to become informed, inspired, and motivated. Educate yourself as much about your relationship as you do about your profession and what you get will be worth more than any promotion or bonus check.

Just Do It:

Within the next two weeks, learn something new to improve your relationship with your mate. Read a relationship book, enroll in a couples retreat, or watch a video on relationships.

The Perfect Example

Example moves the world more than doctrine. The great exemplars are the poets of action, and it makes little difference whether they be forces for good or forces for evil.

HENRY MILLER

YOU have a wellspring of opportunities to learn and grow from the two people who brought you into this world and raised you: your parents. Whether you realize it or not, your relationship with your mate is directly affected by your parents' relationship with each other.

Your mother and father were and may still be your most influential role models for being in a long-term partnership. Even if their example wasn't or isn't a sterling one, you can gain as much insight from it as if it were the most healthy loving relationship you've ever witnessed.

I learned as much about being a couple from my parents' relationship struggles as I did from their successes. Whenever my father went back to his office after dinner, I knew my parents had had an argument. His escape hatch helped him to calm down and regroup so that upon his return, he and my mother could work out their differences. My dad was the master of detachment. His example taught me how to step away from arguments and wait until I'm ready to talk rationally.

One of the best gifts my parents ever gave me was their example of playfulness. As far back as I can remember, my parents would rearrange the family room furniture and turn our den into a miniature ballroom. Being a product of the big band era, my parents knew how to "cut a rug." With the sounds of bands like Glen Miller or Tommy Dorsey blasting from the console stereo, my mom and dad would jitterbug for hours.

I remember cuddling up on the couch to watch them, completely enamored by their rhythm and chemistry. A silly grin would appear on my face as I'd fantasize about the day I would someday dance with my husband in my own home.

My parents gifted me with such a powerful example that not only do my husband and I dance in our home, dancing is how we met. It was while dancing in a 1940s musical revue that I first set eyes on my husband. As an actress in the show, my job was to dance with men in the audience. When the band struck up Glen Miller's "In The Mood," I spotted my husband and pulled him onto the dance floor. As we jitterbugged, there was instant chemistry between us. Images of my parents dancing in our family room flashed across my mind. I knew in that moment that I would marry him. And I did—eighteen years ago.

Think About It:

Whether your parents are still alive or not, they are an invaluable resource for your relationship with your mate. Your coupleness will grow richer from their positive and negative examples.

When History Repeats Itself

You learn from a conglomeration of the incredible past—
whatever experience gotten in any way whatsoever.

BOB DYLAN

ALL of us, at one time or another, look back at past relationships and cringe. Take a stroll down the memory lane of former relationships and you'll recall words you wished you hadn't said, feelings you wished you hadn't felt, and decisions you wished you hadn't made.

Regardless of how much you might like to erase the past, you can't. You can, however, learn from it. You may not realize it, but your past relationships, especially the less than stellar ones, can be your ticket to having a loving, healthy relationship with your mate. If you didn't learn certain lessons in a past relationship, don't worry, you'll get another opportunity this time around. The good news is that if you've learned from your mistakes, you won't repeat history.

Phil was in his early thirties and ready to settle down with someone and start a family, or so he thought. His past four relationships with women had ended after a year or two of dating each of them exclusively. It wasn't until his fifth relationship that he realized why none of them had lasted.

Phil had always started his relationships being open-minded and accommodating. The first few months of dating ran smoothly as he and his partner shared interests, values, goals, and grew closer. By the fourth or fifth month of a relationship, Phil would become controlling, possessive, and opinionated. He would insist on knowing where his mate was going and what she was doing every day. He not only tried to exercise control over her whereabouts, but over the clothes she wore and the makeup she used. Eventually whoever he was dating would feel completely smothered and would abruptly end the relationship.

It wasn't until the end of his fourth relationship that Phil realized he was a major part of the problem. He finally began to look at his own behavior as a contributing factor to his past unsuccessful relationships. Once he looked within himself, he couldn't ignore the fact that the same pattern appeared in all of his relationships. His jealous nature made him want to control his mate, which eventually pushed her away.

Determined not to repeat the same destructive habit in his next relationship, Phil reached out for help. With the aid of a qualified therapist, Phil slowly learned to let go of his control and replace his insecurities with a healthy, well-adjusted view of the new love in his life.

Whether your past relationships have been marriages or dating relationships, don't get into the next one without facing the music from the last one. The only way you can break the cycle of unhealthy relationships is to get healthy yourself.

Think About It:

Think about your past relationships. Admit to yourself if there is anything unhealthy in your present relationship that looks familiar from a past one. If so, face up to what part you play in the dysfunction. If getting professional help is the answer, do it so you can move on with your life and your relationship.

The Gender Blender

Different though the sexes are, they inter-mix. In every human being a vacillation from one sex to the other takes place, and often it is only the clothes that keep the male or female likeness, while underneath the sex is very opposite of what it is above.

VIRGINIA WOOLF

GENDER separation is a convenient way to justify limited thinking about your mate or the opposite sex in general. It's much easier to deal with people when you can say things like, "He's a man, you know" or "That's women for you." Although life seems to run smoother when you compartmentalize it, you may miss out on a lot of its richness by doing so.

I understand that, generally speaking, men tend to react in certain ways and women in others, but what I object to in the classification of the sexes is the idea that women have to stay on one side of the line and men on the other without daring to cross over.

Yes, women, by and large, have a softer more nurturing nature than men. And yes, women like to talk about feelings, or talk just for the sake of talking. Men, on the other hand, are generally more concerned about the final product or outcome of a situation. There is usually a reason for their conversations, rather than for conversation's sake alone.

So much for pigeonholing. The reality of life is that whether you're a man or a woman, you have qualities of both genders within you. If you are a man, you have some feminine qualities and if you are a woman, you have some masculine qualities. For you to grow into the person you are meant to be, depends on your acknowledgment of that fact.

Your personal gender mix of masculine and feminine qualities brings a sense of balance to your relationship with your mate. More often than not, your feminine qualities complement your mate's masculine qualities and your masculine attributes complement his or her feminine attributes.

To deny qualities in you that are from the opposite sex is the same as denying your heritage—that you are Jewish, Italian, or Afro-American. Your heritage belongs to you and so does your gender mix. Whatever proportion your mix is: ninety percent masculine–ten percent feminine; fifty percent masculine–fifty percent feminine; seventy-five percent feminine–twenty-five percent masculine, doesn't matter. What matters is that you realize you are not all man or all woman.

My husband fought his feminine side for the longest time. He worked hard at holding in his feelings, focusing on project goals and being concerned with only the bottom line. The problem was that when he did those things, he was miserable. What he really wanted was to be able to expose his feelings, let go of the outcome, and be concerned about people rather than revenue.

What he finally came to realize was that for years he had been at war with his own femininity. Little by little, he has allowed his softer side to show at work, allowing him to be the whole person rather than the half person society labels him.

The opportunity to show his feminine side arose recently when he bought a 1999 Volkswagen Beetle. The new version of this car comes with a built-in vase, which my husband took only minutes to fill with a yellow carnation, chosen to match the car's color.

He didn't lose any time in driving his new "Bug" to the home of his boss, Greg, who had the same car, only in red. When Greg noticed the yellow flower in the vase, he cleared his throat, dropped his voice an octave and said, "I use my vase as a pencil holder." With a self-accepting tone, one my husband hadn't had until a few years ago, he looked at his boss and said, "I think I'll alternate between mums and carnations."

Accepting your feminine and masculine sides will not only "round you out" as a person, it will make living with your mate a much more fulfilling experience. The pressure to "act like a man" or "be womanly" will be off.

Today my husband is a very strong, high-powered executive in the business world, but when he gets home, he still ties an apron around his waist and makes homemade applesauce!

Just Do It:

Accept that you are part feminine and part masculine. Grow into your "other side" and your relationship will grow along with it. Once you accept yourself for all that you are, your authentic relationship will naturally thrive.

Emotional Smarts

The only questions worth asking today are whether humans are going to have any emotions tomorrow, and what the quality of life will be if the answer is no.

LESTER BANGS

ONE of the things that probably attracted you and your mate to each other was your intelligence. Conversations about your knowledge, your ideas, and your perceptions helped spark the chemistry between you.

If you and your mate were to reminisce about your first few dates, you would most likely remember all the hours you spent talking. Those first long conversations with your partner felt like being on an intellectual archaeological dig. You had a new brain to pick and the information, perceptions, and insights inside of it were intriguing.

As a young child, I remember my mother saying that she and my father had an intellectual relationship. It wasn't until I was older that I understood what she meant. Both of my parents had inquiring minds. Their brains were like human sponges, ready and waiting to soak up whatever information was available. Whether it was from a best-selling novel, *The Wall Street Journal*, or a show on public television, my parents were always eager to learn new information and share it with one another. My mother was right. Much of their marriage was spent in a nuptial conference room having an intellectual meeting of the minds.

A man's or woman's intellectual intelligence is an exciting piece of any relationship and one that must be cultivated for it to stay stimulating. Intellectual intelligence alone, however, cannot carry a relationship. If depended upon too much, your cerebral connection to your mate will make your relationship one dimensional—all mind and no heart.

Daniel Goleman, author of the book *Emotional Intelligence* tells us that there is a different way of being smart. Emotional intelligence includes self-awareness, compassion, and the ability to speak and act from the heart. When mates are able to operate from their hearts as well as their heads, their relationship flourishes.

If you are someone who is used to reacting from a cognitive place rather than an emotional place, you will need to grow into using your heart more often. Without exercising your heart as an emotional muscle, your relationship will be thrown off balance.

When Esther and Nathan first met, their mutual passion for American history made them hungry for more and more time together. For weeks they spent evening after evening comparing what they had learned in college and their masters' programs. Their relationship quenched an insatiable intellectual thirst for them both.

It wasn't until a few years after they were married that Esther realized their intellectual relationship wasn't serving them the way it once had. Having a double-income family with two preschoolers, one dog, and two cats wasn't conducive to bantering historical facts and theories back and forth.

Esther no longer felt strongly about the establishment of the European Hegemony or the Battle of the Bulge. The only battle she cared about was the one she was having every day with her two-year-old son. Her hunger for emotion replaced her appetite for knowledge. She needed to connect with Nathan on a heart level instead of a head level.

Having never learned to shift from his head to his heart, sharing feelings took an enormous amount of effort for Nathan. Born into a family that almost never expressed feelings, his emotional intelligence had been stifled from the time he was a toddler.

Every time Esther tried to extract feelings from Nathan, she became more and more frustrated. She began to think he simply didn't have any—that he was a walking history book void of any emotion.

Esther was at the point of giving up on their marriage when Nathan finally consented to seeing a therapist. It took many months, but Nathan eventually learned how to get in touch with his own heart. Today he is as emotionally intelligent as he is intellectually intelligent. His healthy marriage is living proof of it.

Just Do It:

If operating from your heart is harder for you than operating from your mind, practice talking about your feelings. Purchase a journal and write down five of your feelings during the course of the day. Begin sharing one feeling with your mate a day. Work your way up to sharing all five feelings with your partner each day.

Uncontrollable Changes

He who governs others, first should be the master of him-self.

PHILIP MASSINGER

THERE are probably things about your partner that you'd love to change. Like a piece of soft, supple clay you would love to get your hands on his or her personality so you could mold and shape it into exactly what you want it to be. With a little rounding here and a little pressure there, you could create the perfect mate.

Take my advice and save your sculpting talents for pottery class. The only way your mate will be able to change and grow is if you keep your hands off the clay and out of the kiln.

It's best to acknowledge that both you and your partner have some character defects. And, the best chance your mate has of embarking on a self-improvement project is if he or she does it alone. By all means, cheer from the sidelines, but do it from the bleachers, not the coach's box.

Carrie approached the first year of marriage to her husband, Dan, as if she were a contractor overseeing a home improvement project. Upon acceptance of his marriage proposal, Carrie made a mental list of qualities about her fiancé that, with a little tweaking, would make him the perfect husband for her.

She had always enjoyed Dan's calm and quiet nature, but wished he would open up at parties and be more sociable. Since she loved to entertain, she figured she'd have lots of opportunities to teach him how to relax around large crowds of people.

Although Dan had cut back on his cigarette smoking, Carrie planned for him to see a hypnotist and join a SMOKENDERS support group. She decided to have chewing gum and nicotine patches on hand for him to use if he needed additional help.

Carrie felt Dan didn't have a close enough relationship with his teenage daughter, Claire. She decided that once they were married, she would invite her stepdaughter over regularly to force Dan and Claire to strengthen their father-daughter bond.

It didn't take long for Carrie to realize that, as hard as she tried, she couldn't change her husband. The more she tried to adjust his personality, his habits, and his relationships with other people, the more he clammed up at parties, smoked, and distanced himself from his daughter.

Carrie realized that she couldn't change her husband, only her reaction to him. When she let go of her need to control, Dan not only felt released from her dominion, he felt free to change. It was only after she threw away the nicotine gum, stopped calling his daughter, and let him be himself at social gatherings that Dan believed Carrie trusted him to grow on his own.

Your own growth as well as your mate's depends upon your ability to let go of what you can't control. You can't control or change your mate. You *can* control how you react to him or her. Understand that and your relationship will bloom.

Just Do It:

Make a list of all the things about your partner that you would like to change. Next to each item, write how you can change your reaction instead of your mate.

Unleashing Your Talents

If a man has a talent and cannot use it, he has failed. If he has a talent and uses only half of it, he has partly failed. If he has a talent and learns somehow to use the whole of it, he has gloriously succeeded, and won a satisfaction and a triumph few men ever know.

THOMAS WOLFE

N O matter who you are, gifts have been bestowed upon you. You have God-given talents that are unique to only you, and it is for you to decide whether or not you will unleash your endowment.

There is a direct correlation between your ability to unearth and use your talents and the health of your relationship with your mate. Because your relationship stems from you and your partner, it stands to reason that it will only be as fulfilling as the two of you are fulfilled.

Fulfillment is a funny thing. It's something you strive for your entire life, yet it often alludes you. You may watch your friends, family, and your own mate take flight in their personal development, while you stay grounded, confused and frustrated as to why your path to wholeness is unclear. Living with a partner who understands his or her own gifts and uses them freely can put a strain on your relationship if you think your gift box is empty.

For Sandra, the eleventh year of marriage to her husband, Jack, was like living with a complete stranger. It was during that year that Jack decided to uproot a long lost talent he had buried many years before, and it was Jack's decision that almost put an end to their relationship.

For months, Jack had felt agitated and restless. He had reached a point in his job where he felt stagnant and realized that unless he changed careers totally, he was not going to grow much more in his day-to-day work. Although he had accepted the halt in his professional growth, he wasn't willing to accept a standstill in his personal development. That unwillingness is what propelled him to dredge up a long lost friend from the recesses of his attic—his guitar.

In his efforts to climb the corporate ladder, Jack had closed a door on one of his precious talents—his gift for making music. He had been so focused on his profession that personal artistic growth had never been on his agenda.

For the first time in their marriage, music filled Jack and Sandra's home as Jack played his guitar for an hour every evening. With each nightly jamming session, Jack felt more and more secure and fulfilled in his decision to breathe life back into a talent he thought had been dead and buried forever.

As Jack's enthusiasm for his newfound gift grew, so did Sandra's resentment of it. Instead of supporting her husband in his personal discovery, she complained about the noise and disruption it created. Opening the guitar case became the precursor to an inescapable argument between them.

The tension in their relationship built to such a crescendo that Jack took drastic measures. He wasn't willing to let his gift for music get in the way of his relationship, but he wasn't willing to rebury it either. Desperate to use his musical ability, he sneaked his guitar into his workplace and hid it up above one of the ceiling panels in his office. After the last person in his office left each evening, he pulled down his guitar and jammed for a half hour before leaving for the day.

Although the guitar was no longer in Jack and Sandra's home, the tension between them had taken permanent residence. Sandra's lack of support for Jack's gift of music cut deep into the heart of their relationship. It took months for Sandra to realize that her angst about her husband's talent came from believing that she didn't have one of her own. She couldn't be happy for his new find until she cultivated her own hidden treasure. She had become so involved in raising their children and running their household that her gifts had been overshadowed. Sandra knew she was every bit as gifted as her husband, but she had chosen to put her talents on the back burner. Once she turned off the back burner and lit the front one by enrolling in a dance program at a local college, she began supporting Jack's talents along with her own. The wounds she had inflicted upon their relationship began to heal.

Dancing to guitar music became one of her favorite activities.

Just Do It:

If you resent your mate's talents, turn around and face yourself. What you probably resent is the fact you haven't cultivated your own. You and your partner are both gifted. It's up to you to unwrap your own present.

If the Therapist Fits . . .

When we turn to one another for counsel, we reduce the number of our enemies.

KAHLIL GIBRAN

WE live in a progressive, open-minded era, but still woven throughout our society is the stigma associated with getting counseling, therapy, or any kind of "outside help."

When your parents were first married, they wouldn't have entertained the idea of talking to anyone about their personal relationship concerns and problems. Their issues were thought to be no one else's business but their own. In your parents' day, getting help for their relationship just wasn't done.

Nowadays, a good chunk of the Yellow Pages is devoted to family and marriage therapists and people now have the option of "letting their fingers do the walking" in hopes of saving their relationship. I receive several calls a week from men and women asking me to recommend a therapist. Of the many people I talk with, I hear from a handful of them whose mates don't want to have anything to do with asking a "stranger" for help.

It always amazes me that there are still people whose mates are about to walk out of their lives forever, yet think they can solve their relationship problems without anyone's help. They would rather drop to their hands and knees, grovel and beg their mates to stay with them, which by the way, only ensures their mate's departure, than see a therapist.

Even if the communication between you and your mate is open, honest, and frequent, there will come a time when talking to each other will only get you so far. There may be a period in your relationship when you and your mate are so enmeshed in whatever problem you are dealing with that you won't be able to separate yourselves from it enough to get a clear view of the situation. At times like these, you have choices. You can ignore the problem and watch it reappear later with more intensity. You can point your finger at your partner and allow the act of blaming to drain the life force out of your relationship. Or, you can find a therapist.

I'm not recommending that you *call* a therapist. I'm recommending that you *find* a therapist, which requires searching. The key to getting the most out of relationship therapy is finding the right therapist for you and your mate.

Finding the right counselor is no different than finding the right car, house, or couch for your living room. You go with the one that feels the most comfortable and is of the highest quality. Determining the best fit may mean collecting references and interviewing several people before you decide on the person who works best with you and your mate. It's worth the effort.

Reaching out for help is what growth is all about. Sometimes the act of surrendering enough to ask for help is what causes you to grow the most. If your relationship has stopped growing, it could be time for you to get professional help.

Think About It:

Recognize when your relationship could use help from a therapist or counselor. The person you choose may work with you intermittently throughout the coming years, so make sure he or she is the right fit for you and your mate. Whomever you choose should be licensed by the state. Call the American Psychological Association's Practice Directorate at 202-336-5800 for the name of a state psychological association who can refer you to a licensed therapist.

The Gift of Personal Space

Privacy is not something that I'm merely entitled to, it's an absolute prerequisite.

MARLON BRANDO

PROTECTING your personal space within your relationship is crucial. Placing distance between you and your mate is as important as the intimacy between you. It doesn't matter if it's space to work on a creative project, space to get dressed in privacy, or space to sit with a quiet mind. You need it.

Feeling so connected to your partner that you feel like soul mates, kindred spirits, or two-as-one is a remarkable feeling. What isn't remarkable is when you are so enmeshed in your mate that you can't remember where you end and your partner begins.

As emotionally, physically, and spiritually close as you feel to your mate, you are still a separate, unique individual. For your relationship to be balanced and healthy, you must honor your own personal space.

Linda and Max dated each other exclusively for three years. Other than the time they were apart during business hours, they spent every waking minute together. They ate together. They jogged together. They grocery shopped together. They even washed their cars together.

Although Max loved being with Linda as much as she loved being with him, it didn't take long for him to start craving his own personal space. From the time he was in high school, he had an interest in painting. With the pressures of college and then his career, he had never had the time to pursue his undeveloped talent. Once he began dating Linda, every free moment was taken.

Instead of talking about his buried passion with Linda, Max hid it from her. By the time he burst forth with his desire to paint, it was too late. He had allowed himself to feel suffocated and trapped inside their relationship. He wanted his freedom and he wanted it immediately.

For your relationship to grow, *you* have to grow. One of the best ways for you to grow is to spend time alone with yourself. You must have personal space to hear yourself think, talk, pray, and do what it is you feel called to do.

Don't worry. As long as you balance your alone time and your time with your mate you won't lose touch with or alienate him or her. You will, however, feed your passion, become more intellectually stimulating, and understand yourself better. Remember, you bring who you are to your relationship. If you don't respect your right to personal space, you'll never find out who you are.

Just Do It:

Devote at least one half hour per day to time for yourself. Spend it doing anything that is important to you, for you.

Parasitic Relationships

Immature love says: "I love you because I need you."
Mature love says, "I need you because I love you."

ERIC FROMM

YOU go to the pharmacy when you need to fill a prescription. You go grocery shopping when you need to get food. You go to the bank when you need to withdraw money. You move through your day filling one need after another. Whether it's the basic need to eat or the need to spend money on something frivolous, you're used to filling your own needs.

While it is important to recognize and get your needs met, one need you want to avoid at all costs is the need to be in a relationship. If you want to spend the rest of your life with someone because you need to rather than want to, the relationship is doomed.

Needing to be in a relationship is usually fueled by low self-esteem. If you get into a relationship expecting the other person to fill the emptiness inside of you, at first your poor self-image will fade because you will rely on another person to make you feel good about yourself. However, the last thing your mate wants is to be depended upon to make you happy. Before you know it, he or she will see you as a parasite rather than a partner. By relying on your partner for your happiness you have abdicated responsibility for yourself.

In her book, *A Course in Love: Powerful Teachings on Love, Sex, and*

Personal Fulfillment, Joan Gattuso tells us that needy isn't attractive. She says, "Relationships are not about filling your needs. A needy person is like a human bloodsucker, seeking nourishment, fulfillment, and completion not in himself or herself, but in you. It is a draining, damaging, dysfunctional means of interaction."

You've probably heard the expression, "Two halves make a whole." In relationships, that doesn't work. If you take two people who are looking for their other half, and put them together in a relationship, you won't get a whole relationship. You'll get two desperate people searching for wholeness from a source unable to supply it.

You don't have to be a complete, enlightened, self-actualized human being before you get into a relationship. You need to at least be on a path to wholeness and know that your personal growth derives from you and no one else. Your relationship with your mate has a better chance at lasting a lifetime when you take responsibility for your own happiness.

Think About It:

Ask yourself this question: Is my mate responsible for the condition of my self-esteem? If the answer is "yes," you've become needy. Remember that needy isn't attractive. Work toward wanting to be with your mate because he or she complements who you already are rather than needing to be with your mate because you think he or she makes you who you are.

Say It Again, Sam

A princely marriage is the brilliant edition of a universal fact, and as such, it rivets mankind.

WALTER BAGEHOT

EVERY living thing, no matter what it is, needs new life breathed into it occasionally. Whether it's a plant that needs repotting, a tree that needs repruning, or a lawn that needs reseeding, living matter has to be resuscitated now and then.

Your relationship is a living entity with a spirit and energy of its own. If something isn't done periodically to reignite the pilot light of your relationship, its flame will eventually grow dim, flicker, and die out.

One of the best ways for you and your mate to rekindle your relationship is to renew your wedding vows. Regardless of how long you've been together, recommitting yourselves to each other is a fun and meaningful way to regenerate your coupleness.

There are no rules or regulations for this matrimonial rerun. Because it's your show, you can make it as simple or elaborate as you like. There are also no set standards on how often you can repledge your love for one another. Whether you do it once every ten years, once every five years, or once every twelve months is completely up to you.

There are several rationale for revisiting the altar. Maybe your parents designed your first wedding and you would like the chance to plan your own.

Perhaps you're married for a second time and because you had a big wedding the first time around, you want to make up for your initial prudence. Maybe you and your mate eloped and now that you've been together for years, you could care less about privacy and want to recommit yourselves in front of your friends and family. Possibly you and your partner have been through a crisis and want to claim victory by celebrating your union.

Whatever your reason for restating your vows to each other, the result is the same—a solidified, unified, and rejuvenated relationship.

Having each been married once before, my husband and I decided to have a small second ceremony. Rather than a formal reception, we chose to have a picnic in our backyard immediately following the church service. We've never regretted having a simple wedding, but when our tenth anniversary rolled around, we were itching for an extravaganza.

We told ourselves we had been through a lot and deserved nothing short of a Tony Award–winning production. Having made it through our son's neurosurgery, the death of our parents, and the loss of our house to a fire, we felt we had a reason to make merry.

So it was with justification that we jetted off to Jamaica to renew our vows in the Caribbean. Our private ceremony took place in a gazebo surrounded by tropical plants, with a breathtaking view of the sea. Because we had spent our honeymoon at this particular resort, our exchange of vows took on extra significance.

A videographer captured every tear, every hand tremor, and every kiss as we recommitted our love for each other. Instead of rings, my husband surprised me during the ceremony with the presentation of two gold necklaces and pendants, on which was written "Kathy and Dick" on one side and "The First Ten Years" on the other. As we put the matching necklaces around each other's necks, we felt gratitude for all that we had been through together and for all that was yet to come. The act of renewing our vows was the perfect springboard to propel us into our next decade together.

Just Do It:

If you haven't done it within the last five years, make a commitment with your mate to renew your vows within the next five years. Once you've done it, you'll feel refreshed, restored, and ready to face whatever life presents to you as a couple.

Parting Doesn't Have to be Sweet Sorrow

If love . . . means that one person absorbs the other, then no real relationship exists any more. Love evaporates; there is nothing left to love. The integrity of self is gone.

ANN OAKLEY

LET'S assume you and your mate plan to spend at least the next thirty years together. It doesn't take long to figure out that thirty years with the same person is the equivalent to 360 months, 1,560 weeks, or 10,950 days together. When you look at it that way, time away from your mate seems pretty appealing.

If you and your partner are soul mates, kindred spirits, or have known each other from a former life, you still need to be apart from each other occasionally in order for your relationship to reach new heights.

Spending time away from your mate reminds you that you are an individual, with your own decisions to make, opinions to form, and thoughts to contemplate. Whether you take as little as a day or as long as a week away from your mate is completely up to you. It's not the time away from your partner that matters as much as it is your motives for taking the time away. If you spend time apart from your mate to escape your relationship rather than to enrich it, your respite from your partner will backfire. If, on the other hand, you leave your partner knowing that you will return refreshed and ready to

129

pick up where you left off, with a renewed sense of self, the reprieve from your mate will enliven your relationship.

This past year my husband decided to spend time alone to reexamine himself. He had spent most of the previous year entrenched in his roles as husband, father, and primary breadwinner. He needed a break from his workplace, his family, and quite frankly, from me. Although he adores me and our children, he recognized that if he didn't cut loose from it all, he would sacrifice a piece of himself to the war zone of everyday life. Not only his health, but the health of our relationship depended on his taking some time away.

So it was with a sense of self-love that he spent five days and four nights in Sedona, Arizona, resting, sunning, and painting. With each day's phone call, I heard a stronger more vibrant voice; the voice of a man who was grateful for time alone, but who couldn't wait to get back in my arms.

For your relationship to grow and prosper, you and your mate have to do the same. You can't grow if you're root-bound by work, home, and parental responsibilities. Even if it's for a short amount of time, spending time alone away from your partner can be just the fertilizer your relationship needs.

Just Do It:

Once or twice a year, spend at least a day away from your mate. You have to know who you are in relation to yourself before you can be in a healthy relationship with anyone else, especially your partner.

Grow Toward Understanding

If one does not understand a person, one tends to regard him as a fool.

CARL JUNG

I don't get it." "What are you talking about?" "*No comprendo.*" "Are you on drugs?" If you have ever said any of these phrases, you know what it feels like not to understand someone. If that someone frequently happens to be your mate, your relationship is skating on thin ice.

Understanding your mate doesn't mean you have to agree with him or her. It simply means you have to try to see how he or she might think or feel a certain way.

The word "understand" is a compound word; one that is made up of two separate words: *under* and *stand*. Flip the words around and they become "standunder." If you think about it, that's really what understanding is all about—standing under someone in support of their ideas, opinions, and feelings. The opposite word would be "overstand," and standing over someone denotes control or power—not my idea of a component of a lasting relationship.

Paul could never understand why his wife, Joyce, got stressed out over hosting Thanksgiving dinner in their home every year. The night before the dinner, Paul watched Joyce fret and worry about whether or not the turkey

131

would be moist, the potatoes would be lumpy, or the dinner table would seat enough people. Each holiday he'd say to Joyce, "What's the big deal?" or "You did this last year," or "Who cares about lumpy potatoes." With each flippant response from her husband, Joyce felt more and more misunderstood. A Thanksgiving eve argument became a holiday tradition.

Paul certainly didn't have to agree with the way Joyce was handling her emotions about Thanksgiving. In the same situation, he would have reacted differently. Unfortunately, year after year Paul missed his golden opportunity to understand why his wife might feel the way she did. For most of her life, Joyce's mother had hosted Thanksgiving dinner. Now that the holiday scepter was passed to her, she felt nervous and pressured to keep up the family traditions. All she really needed was for Paul to empathize with her nervous tension. He didn't have to say, "I agree with you totally. I think everyone should freak out over dry turkey breast." He should say, "Knowing how much this means for you to have your family in our home, I can see why lumpy potatoes would worry you."

The desire to understand your mate is an admirable aspiration for your relationship—one that is lofty but not unreachable. Along with this newly acquired relationship goal will come a new and improved vocabulary, including phrases like "I see what you mean," "Now I get it," "I can imagine how you feel," and the magic words, "I understand."

Think About It:

When you and your mate argue, remind yourself that you don't have to come to an agreement. You can hold onto your point of view and still understand why your partner might think or feel a certain way.

Life's Pickle in the Middle

At last now you can be
What the old cannot recall
And the young long for in dreams,
Yet still include them all.

ELIZABETH JENNINGS

ONCE you and your mate have made a commitment to each other, spending the rest of your life together is what you expect to do. What you don't expect, however, is to be hit by midlife, a period that throws you off balance and threatens the stability of your relationship.

In her book, *Understanding Men's Passages: Discovering the New Map of Men's Lives)*, Gail Sheehy refers to a byproduct of today's society that she calls "Gender Crossover." This is what happens during the time in life commonly known as midlife when men and women experience a restlessness about life's meaning and worth. Although you and your mate may be going through this passage simultaneously, your reactions to it can be diametrically opposed, putting your relationship at risk.

Sheehy tells us, "Partners at the same developmental stage are often out of sync. When healthy, educated women reach their fifties today, they generally feel a great release of energy. They are likely to say, 'Hey, I have thirty or forty years ahead of me! Let's go!' Men facing the same passage, if they view it as a loss of power or potency, become threatened that they are less needed by women. This imbalance has created one of the newest and most challenging passages for married men and women in middle life today."

Sarah and Chuck were both energetic people who took advantage of as much as life had to offer. Chuck, an engineer for an automobile manufacturing company, loved his work and had enjoyed a steady rise up the corporate ladder for thirty years. Sarah, a part-time research scientist, enjoyed the balance she had struck between her work and the raising of their two sons.

The scales of harmony tipped when this couple reached their mid-fifties. As often happens in large corporations, Chuck's company was bought out by a larger company. His position was immediately eliminated in the takeover, leaving him with a comfortable severance package, but a fragmented ego.

Sarah and Chuck were fortunate in that Sarah was able to make an easy transition from a part-time researcher to a full-time researcher, relieving the financial burden that would have otherwise strained their relationship. Although the pressure was off financially, the pressure cooker was on high for them emotionally.

It was hard enough for Chuck to adjust to his career disaster, let alone watch his wife expand into her profession at a time when he wanted her pace to slow down and keep time with his. It took a full year of counseling before Chuck felt peaceful enough about his own self-worth to relax into a different lifestyle with his wife.

Gail Sheehy reminds us that, "The Gender Crossover escalates into a crisis only when the man does not feel sufficiently strong and capable or has bought into the myths of manhood dictating that the man must always be dominant in all spheres. He will then have difficulty watching his wife discover her own strengths and capabilities."

Just Do It:

In order for your relationship to grow through midlife, you and your partner must release your grip on the stereotypical lifestyle of "man makes money until retirement age" and "woman waits patiently" until they drive their recreational vehicle into the setting sun. Exercise emotional and financial flexibility during your pre-golden years.

Ask and You Shall . . . Grow

Any solution to the problem changes the problem.

R. W. JOHNSON

FROM the time you were old enough to raise your arms toward your parent and say "up" you've known how to ask for help. How else do you think you learned how to tie your shoe, ride a bike, or drive a car. At some point, your call for aid changed from asking for help with basic needs to not asking for help because you were too proud or embarrassed to ask.

Life has a way of presenting situations that require making choices. When you make the right choice, life keeps humming along. When you make the wrong one, you're faced with a dilemma. Do you deny the problem by pretending nothing's amiss? Maybe you go so far as to admit to yourself that you have a problem, but vow never to let anyone else know what you're going through. No one ever needs to know because you can handle it yourself, right?

Sticking your head in the sand about a problem in your relationship, or assuring yourself you can deal with it without anyone's help is damaging to the life you've built with your mate. If you had a problem at your job and your responsibility was to make sure business ran smoothly, you'd be the first to call someone to help you solve the problem. You'd have to in order for the business to survive.

That's exactly what you have to do in order to protect your relationship. Recognizing you have a problem is the first step to solving it. You need to pull your head out of the sand and look at the situation dead in the eye.

What's so wonderful about problems is that attached to them are usually many options. Relationship problems are no exception.

Whether your relationship is plagued with miscommunication, boredom, or infidelity, there is someone you can reach out to for help. Nowadays, the world provides several resources to help couples live in harmony. There are secular and nonsecular relationship workshops, seminars, and retreats offered all around the country. If you want one-on-one guidance, your community most likely offers a network of family, marriage, and relationship therapists.

Frank and Judy who had been together for fifteen years, spent the past five years of their relationship feeling not listened to by each other. No matter what either of them said, they felt they were speaking a foreign language. It wasn't until they went to a therapist who directed them to a workshop on listening that they were able to work through their dilemma.

There is no shame attached to asking for help. You won't be judged for reaching out, you will be rewarded.

Just Do It:

Make a list of up to three problems you think you need to deal with in your relationship. Pick one to solve. Create a list of people you can reach out to who can help you deal with the situation. Reach out to one of them and ask for help.

CHAPTER FIVE

Romance and Fun: A Lifestyle Change

NOT much time has to pass before fun becomes a foreign experience in a marriage. When I teach workshops and explain that couples absolutely must make time to have fun together, many of the participants tell me they can't remember the last time they made merry with their mate.

The day you and your mate exchanged wedding vows, I am certain you did not make a promise to set out on a path of lifelong drudgery. On the contrary, your minds were already racing ahead to the joy you were about to experience at your wedding reception and honeymoon.

With a commitment of a lifelong relationship comes heavy responsibility: children, dual incomes, college funds, etc. If you don't, however, balance your awesome duties with some awesome fun, you're going to have an awesome lawyer's bill from your awesome divorce.

You can certainly have fun without romance, but it's nearly impossible to have romance without fun. Because of that, it's crucial to feed your relationship a romantic snack once a day. You can save the full course dinner for special occasions, but without being tossed at least a romantic crumb every day, your marriage will die of starvation.

You may consider yourself romantically handicapped, challenged, or impaired but you can become whatever you want to be, and there is nothing more worthwhile for your marriage than becoming a romantic. If you already consider yourself a romantic, you can always improve on a good thing.

Romance is not meant to be a one shot endeavor. It craves to be embraced and woven into the fabric of your marriage. Given the courage and knowledge, you and your mate have all you need to embark on a romantic journey together. I can give you the knowledge, but the courage is up to you.

Romantic Simplicity

We ascribe beauty to that which is simple; which has no superfluous parts; which exactly answers its end; which stands related to all things; which is the mean of many extremes.

RALPH WALDO EMERSON

I F you're like most people, you'd love to be romantic, but you think you don't have the time, money, or creativity. The idea of romancing your mate can be very intimidating, especially if you think that in order to do so, you have to whisk your partner away to some exotic island or hire a limousine to escort you and your mate to a five-star restaurant.

Because any romantic gesture carries the message, "You make a difference in my life, so I want to make a difference in yours," the size of your gesture is irrelevant. What makes a romantic gesture romantic is the simple act of doing it.

I knew a woman whose husband was romantically challenged. This poor lady was starving for something . . . anything that hinted of romance in her relationship. She was tired of always being the one to send flowers, make romantic candlelit dinners, and stock up on greeting cards.

One morning she realized her single-handed efforts were beginning to pay off. As usual, she awoke after her husband had left for work and shuffled into the bathroom to start her morning routine. There before her was the surprise of her life. Her husband, who she thought didn't have a romantic blood cell in his body, had dumped everything out of her makeup bag and made an "I love you" message out of her lipstick, mascara, brushes, eyeliner, and compact cases. Spread across the bathroom counter was the letter *I*, a heart with an arrow through it, and the letter *U*. She was so thrilled with his romantic overture that she grabbed her camera and took a picture of it.

Knowing what I do for a living, she sent me a photo of her husband's display of romance. I now take this photo with me whenever I lecture on romance in order to show people how a simple gesture that took little time and cost nothing made a a big enough impact on someone to actually take a photograph of it!

Romance doesn't have to be an extravaganza. A simple romantic gesture, as well as an expensive, time-consuming one relays the same message: You make a difference in my life. If romance is a challenge for you, face it with simplicity.

Just Do It:

Don't let romance intimidate you. Once this week do something simple—the simpler the better—to prove to your mate that he or she makes a difference in your life.

Invaluable Tools

Man is a tool-using animal . . . without tools he is nothing,
with tools he is all.

THOMAS CARLYLE

E VERY home should have a toolbox for dealing with emergencies: a hammer, screwdriver, etc., to cope with the little chores that inevitably emerge. Aside from a toolbox for household emergencies, you need to have a "tool kit" designated strictly for romance. This space is meant for romantic tools: anything from greeting cards to sex toys, from personal photographs to brochures of romantic getaway places. Depending upon how personal the tools are in your romance drawer, it may be advisable for you to keep your romance enhancers under lock and key.

Our romantic tools are located in the two drawers of my nightstand and are a marvelous resource for my husband and me. Over the years we've collected a variety of massage oils, lotions, and lickable dusting powders. Amongst the tactile materials, we keep our aromatic doodads like candles, perfumes, and sprays. The bottom drawer of my nightstand contains a collection of sex boutique goodies from sex toys to books on sexuality.

Mixed among our sexual paraphernalia is a very special tool, a book called *Our Love Story: A Record Book*, written by Helen Exley. As she tells us, "Everyone has an individual story to tell about their own particular romance. When completed, this book will tell your personal story, and in years to come it will remain as a lasting record of the wonder of falling in love and your precious times together." I keep this book in our romance drawer and write in it whenever my husband and I create a special memory.

Building up a romance space is a relationship-savvy thing to do for two reasons: It allows you to centralize everything that can help you and your mate stay physically and emotionally connected and it makes romance easily accessible in a world that is good at making romance hard to come by.

Whether you use a drawer, a cupboard, or a lockbox, have fun creating your romance resource file. I knew one artistic woman who bought a small armoire, painted it, and lined it with scented paper. She and her husband kept everything in it that had to do with keeping their love alive. Their romance cabinet became their relationship tool chest.

Just Do It:

Start a relationship drawer—your own relationship toolbox of sorts. You do it for your hammers, screwdrivers, and pliers. Why not for your relationship? Begin by lining a drawer with scented paper and make your first tool a favorite picture of you and your mate. Little by little fill your drawer with romantic resources.

Escape to . . . Wherever

Of all the alternatives, running away is best.

CHINESE PROVERB

IN many instances romance is associated with getting away. Putting yourself in a different environment, whether it be on a secluded island, in a bed-and-breakfast, or a local hotel, is often a precursor to romance.

For many couples, getting away is the only prescription for what ails their relationship. After their first night at a bed-and-breakfast, Jackson and Ruth became b&b addicts. "We've decided that no matter what is going on in our lives, we're going to get away to a different bed-and-breakfast every three months," said Ruth. "By the time we celebrate our fiftieth wedding anniversary, we want to be able to say we've stayed in a b&b in every state in the country."

For Dinah and Hugh, a weekend away is never long enough. "Getting away for a romantic weekend is nice, but just as we start to feel close and connected, it's time to check out of the hotel or inn," said Hugh. "Going away for one or two nights almost frustrates us more than not going away at all. We decided that if we're going to go through the trouble of hiring a babysitter and taking time off of work that we have to escape for at least five days."

Parents of ten children, Olivia and Taylor have a different slant on what romance means. In twenty-six years of marriage, neither of them can remember one single instance when they've both been alone together in their own home. To them, the ideal romantic situation is to be able to spend time in their house together without having to respond to anyone but each other.

Determined to make their dream a reality, they hired two baby-sitters, packed their children's bags, and sent the entire crew to a hotel while they stayed home alone together. "It was wonderful," said Olivia. "We had our whole house to ourselves and we knew our kids were in their glory swimming in a hotel pool and ordering room service."

Whether you send people away or leave home yourselves, you and your mate must change your environment enough to allow romance to touch your relationship. Go ahead. Escape with your partner to wherever and become romanced by romance.

Just Do It:

Listen carefully enough and you'll hear romance calling your name. Its whispers are beckoning you to escape to somewhere . . . anywhere with your mate. Go ahead—get your calendar and set the date. Hire a baby-sitter and start packing.

The Romantic Movement

The power of a movement lies in the fact that it can indeed change the habits of people. This change is not the result of force but of dedication, of moral persuasion.

STEVEN BIKO

ROMANCE and fun are synonymous. If you're being romantic, chances are you're having fun. If you're having fun, somewhere in your play I'll bet there is at least a hint of romance.

What makes romance so much fun is the element of the mysterious, the unexpected . . . the unknown. Unless, of course, you've boxed yourself into a romantic rut. Even romance can become dull, usual, and ordinary.

Angelo prided himself on being a romantic husband. For seventeen years, he sent his wife, Nora, a dozen red roses on their anniversary. On Valentine's Day, he always presented her with a two-pound heart-shaped box of chocolates. His romantic sentiments were as constant as the rising and setting sun. The problem was they were also habitual, and habit is anything but romantic.

The key to a successful romantic relationship is change and surprise. What makes romance so titillating, so anticipatory, and so yearned for is the idea that you never know what's coming next.

Married for twenty-eight years, Carmen viewed each wedding anniversary as a bright new opportunity to tell the world how much he loved his wife,

146

Rosa. His yearly public proclamation meant so much to Rosa that she kept a scrapbook as a reminder of each year's romantic display.

One year Carmen hired a skywriting pilot to write "Happy Anniversary, Rosa" across the sky during a Cleveland Indians baseball game. Another year he painted a thirty-foot banner and hung it on a bridge over a freeway that Rosa traveled on her way to work. Stunned by the sight of her name on a banner, she almost drove off the rode as she sped by her husband excitedly blowing her kisses from a bridge.

Carmen's romantic success came from his determination to change his approach every year. He wasn't willing to bore his wife with the same old box of candy or bouquet of flowers.

If you're used to giving your mate greeting cards to express your love, wait twelve months before you give another greeting card. Express your love differently. If you're accustomed to sending flowers on special occasions, send anything *but* flowers. If your brain turns to mush at the thought of breaking your romantic rut then go to a library or bookstore and get the book *1001 Ways to Be Romantic* by Gregory J. P. Godek. It is the best guide I know for romance and fun.

When you plan a surprise for your mate, you automatically make romance. When you make romance, you automatically make fun.

Just Do It:

How have you romanced your mate in the same way over and over again? Decide not to do whatever it is you've been doing for an entire year. Do something completely different to romance your partner.

Teach Your Children Well

Life is amazing: and the teacher had better prepare himself to be a medium for that amazement.

EDWARD BLISHEN

I F someone asked you, "Would you like to see your children in a romantic, loving adult relationship someday?" your answer would most likely be a resounding, "Yes!" Who wouldn't want that for their children?

The best way for you to increase the odds of that happening for your children is for you to have a romantic, demonstrative relationship with your mate. Your children—whether they are toddlers, school age, or adults—are watching every move you make. If there is tension between you and your partner, they pick up on it, and if romantic sparks are flying they can detect those, too.

One of the best ways to model romance for your children is to include them in the planning, whether it be a getaway weekend or a small surprise. When our children were ages three and six, I made a huge impression on them by letting them help me with a romantic surprise for their father. For Valentine's Day that year I sneaked into my husband's parking garage where he works and filled his car with thirty-five balloons. In each balloon was a note I had written saying why I loved him. The only way he could drive home that day was to read each note by first popping every balloon with a needle, which I had taped onto his windshield.

My children helped me with this romantic ruse by stuffing the notes inside the balloons. They of course asked me to read each reason why I loved their father before they would hide the notes. With the reading of every reason, their smiles grew bigger and their sense of security grew stronger. My children are now fifteen and twelve and they still remember the day Mommy surprised Daddy with a carful of balloons.

Even the smallest attempts at romance don't go unnoticed by children. My son and daughter comment on the littlest things I do for their father. For instance, when I pack my husband's lunch every day, I always include a banana. Although my husband likes bananas, he enjoys the messages I write on the peel more than the fruit itself. As soon as we run low on bananas, my daughter, Katie, is the first to remind me to get another bunch—and she hates bananas.

You and your mate are your children's most influential role models. Your relationship will be the first one they look to for guidance on how to be in an adult relationship themselves. Being your children's template for their future love lives is an awesome responsibility and one you can have a tremendous amount of fun creating.

Just Do It:

Do something romantic for your mate today and include your children in on your scheme. Whether you make an "I love you" call, hide a surprise note for your partner, or give your lover a single rose, allow your children to be a part of your romantic game plan.

Laugh, Laugh, and
Be Merry

If we may believe our logicians, man is distinguished from all other creatures by the faculty of laughter. He has a heart capable of mirth, and naturally disposed to it.

JOSEPH ADDISON

ROMANCE, fun, and laughter are the trinity of a happy marriage. Where you have one, the others are not far behind.

One of the most precious gifts your mate brings to your relationship is his or her laughter. Whether your partner's laugh manifests itself as a series of chuckles, snorts, belly bellows, or inaudible, tear-producing shoulder shakes, new energy is infused into your relationship with each guffaw.

In her book *Laughter Therapy: How to Laugh About Everything in Your Life That Isn't Really Funny*, Annette Goodheart, Ph.D., tells us, "Laughter can be beneficial to our well-being because it heals and connects. It offers a universal form of communication that dissolves all barriers of language, age, nationality, race, and creed. When people laugh together, they feel closer."

Regardless of whether or not your mate laughs easily and often or is guarded about his or her mirth, cherish every moment of your partner's laughter.

There are laughers in this world and nonlaughers in this world. My husband laughs, but because of his intense nature, he tends more toward being a nonlaugher. Because I grew up with a father whose trademark was his knee-slapping cackle, I entered adulthood expecting everyone, including my husband, to react to life's humor with the same frequent, boisterous laugh.

After fifteen years of marriage, I've finally accepted that it takes a lot more for my husband to "bust a gut" than it does for me. When something does strike my husband as funny, however, I make sure I'm available to revel in the spectacle of his laughing jag.

His bouts of laughter usually begin by him cupping his hand over his mouth, squinting his eyes, and shaking convulsively. By the time his laughter has reached its peak, every vein in his forehead is bulging. Although this pose isn't a particularly attractive one, it's an image I savor and hold dear in my mind until the next attack of laughter enriches our relationship.

Whether you or your mate is the one doing the laughing, you can't deny that while it's happening you're having fun; and more fun is what every relationship in this world needs. Ask yourself, "Am I having fun in my relationship?" and if your answer is no, I bet one of two things is happening. You're either not laughing enough or when you are laughing, you and your mate aren't taking the time to revel in the merriment.

Just Do It:

From now on, when your mate laughs I want you to stop whatever you're doing and watch the show. Get it on videotape if you can! What your partner is displaying for you is nothing short of pure joy. He or she is gifting you with a few moments of gaiety that, if you let it, will recharge your relationship.

Forgetting to Remember

The true art of memory is the art of attention.

SAMUEL JOHNSON

I F ever there comes a day when you think you are falling out of romantic love with your partner, don't kid yourself. True, you'll no longer feel as strong a heart connection to your mate, but this feeling of separation will have as much to do with what has happened in your mind as well as in your heart. In other words, when you think you've fallen out of love, chances are you've forgotten out of love instead.

In the beginning of your relationship, you carry in your consciousness mental pictures of the wonderful, romantic moments you've shared with your partner—your own cerebral photo album. Your relationship grows, and so do the memories of each day together. When you and your significant other are apart, you depend on those mental pictures to fill the void between you.

But as time passes, your mind begins to need more than its own images to remind you of romance. In competition with your memories is an outside world clamoring for your attention.

Your own home is one of the biggest competitors. If it's not the television, it's the radio. If it's not the radio, it's the phone. If it's not the phone, it's the computer.

Although your home has a number of things in it to divert your attention from your relationship, it can also house powerful reminders of your commitment to each other. Look around. What rooms do you live in most? Wherever you and your partner spend the majority of your time is where I want you to display a picture of you as a couple.

I know of a husband and wife who filled their home with photos. Not only did it make a huge impact on their relationship, it made an impression on anyone who visited them.

One year, their house was selected to be in their city's annual house tour. During the tour, people commented how heartwarming it was to see so many romantic pictures of this couple together.

Another couple, Jessica and Paul, not only wanted to remind each other of their love, they were determined to remind their children of it as well. For Christmas one year, they framed a 5 × 7 photograph of the two of them and gave it to each of their children. The photos sit on their children's nightstands as a remembrance of how much their mommy and daddy love each other.

Think of all the ways you remind yourself of what has to be done every day. You make lists. You write notes to yourself. You ask other people to remind you. You may even leave voice mail messages for yourself. You do whatever it takes to remember to make that call, run that errand, or get to that appointment.

Your memory bank can hold a lot of information, but it's only so big. Make sure you leave room for the romantic memories between you and your mate. The next time you think you're falling out of love with your partner, think again. Chances are, you've just forgotten.

Just Do It:

Find three different romantic photos of you and your mate. If you don't have any, take some. Frame the pictures and display them in strategic places in your home, preferably where you spend much of your time.

Theme Sparks

Passions are the only orators which always persuade.

FRANCOIS, DUC DE LA ROCHEFOUCAULD

I F you find it difficult to choose a theme around which to romance your mate, develop one around your partner's passion. If your mate likes horseback riding, use an equestrian theme. If he or she loves to cook, add a culinary flair to your romantic endeavor.

The husband of one of the couples who attends the annual Marriage Movement Romance Workshop has used this technique to impress his wife, Geraldine, by capitalizing on her passion for antique rhinestone jewelry. One year Max presented her with a necklace in an unorthodox way during the workshop.

Max asked one of our outside speakers for the day, an owner of a local sex boutique, to present his wife with a rhinestone necklace during her talk to the workshop participants. He was as surprised as his wife when the owner of the sex boutique displayed not only a variety of marital aids, but a particular one wrapped in rhinestones. It didn't take long for Geraldine to realize that the wrapping was meant for her.

Romancing your mate by incorporating his or her passion makes a greater impact than if you were to romance him or her in a more generic, perhaps expected manner. One of my husband's passions is race car driving. He loves watching it and has always wanted to drive a Formula One car himself.

154

For his forty-sixth birthday, I enrolled him in a racing school in Wisconsin. I kidnapped him from work on a Friday afternoon and drove him to a bed-and-breakfast near the racetrack. Before dinner that evening, I asked the maitre d' to slip the racing school brochure and agenda into my husband's menu. Believe me, he never had so much fun ordering an appetizer as he had that night. By mixing romance with his dream of a lifetime, I created a memory he will always treasure.

Your mate's personal passions are already wired for romance. All you have to do is turn on the switch!

Just Do It:

Once in the next twelve months execute a romantic adventure around one of your partner's passions. Romance takes on a whole new identity when it's custom designed.

Are We Having Fun Yet?

The true object of all human life is play. Earth is a task garden; heaven is a playground.

G. K. CHESTERTON

AFTER years of teaching men and women how to live happily together, I am convinced that those who play together, stay together. Think of play for now as being nonsexual. I want you to remember what it felt like to play from a child's point of view.

As you conjure up memories and feelings of childhood play, let your mind wander to the days of lighthearted spontaneity. You had no constraints on your imagination back then. It never entered your mind what people might think of you as you did a huge belly flop into the pool or cartwheeled across the front lawn. Your play came from your desire to have fun at all costs. If you saw an opportunity to laugh or giggle you seized it.

At some point, you realized that playing with another person doubled your pleasure and so games became a part of your playful repertoire. Hide-and-seek, tag, and just foolin' around gave you so much joy.

What exactly was it that forced you to grow up, act your age, and stop being silly? Whatever it was has kept you from having an alive and vibrant relationship with your mate. Who are you kidding to think that the little boy or girl who once lived in your body has disappeared? He or she sits in a corner of your soul just waiting for an invitation to play.

Playfulness is an ageless activity. I recall one summer, sitting by a pool and watching a couple in their seventies play with each other in the water. The husband stealthily glided through the pool as he prepared to catch his mate. His wife, realizing she was being chased, defended herself from being captured by frantically splashing. Several people in the pool stopped their activity to enjoy their frolicking as the husband finally won the chase.

Look around you. You have opportunities every day to be playful with your mate. Take a second to tickle your partner or chase him around the room. Instead of handing your mate the car keys, toss them to her. Rather than walking to the kitchen or dining room for dinner, grab your partner and dance the tango to the table. Be outrageous. Lighten up or you'll miss all the fun!

Just Do It:

Visit a playground, a school, or anywhere you can to observe children. Watch them and they will remind you how to play. Before the day ends, do one playful thing with your mate.

It's How You Play the Game

For nothing can seem foul to those that win.

WILLIAM SHAKESPEARE

IT is not unusual for there to be a certain amount of competition in your relationship with your mate, even in the midst of fun. If you both play the same sport or work in the same profession, there's likely to be a touch of rivalry between you.

Admittedly, a little competition is a healthy motivator. You're more likely to work harder toward reaching a goal when someone else is racing you to the finish line.

If, however, you're one of those people who must win at everything, including your weekly tennis matches with your partner, then you better check your cutthroat nature at the door. If you can't take the disappointment of your loss and turn it into pride and respect for your mate's win, then you have a problem.

Carl and his girlfriend, Eve, met on the golf course, and had fun playing eighteen holes of golf once or twice a week. That was until Eve started shooting five strokes under Carl. Carl didn't mind losing to Eve occasionally, but when her score dropped several strokes below his most of the time, it wasn't fun anymore—for either of them.

Whenever Eve won a match, Carl couldn't rise above his own feeling of inadequacy. Instead of acknowledging her success, he continued to focus on his lack of it. Sadly, they stopped enjoying the game that brought them together in the first place.

When your mate beats you at a sport or game, it's only natural for you to feel a little envious at first. What's not natural, is for you to dwell on that feeling until you're more upset by what you *haven't* achieved than happy for what your mate *has* achieved.

When your partner "wins," it is an opportunity for you to add another brick to the foundation of your relationship. If you are genuinely happy for your partner, he or she will feel it instantly and the two of you can bask in the glory of the achievement. Once you learn to celebrate your mate's victories, you clear a path for your mate to revel in your successes. In other words, you both will win at whatever game you play.

Just Do It:

The next time you are in a competitive situation with your partner, let go of the feeling of having to win. Do your best, but if your mate's best is better than yours, let him or her glow in the limelight. Be proud of your significant other. Remember, this talented, fun-loving, shining star is with you!

Prepare to Meet Romance

The end may justify the means as long as there is something that justifies the end.

LEON TROTSKY

ROMANCE can be spontaneous. The quickly lighted flame of a candle. The push of a stereo button for mood music. An effortless turn of an electric dimmer switch. For anyone who is short on time, and that's most of us nowadays, a romantic atmosphere can be created with minimal effort.

For those of us who want to savor the process of romance, who want to enjoy the planning stages, romance can be as much a means to an end as it is a final product.

I've orchestrated many a romantic escapade in my marriage. The memories I've made while organizing each one mean as much to me as the memories I've made enjoying the fruits of my preparatory labor.

One of my favorite romantic memories is when I planned a red Valentine's Day lunch for my husband. Red being the signature color for romance, I decided to use it to the hilt.

From start to finish, it took me a week to plan for our "red letter" day. Every day for the week prior to Valentine's Day I left a note in my husband's lunch that had the word "red" in it. By the time I invited him home for lunch on Valentine's Day, he felt flushed; red in the face with anticipation.

Instead of serving lunch in an expected place such as the kitchen or dining room, I decided to serve it on our hope chest in the bedroom. I purchased red lace fabric for the tablecloth, used red napkins, and bought red sheets and pillowcases for our bed.

I was so determined to stay true to the red motif that everything I made for lunch was red. I boiled pasta in water that was tinted with red food coloring and topped it with red sauce. I made tomato soup and baked red bread. I even made a red key lime pie for dessert.

Knowing that romance for men usually includes a taste of sexuality, I dressed myself in a red corset, garter belt and hose, and played the song "Lady in Red" as he entered our bedroom.

Our afternoon was glorious and one I will never forget, however, I enjoyed the week of planning and scheming as much as the final production. One of the memorable moments from that week happened the morning of the illustrious lunch. Wanting to be superorganized about my Valentine's Day presentation, I laid everything out on our kitchen table before I put my props in place. Displayed on the table were red candles, the red tablecloth, and a few sundry sexy goodies such as pasta in the shape of women's breasts and red fur handcuffs.

Within seconds of surveying my lunchtime props, the doorbell rang. At the door stood the man who delivers replacement bottles for our spring water cooler located in our kitchen. As the delivery man replaced our water, I was mortified as I stared at the sexual paraphernalia sprawled across our kitchen table. Before I had a chance to lay across the table or quickly scoop up the items, he perused the display, looked at me, smiled like a Cheshire cat, and said, "Have a nice day!"

Although we now enjoy spring water from an entirely different water supply company, that embarrassing moment was part of what made my homemade romantic memory so memorable.

Certainly, if time is at a premium, instant romance is a better option than doing nothing at all, but once in a while treat yourself to the fun of the strategic romantic experience. Planning the execution of a romantic fantasy is a thrill you won't want to miss.

Just Do It:

Set a date on your calendar between today and the next eight weeks to plan a romantic fantasy for your mate. Be sure that the preparations take at least a few days in order for you to feel a sense of anticipation. When the unveiling of romance arrives, you'll benefit from the means as well as the end.

In the Mood

Romanticism is not just a mode; it literally eats into every life.

ANITA BROOKNER

Y OU have opportunities every day to make romance a part of your daily life. Whether it shows up in what you wear, where you eat, or how you smell, romance is as easily available as your imagination.

There is something, however, that even an active imagination can't withstand—a romantic mood killer. The ever popular song "I'm in the Mood for Love" reflects the fact that there has to be certain conditions for that "mood" to prevail. There are also certain conditions under which a romantic mood can bite the dust.

Romance has to be preceded by a certain mindset. There is a carefree, "toss it to the wind" attitude that accompanies a romantic mood. If you're fixated on your finances, your work, or your physical appearance, there won't be much of a chance for romance to flower.

Mary Ellen was one lucky woman to be married to Gene. A full-fledged romantic, Gene was always thinking of ways to romance his wife. It wasn't unusual for Gene to surprise Mary Ellen by kidnapping her and taking her to an intimate restaurant or quiet bed-and-breakfast for an overnight getaway. Unfortunately, nine out of ten times Mary Ellen would dip into her grab bag of mood killers and sabotage Gene's romantic plans.

If she wasn't talking about the ten pounds she wanted to lose, she was complaining about a coworker or that she hadn't been able to get a landscaper to replace the trees that had died over the winter. Inevitably, Mary Ellen took a golden opportunity to be romanced and turned it into a mundane moment. Plainly speaking, she ruined the mood.

When your partner makes romantic overtures, no matter what form they take, do yourself and your relationship a favor. Go with the flow. Let your partner romance you and take you away from the inconsequential in life. Whether he or she has arranged for an evening by the fire or a walk on the beach, don't meddle with the mood by obsessing on something that in the scheme of life doesn't matter anyway.

Once a romantic mood gets in full motion, it can take you for an unforgettable ride. But you can't enjoy the trip if you keep stepping on the brake.

Just Do It:

The next time your mate makes the slightest attempt at romancing you, let him or her do it. Table your fixations on the minutiae of life long enough to experience the joy of romance, whether it lasts for an evening or for only a moment.

Presenting . . .

Gifts must affect the receiver to the point of shock.

WALTER BENJAMIN

WHATEVER you do to romance your mate, the impact of your efforts is directly related to your presentation. If, for example, you attempt to make fast food into a romantic dinner and serve it directly from the paper bag you've picked up at a drive-through window, trust me, your mate will be less than impressed. On the other hand, you can take something as unromantic as a bucket of fried chicken and with a little help from a colorful tablecloth, a candle or two, and a park at dusk, you've got the makings of an amorous environment.

Take a standard store-bought greeting card for example. Although a staff of people at a greeting card company has done all the work for you by designing the card's cover and writing its message, you can still use a prefabricated message and come across as the harbinger of love. Presentation is the key.

You'd think that Bridget's husband, Curtis, would be tired of receiving greeting cards from her by now. On the average, he receives three a week, and has since the time they were married four years ago. What makes getting a card from his wife so delightful is not the card, but how it is presented.

"I look forward to how I'm going to get the cards every week just as much as I look forward to reading them," says Curtis. "One day I'll find a card in my briefcase. The next time I'll find it taped inside the lid of the toilet seat. Life with my wife is a real kick."

I'll never forget our eighth wedding anniversary. I was teaching an evening women's workshop at a local hotel when halfway through the evening, I heard a knock at the conference room door. Suddenly, in walked my husband dressed in a tuxedo carrying a dozen pink roses. I was flabbergasted. The roses were gorgeous, of course, but what shocked me most was the manner in which he presented them to me. Needless to say, the women in the workshop were highly impressed.

Given in a mundane, perfunctory way, not even expensive jewelry will make the same lasting impression that a simple gift like flowers or a greeting card will make when given with an eye for presentation. The gift of romance is not in the gift itself, but in *how* it is given.

Just Do It:

The next time you give your mate anything, *design a plan for how you will give it to him or her. Put more emphasis on how you pres-*ent *your partner with the gift than the gift itself.*

Romantically Impaired

A little knowledge that acts is worth infinitely more than much knowledge that is idle.

KAHLIL GIBRAN

OWADAYS, if you are less skilled than the average person at something, you assign yourself the label of being "challenged" whether it be technically challenged, directionally challenged, or as my bald husband calls himself, follicly challenged.

Whenever I give talks about romance I often pose the question "How many of you feel you are 'romantically challenged?' " Invariably, ninety percent of the hands go up. When asked why they feel inept in the romance department, most women say it's because they are so busy that they never make the time for romance. Most men tell me that they simply don't have a clue what "romance" means to a woman so they don't even make an attempt.

My husband and I teach a romance workshop to couples every year the weekend before Valentine's Day. For the past seven years we have conducted the workshop at a different bed-and-breakfast within two hours of Cleveland and have never had a problem filling the inn with men and women eager to become romantically proficient.

One of the reasons our romance workshops are always sold out is because we know exactly what romance means to men and what it means to women.

Ellen Kreidman, Ph.D., author of *Light His Fire* and *Light Her Fire*, explains the difference between how men and women view romance. "One of the most important differences between men and women is that while men need to know women find them sexually attractive in order to give them the emotional fulfillment they crave, women must feel emotionally fulfilled before they can react to their mates' physical needs."

With that information in hand, we design our romance workshops to teach men how to fulfill women's emotional needs when romancing their mates and we teach women how to add the taste of sexuality that men look for in romantic gestures.

Over the years we've invited massage therapists to the workshops in order to demonstrate the importance of touch in a romantic relationship. We've asked various travel agents to talk about easy and affordable romantic getaways. For several years the owner of a local sex boutique has visited the workshop and displayed her wares in order to broaden couples' sexual horizons. Last year, for the severely romantically challenged we invited the owner of a company in southern Ohio called "Romancing Your Love" to talk about his romantic planning calendar service. This company reminds the romantically challenged about important dates such as birthdays and anniversaries and plans for everything from a romantic dinner to elaborate travel destinations.

Nowadays neither a man nor a woman can hide behind the handle "romantically challenged" and get away with it for very long. There are just too many resources out there to make being a romantic anything but a challenge.

Just Do It:

If you consider yourself to be "romantically challenged," a bookstore can be the thing you need to make a change. There is a plethora of books on the subject of romance. Many give you specific ideas on what to do to romance your partner. Your job is to choose an idea and just do it!

The Alternative Called Nothing

The art of pleasing consists of being pleased.

WILLIAM HAZLITT

O VER many years of encouraging people to romance their partners I've heard every excuse in the book why they don't want to. One of the most common excuses is that men and women are afraid of rejection. "What if my husband laughs at me?" "What if she criticizes my efforts?" What if, what if, what if. What if you don't do anything? You'll continue to live in a dull, lackluster relationship and die after years of being a charter member of the ever-popular club of the walking dead.

If you were to look me in the eye and tell me that you've romanced your mate but he or she has never appreciated it, I'd still tell you to stay true to your mission of romance, no matter how uncomfortable it feels. Sometimes you have to feel uncomfortable to reap the rewards of something that is absolutely worth it.

Maxine, a woman in one of my workshops, dug her heels into the ground every time I suggested she surprise her husband with a romantic gesture. "I'm not doing it," she'd say. "The last time I spent the day preparing a romantic candlelit dinner, he was two hours late." But in the same breath, she'd complain about being in a boring marriage of twenty-two years.

I told her that if she didn't romance her husband, she'd still be in a boring marriage, and in ten years, it would be one of thirty-two years. If she did romance her husband, she'd at least have fun planning her romantic gesture and even if he didn't react exactly the way she would like, she'd feel better for having done *something* in her relationship rather than nothing.

A week after she was given the romantic gesture assignment, she came back to class with her tail between her legs. "This stuff really works," she said.

"Yeah," I said. "But you have to work at it."

Working at romance doesn't mean trying it once or twice and when it doesn't go the way you expect, giving up. It means being a vigilant romantic, doing whatever it takes to keep the chemistry going between you and your mate.

When persuading men and women on the vital importance of romancing their mate, I often use this analogy. "If your child were trapped inside of a burning house, what would you do?"

They immediately say, "I'd do whatever it would take to get my baby out of that house, even at the risk of my own life."

Why would you do anything less for your relationship? Your relationship *is* your baby and without it, you would never have had your children. Romancing your mate is as important as rescuing your child. If you don't do it, your relationship will eventually perish.

Just Do It:

If the reason you don't romance your mate is because you're afraid of rejection, feel the fear and do it anyway.

CHAPTER SIX

Embrace Your Sexuality

F ROM the moment of conception, you were a sexual being. Whether your X chromosome linked with a Y chromosome or with another X chromosome, your sexual essence was formed long before you were delivered into the world.

Had you been guided by your natural instincts, without the influence of family, peers, and society, you would have grown into adulthood completely uninhibited about sex. There would be no self-imposed pressure, guilt, or repression surrounding your sexuality. You would feel as free to embrace your sexual self as you feel free to sleep, eat, and breathe.

Whether or not you accept and enjoy your sexuality can depend upon how the idea of sex was introduced to you as a child. If "sex" was a dirty word in your household or if you were admonished for exploring your own body, chances are you've approached your sexuality with caution over the years rather than with abandoned curiosity.

The media wields as much, if not more, influence over your sexual self as does your upbringing. Television, movies, and magazines bombard you with sexual messages that can do everything but affirm your desire to be a healthy sexually-open human being. Sex is instead often seen in the context of violence, manipulation, and shame. Constant negative messages around something that is meant to be a God-given gift will disrupt anyone's sexual self-image.

Take an already shaky sense of sexuality and incorporate it into an adult relationship where it has to withstand the pressures of distractions and you've got a problem. So how do you embrace your sexuality after two, three, or four decades of not doing so? You do it like you would do anything else that is new to you. You learn.

Let me assure you. You are not asexual. Even if your sexual desire is like a faint, dying ember beneath ten pounds of ash, it's still there, waiting to be stirred back to life. It will never be completely extinguished.

To rouse your libido you have to do three things: learn, experiment, and practice. Embracing your sexuality isn't about becoming a sex god or goddess. It's about exploration and mutuality. It means that as long as you and your partner agree to it, anything goes.

Read this chapter with an open heart, an inquisitive mind, and an anticipatory libido. Remember, you were a sexual being before you were anything else. To deny your sexuality is to disclaim your nature and eventually your relationship with your mate.

Invest in Sex

October. This is one of the peculiarly dangerous months to speculate in stocks. The others are July, January, September, April, November, May, March, June, December, August, and February.

MARK TWAIN

I N today's world, financial investment opportunities abound. As enticing as stocks, bonds, and mutual funds are, I can't think of a better way to invest your hard-earned dollars than in your sex life.

How much money do you spend every year to improve the sexual intimacy between you and your mate? My guess is you don't drop nearly as many bills on fueling your sexual fires as you do on fueling your lawn mower.

You might as well accept the fact that pumping new blood into your libido is going to cost you, whether you invest in a book, a video, a sex toy, or a piece of lingerie. The return on your investment will be worth every penny.

In her book, *101 Nights of GRRREAT Sex*, Laura Corn teaches you how to "window shop for sex." By using her tear-out guide to eroticism, you get nearly two innovative ideas a week on how to seduce your partner. The book costs about the same as a tankful of gas for a large van and is one of the many resources available to pump up your passion.

In my hometown of Cleveland, we have a chain of stores called, Ambiance: The Store for Lovers. Located within an hour of any suburb in the area, these stores offer anything needed to spice up a sex life. From relationship books, to massage oils, from lingerie to vibrators, this store has it all.

As soon as our sex life gets the least bit rusty, musty, or dusty, my husband and I go shopping. We gladly spend $30 to $50 each time we visit our candy store of love, knowing we'd spend as much on a quick trip to the grocery store. Salad dressings and laundry detergents are nice, but not nearly as fun as what we bring home from Ambiance.

If you're not fortunate enough to have a "store for lovers" in your neighborhood, then get yourself to a computer that's online. Sex sells, and no more anywhere than on the Internet. Type in the word "sex" and you'll have an instant shopping mall of erotica. Numerous Web sites offer products as well as fresh ideas to incorporate into your relationship.

Whether through the Internet, retail stores, catalogues, or libraries, there is an inexhaustible supply of ideas to help you add flavor to your sex life. Take advantage of them and you'll cash in on your investment.

Just Do It:

Sit down with your mate and review your monthly budget. Whether you have to pull from your savings, or spend less on something else, invest at least $15 a month on your sex life. You can't afford not to!

The Anatomy of a Dinner

Let the stoics say what they please, we do not eat for the good of living, but because the meat is savory and the appetite is keen.

RALPH WALDO EMERSON

S EX and food have a lot in common. They both fuel your body, your mind, and your spirit. Just as you have a choice of what kind of utensils to use whenever you eat, such as a fork, spoon, toothpick, or chopsticks, you have the pick of five senses whenever you get hungry for sex.

Although I employ as many senses as I can when making love, one of my personal favorites is the sense of taste. Assuming your mate has practiced personal hygiene, tasting his or her skin can be a delightful experience. With the advent of flavored body paints, gels, and powders, your partner can provide a feast as good as any banquet.

Joann had enough flavored body paints stashed in her bottom dresser drawer to fill a spice rack. Which paint she'd use on her husband, Daryl, depended on what she had a taste for. If she had a hankering for something sweet, she'd dust her husband with honey-flavored dusting powder and lick it off from the arch of his foot to the dimple in his chin. If she craved the taste of chocolate, she'd plaster his body with a rich, smooth chocolate body paint. Lovemaking for Joann was a smorgasbord.

You might consider certain parts of your partner's body as off-limits, without the help of flavoring. If things like toes, feet, armpits, genitalia, and rectal areas are not what you find particularly appetizing, invest in flavored body paints. Keep in mind that although you might not crave the taste of your mate's toes, he or she craves to be tasted.

Exploring your partner with your tongue is truly an adventure. Traveling up, down, and around your mate's curves and swerves can, however, take its toll on your tongue. Flavored oils and gels can make your road an easier one to traverse.

As enticing as the sights and sounds of sex are, you do your relationship an injustice by not partaking of your sense of taste when making love. Taste your mate with a lick and promise, and you might be tomorrow's dinner.

Just Do It:

The next time you make love to your mate, taste him or her. Whether you choose to flavor your partner or not, enjoy your tongue's tantalizing trip.

The Spousal Arousal

Is that a pistol in your pocket or are you glad to see me?

MAE WEST

HALF the fun of the act of sex is the dress rehearsal. The build up to anything, whether it be a roller coaster ride or intercourse, is what quickens your pulse or stirs your loins.

Although foreplay is important, don't wait until you are in bed to begin. Start early. Be the big tease.

For Becky and Justin, seduction was the foundation of their sex life. They put as much energy into tempting each other with their sexuality as they did making love. Their foreplay wasn't confined to minutes or hours. It lasted one or two days.

One of them would initiate his or her game plan for arousal by setting bait. The lure could be in the form of a note on the bathroom mirror or a sexy message on voice mail. Whatever it was, it sent out a signal to let the other know he or she was the object of seduction.

Becky always packed a lunch for Justin and wrote an erotic message on his piece of fruit whenever she wanted to tease him. That, combined with a sexy e-mail message and an enticing fax, usually drove him to distraction.

Justin knew exactly what to do to whet Becky's sexual appetite. All he had to do was pull on her heart strings by writing a romantic note and attach it to a photo of the two of them. If he really wanted to drive her crazy, he'd write her a poem. Once he spoke to her heart, he went in for the kill by dropping hints about what he was going to do to her in bed.

Becky and Justin know the secret to an active sex life—foreplay to the nth degree. By taking seduction out of the bedroom and incorporating it into everyday life, their sensuality wasn't confined to any one place or time.

The lead-up to sex can be as stimulating as sex itself, but you've got to play the game. Don't merely have intercourse with your mate. Seduce him or her. Be on the prowl for your partner and you'll enjoy the catch.

Just Do It:

The next time you feel like making love to your mate, postpone it. Tease, tempt, and tantalize your partner first. Turn foreplay into a one- or two-day event. Your lovemaking will be worth the wait.

The Call of the Wild

Electric flesh-arrows . . . traversing the body. A rainbow of color strikes the eyelids. A foam of music falls over the ears. It is the gong of the orgasm.

ANAIS NIN

THE sounds you make when you're having sex can add to the blinding thrill of lovemaking. Circumstances can dictate that you make love without making a sound. If your children are awake in the next room or your house guests are in earshot, screaming at the top of your lungs, "Yes, do it to me, baby" is probably not a good idea.

If, however, you are making love in a place where no one can hear you, scream, moan, groan, yelp, or sing the Alleluia Chorus if you feel like it. Think how wonderful the climb to an orgasm feels, let alone the orgasm itself. To expect yourself not to release your feeling of ecstasy by making some sort of noise is nothing short of torture.

Aside from preventing yourself from expressing pleasure, taking a vow of silence during sex does an injustice to your partner and your relationship. One of the best ways for your mate to know he or she is pleasing you is to hear it from you.

Words are wonderful, but sounds can mean more than words. When you're in the throws of an orgasm, chances are you aren't going to be composed enough to articulate your gratitude perfectly anyway. Let your sound effects express it for you.

Howard loved the noises his wife, Stephanie, made whenever they were making love. Her guttural, almost animalistic sounds, were as stimulating to him as anything else in their lovemaking. As she'd ascend, she'd begin with a low moan and end with a roar. Howard nicknamed Stephanie his "wild cat."

Sex isn't supposed to be quiet. What is happening inside your body could easily be translated into a biological fireworks display. You can't expect to zip your lips when every cell in your body is screaming, "This feels incredible!"

If making noise during sex is something you've always wanted to do, but have felt self-conscious, start small. Pay attention to your breathing. Instead of holding your breath or breathing quietly, relax and give into heavy breathing. As you get used to exhaling heavily, add sounds. The more you do it, the more natural it will feel until you gradually work your way into moans, groans, and screams of ecstasy.

You wouldn't think twice about screaming at a Super Bowl game, at your child's sporting event, or if you were told you had won a million dollars. Why hold in your jubilation when making love with the person you care about more than anyone else in the world?

Just Do It:

The next time you and your mate make love, make noise. You'll enjoy the feeling of release and your mate will enjoy hearing your pleasure.

Aqua Sex

So let man consider what he was created;
he was created of gushing water
issuing between the loins and the breast-bones.

QUR'AN

WHETHER you realize it or not, every single day you take part in one of life's most sensual rituals—washing yourself with water. The Romans, remembered in history for their ceremonial baths, knew the erotic power of water. Taking baths for them was not only a matter of getting clean, but a matter of pleasure—sexual pleasure.

Stepping into a warm shower or bath sets off an involuntarily reflex to say, "ahhh" or "mmmmm." The warm soothing water, whether pulsating against your skin or enveloping your body, relaxes you and highlights your sensual nature. I can't think of a better place for you to give in to your sexuality than in the bathtub or shower.

Because your sexual essence comes to the forefront while washing yourself, it only makes sense to double your pleasure and invite your mate to join you once in awhile. Opportunities for intimacy abound with warm water and suds at your fingertips.

My husband and I enjoy taking showers together so much that we had a shower stall custom-designed with intimacy in mind. Stocked with a variety of shower gels, sponges, and our own built-in tile bench, we do more in the shower than get clean.

Five out of seven days, our shower is used for washing the dirt off our bodies. Because my husband leaves for work at the same time that I take our children to school, showering together every day is not feasible. We save "aqua sex" for the weekends.

On either Saturday or Sunday, my husband and I "bathe" together. For thirty minutes, we leave our worries outside the bathroom door and focus on the incredibly sensual feeling of lathering up each other's hair and body.

You don't need a glamour bath to enjoy the simple pleasures of "aqua sex." If you have a small stall shower or a tub shower, even better. So what if you bump into each other or have to maneuver around one another to rinse off the soap. That's what intimacy is all about.

If you and your mate haven't taken a shower together recently or have never done so, it's time to get wet!

Just Do It:

Within the next two weeks, take a trip with your mate to a shop that sells shower gel and accessories. As a couple, decide how to stock your shower or bathtub. Spend time feeling different sponges and smelling different gels. Take bathing as seriously as the Romans did, and you'll get a lot more than clean.

Wham, Bam, Thank You, Ma'am (or Sir)

The feeling of being hurried is not usually the result of living a full life and having no time. It is on the contrary born of a vague fear that we are wasting our life. When we do not do the one thing we ought to do, we have no time for anything else.

ERIC HOFFER

N O one likes the feeling of being dismissed. Whether you want to call it "tossed aside," "disregarded," or "forgotten," being left behind is no fun.

The end of your lovemaking is as important as the beginning and the middle. How you treat it leaves more of an impression than anything you do from start to finish. You can have a mad, passionate "romp in the hay" with your mate, but switch gears too fast and you'll leave an unhappy partner in the dust. Go from orgasmic ecstasy to turning on the television or making a phone call, and your mate will not only feel confused, but used.

If you're one of those people who gets so energized by sex that you feel like wallpapering ten rooms or mowing the back forty, relax. The last thing you want to do is bound out of bed before putting closure to your intimacy.

There is no recommended time period for an after sex cool-down. However long it takes you, it takes you. Whatever you do, don't check your watch or clock. You'll know instinctively when it's time to move on to other things.

Pay attention to your mate's mood and body language. If your partner wants to nuzzle, embrace, or relax in your arms, then he or she isn't ready for closure. Unless you're having a quickie and you are dealing with obvious time constraints, don't rush it. Let yourself, as well as your mate, enjoy the afterglow of intimacy.

Sometimes you'll want to talk about what you just went through: what felt good or satisfied you the most. Sometimes you won't want to talk at all. Lying together in silence can be just the icing on your cake your lovemaking needs. Whether you talk or not, fight to stay in the present moment. Letting your mind race to whatever is next on your agenda will do nothing but shut down the sexual energy you and your mate spent time to create.

Falling asleep immediately after lovemaking is another no-no. Although the post-sex period can make you feel like you've been injected with an anesthesia, floating off into la-la land immediately afterward is as detrimental to your sex life as jumping out of bed and doing twenty-five jumping jacks.

It's up to you and your mate to protect your after-sex stage of intimacy. Granted, it's not as glamorous as the build-up and peak of orgasm, but it deserves as much of your attention. Take care to tenderly end your lovemaking and your lovemaking won't end!

Just Do It:

The next time you make love with your mate, enjoy the afterglow. As you declimax, refrain from talking about anything except your lovemaking. Fight the urge to rush onto your next activity or the temptation to fall asleep. Follow your intuition, and you'll know when you've come to closure.

Coming Attractions

Wickedness is a myth invented by good people to account for the curious attractiveness of others.

OSCAR WILDE

PHYSICAL attraction fuels your libido. But what happens when your libido gets stimulated by your attraction to someone other than your partner?

Whether you want to admit it or not, you are attracted to different people every day. There's a person standing behind you in line at the grocery store. You think to yourself, "Now there's a looker." As you flip through the pages of a magazine while waiting in the doctor's office, your eyes lock onto some photographs of attractive people. A nice-looking employee at work catches your eye. You find a new neighbor particularly appealing. Attractive people are everywhere.

Chances are, along with your sexual stirrings comes a twinge of guilt for feeling this way. Let me put your conscience at ease. If you think you're going to be in a long-term committed relationship and not be attracted to other people, you're deluded. Physical attraction to others is a good sign—it means your sexual drive is in working order.

If, however, you follow through on your feelings of attraction and pursue the person who piques your interest, you put your relationship with your mate at risk. So what do you do with momentary feelings of attraction? Real-

185

ize they are just that—momentary. Allow them to pass through you, understanding that you are not in any way being unfaithful for having them. In fact, if channeled in the right direction, your attraction for another can be used as coal to stoke the fire in your own relationship.

Stephanie had a "thing" for bald men. In fact, her husband's bald head is what attracted her to him. She noticed that over the course of her fifteen-year marriage she had been drawn toward several men who were bald. Her guilty feelings kept her from understanding why the pull was so strong. Once she realized the connection between her attraction and the fact these men were bald, she relaxed and gave herself permission to feel this way and enjoy it. Now whenever Stephanie feels attracted to another person, she recognizes it, and directs her attention and sexual energy toward her husband.

Instead of fighting the fact that you have natural sexual urges, accept them as a God-given gift. There is nothing inherently bad or evil about being attracted to a variety of people during your lifetime. In other words, it's not the sexual energy that matters, it's what you do with it that counts.

Just Do It:

The next time you feel attracted to someone other than your mate, notice how you feel. Tell yourself that what you're feeling is natural. Then use that sexual energy to fuel the fire of your own relationship.

Dare to Disrobe

Brevity is the soul of lingerie.

DOROTHY PARKER

THE mood that pervades your lovemaking often depends on how you approach your intimate time with your mate. Although it's easier to quickly unzip, unbutton, pull off, and drop your clothes before embracing your partner, undressing is a golden opportunity for you to set the sexual stage. The manner in which you disrobe is a telling prelude to intimacy. Remember, presentation is everything!

Don't underestimate what appears to be a merely functional act of undressing. This process can do a lot to stir up the sexual chemistry between you and your mate and can make the difference between lovemaking being good or being really hot.

You have a lot more options than you may think in how you take off your clothes before having sex. You can tease your partner by prolonging your unveiling, taking off only jewelry or accessories at first. When your mate tries to finish the job, tell him or her that you're in control and you will decide what comes off when.

Undressing can be your chance at directing your own erotic mini-production. With the help of lighting, candles, and music, you can perform an enticing strip tease for your lover. You may feel self-conscious at first, but your mate's awe and delight will quickly ease your discomfort.

In the classic sex manual, *Joy of Sex*, Alex Comfort, Ph.D, tells us the impact removal of clothes has on the first steps to lovemaking. He explains, "Clothes and their removal as a kick have, if one wants to be serious about it, a whole biology in terms of 'releasers,' a releaser being what turns somebody on. The releasers for the male are garments that emphasize breasts and buttocks or, like tight panties, simplify the outline of the female. Women are not so dependent on this sort of concrete signaling—having the right man is their chief releaser, a social and emotional one—but many of them have preferences. A well-filled jockstrap, or a man naked from the waist down, can act as part of the preliminary scenery."

Regardless of the type of clothes you peel off, it's the act of unmasking that counts. Jill surprised her husband, Hank, one evening by retiring a few minutes earlier than he and leaving a trail of shoes, socks, earrings, and slacks leading up to the bedroom. When Hank found Jill, she was wearing what was left of that day's attire, ready and waiting to set the mood for making love. Jill took the ordinary act of removing clothes and transformed it into a steamy exposé.

To make love to your mate, you have to take off your clothes anyway, so you might as well make the most of it. Get mileage out of your disrobing and your relationship will benefit.

Just Do It:

The next time you and your mate make love, take your clothes off in style—sensual style. Instead of rushing to unzip, unzip one zip at a time. Rather than taking off your pants, give them a nudge and let gravity do the rest. Undress for your partner instead of simply in front of him or her.

Permission Granted

I know not what you believe of God, but I believe He gave yearnings and longings to be filled, and that He did not mean all our time should be devoted to feeding and clothing the body.

LUCY STONE

YOU are a multifaceted human being. You were created to be emotional, intellectual, spiritual, and, yes, sexual. Your sexuality is an integral part of who you are. Not embracing your sexuality is not being who you were created to be.

Locking sexuality and sensuality out of your relationship with your mate is like imprisoning a piece of your soul. If your soul isn't free to be all it is meant to be, neither is your relationship.

If you won't give yourself permission to embrace your sexuality, let me grant it to you. If my permission isn't good enough, how about God's? Not only does your creator permit you to be sexual, He expects it of you as evidenced by the natural involuntary stirrings you experienced as a child. Would you be created with urgings to explore your body unless it was part of the master plan?

For you to reach adulthood after having spent years exploring your sexual feelings as an adolescent, just to close them off from your partner is for you to deny yourself and your relationship the precious God-given gift of sexuality. Take your creator's advice through the word of the Holy Bible, Song of Solomon, 1:2–4:

> O that you that would kiss me
> with the kisses of your mouth!
> For your love is better than wine,
> your anointing oils are fragrant,
> your name is oil poured out;
> therefore the maidens love you.
> Draw me after you, let us make haste.

What He is telling you, in black and white, is to love your mate with every sense he has bestowed upon you. Use your lips to kiss, your tongue to lick, and your hands to stroke. Your lover's flavor is better than wine, but unless you taste it, you'll never know. Your partner's scent is fragrant, but unless you inhale it, it will escape you.

Your sexuality is your birthright. You inherited it with the commission to use it passionately. Embrace it the way you would embrace your intellect, your emotions, or your spirit. It is as much a part of you as is your arm or your leg. Allow it to live through you and your relationship will reflect God's work.

Think About It:

Think about what it would be like to be asexual, without yearnings, longings, and urges. It wouldn't be much fun, would it? Show your gratitude for your sexuality by using it to the fullest.

The Gift of Vibration

Physical pleasure . . . the bad thing is that most people mis-use and squander this experience and apply it as a stimu-lant at the tired spots of their lives and as distraction instead of rallying toward exalted moments.

RAINER MARIA RILKE

WITHOUT stimulation, sex is sexless. Stimulation is the cornerstone of lovemaking. With the gift of five senses, you have innumerable ways to impassion your partner. You can do it with fragrances, music, choco-late, lighting, and of course, your own personal hands-on touch.

As a means of stimulation, your own two hands are one of your best resources. But by far, the king, the ruler, the cream of the crop of stimulators is the battery-operated or electric vibrator. If you haven't used this lover's lit-tle helper, you *must* introduce it into your sex life.

Unfortunately, there is a stigma attached to vibrators. Contrary to popu-lar opinion, a vibrator is not designed to replace the sexual prowess of men. In their book, *The New Good Vibrations Guide to Sex*, Cathy Winks and Anne Semans tell us that vibrators are meant to enhance the sexual chem-istry between two partners. They say, "Chances are, if your partner knows something brings you that much pleasure, she or he will want in on the action. Seize the opportunity to expand your sexual repertoire, rather than confine it. Instead of assuming that your partner will be threatened or disinterested, take the time to find out how she or he feels. Vibrators may be just the thing to help you break out of a dull routine."

For couples who are used to reaching orgasms manually, the vibrator is a welcomed invention. For men whose mates take longer to reach orgasm when being stimulated by hand, a vibrator can be a wonderful tool. The energy he saves from not having to bring his mate to orgasm manually can be used to excite her in other ways.

A vibrator is not patented only for women. Men can enjoy its oscillating, pulsating effects as well. Used on the genital or rectal area, it will send an already aroused man into a state of euphoria.

Kept by the bedside or in a glove compartment, a vibrator can give you pleasure in the privacy of your own home or while you're on the road. Whenever Michelle and her husband, Nate, went on a romantic weekend getaway, they always stashed a battery-operated vibrator in the glove compartment. As soon as Michelle got tired of reading or looking out the window, she'd reach for her "friend" and a blanket for privacy.

It drove Nate wild to hear and watch his wife reach climax in broad daylight with unsuspecting drivers on all sides. By the time they arrived at their destination, they were primed for passion.

If you haven't done it already, introduce a vibrator into your sex life. I promise you that you won't regret it.

Just Do It:

If you've never used a vibrator in your lovemaking, it's time to do it. Within the next two weeks, pick one up at a local sex boutique. If you're uncomfortable selecting one yourself, call ahead and ask the clerk questions about which type would fit your needs. Ask him or her to reserve the vibrator for you so that you can make a quick purchase when you get to the store.

The Blue Dolphin

Reality leaves a lot to the imagination.

JOHN LENNON

THERE are two types of sexual fantasies. The first kind are those that, if played out, could inflict permanent damage on your relationship. These are the ones where you or your mate think about being seduced by another man or woman, envision your partner making love with another person, or fantasize about anything else that, if enacted, could ruin the trust and health of your relationship. What makes these fantasies so erotic and stimulating is the fact that what occurs in them is forbidden and best not ever happen.

The second kind of fantasy is the kind that is based on anything sexual you and your mate consent to doing together. No one else in your fantasy takes part in lovemaking except the two of you. These fantasies are ones you would truly love to turn into reality, but because you are shy or nervous about making them come true they never materialize. If played out, these sexual dreams will do nothing but excite and electrify your coupleness.

For as long as Veronica could remember, she had wanted to have an orgasm in public. The thought of being with a lot of other people while building up to a climax was a tremendous turn-on for her. It wasn't until twenty years into her marriage that she revealed her fantasy to her husband, Zach, who was astounded by his wife's sexual secret, but ecstatic about its unveiling. From the moment she risked sharing it with him, he was determined to become the magic genie who would make her wish come true.

And so it was on their twenty-first wedding anniversary, prior to leaving for a romantic getaway, that Zach handed Veronica a box in which was the key to unlock her long-awaited desire. As she opened her gift, she felt a shiver run down her spine in anticipation of her fantasy finally coming to fruition.

Inside the box was a vibrator in the shape of a miniature rubber blue dolphin. Fastened to it were elastic straps designed to fit around her waist and thighs. A remote-control dial controlled the dolphin's vibration and could be attached to her waistband or belt.

Zach was as excited, if not more excited, about Veronica's fantasy becoming a reality than she was. He couldn't wait to watch his wife be catapulted into ecstasy in front of unsuspecting strangers. Together they decided that the best place for Veronica's dream orgasm was a dimly lit romantic Italian restaurant near where they were staying for the night.

Veronica walked into the intimate setting with her husband by her side and the blue dolphin in place. Once the waiter took their order for dinner, Veronica tested out her vibrator by turning it on low and slowing increasing it to full throttle. Although she felt and heard dolphins' hum, no one else in the restaurant, other than her husband, had a clue what was happening under their dinner table.

It took only a few minutes for Veronica to get over her feeling of self-consciousness. Once the dolphin started to work its magic on her, she became relaxed and almost limp under its spell. With each visit from the waiter, Veronica lowered the vibration on her aquatic friend, making the next buildup even more intense. Meanwhile Zach's appetite for food took a backseat to his appetite for sex. He was so aroused by his wife's self-pleasure that he barely touched his pasta primavera.

Veronica could easily have had an orgasm right after the salad was served, but intentionally prolonged her satisfaction until immediately before dessert. As their waiter refilled their coffee cups, she adjusted her vibrator to low for the very last time. Once their server turned on his heels, Veronica decided to let her ecstasy burst forth. Flushed with desire, she locked onto her husband's eyes as she climaxed and made her sexual fantasy come true.

That night was a turning point in Veronica and Zach's physical relationship. By sharing and acting out the fantasy she had kept hidden for so many years, she broke through the barrier of sexual inhibition. From that point on, they felt free to act out anything their hearts desired, as long as it was only between the two of them.

Tell your mate your secret sexual fantasies and you're halfway to sexual freedom. Act them out together and liberty is yours. Dreams really do come true.

Just Do It:

Talk with your mate about a sexual fantasy you would like to turn into a reality. Plan its execution down to the last detail. Mark your fantasy on the calendar. Make it happen.

Shackles of Love

My reason is not framed to bend or stoop; my knees are.

MICHAEL DE MONTAIGNE

SOMETIMES all it takes to change your lovemaking from enjoyable to ravishing is a little twist. In this case I mean a twist of a scarf or a tie. Gentle bondage is something that, if you've never tried, is worth the attempt.

Done with the utmost care and sensitivity, this form of restraint can give just the erotic edge you need to send you or your partner into orgasmic flight. What makes bondage so tantalizing is the idea that one of you is being forced into pleasure. Because your hands and feet are tied, the feeling that you can't control what is being done to you, although you really can, is what heightens your sexual response.

The key to using bondage successfully is to allow your partner the ability to get free from your love hold at any time. If there is the slightest fear or anxiety attached to bondage, it will turn sour. Many partners enjoy pretending to be forced into submission. For those men and women, I suggest they agree on a code word to use to let their mate know when they want to be released. Whether you use a silk scarf, a soft rope, or a bathrobe tie, always make sure you tie it loosely enough around your mate's hands and feet so he or she can move with ease or get free at a moment's notice.

For the partner who is doing the restraining, the pleasure is no less intense than for the one who is being restrained. As one woman who loved tying up her husband shared, "It's like being a kid in a candy store. With everything out on display and looking so delectable, it's hard to decide which goody to choose." Normally a high-powered, decision-making executive, this woman's husband became putty in the hands of her authority.

Shelly and Frank liked to incorporate bondage into a slave and master fantasy game. One of them would be the conqueror whose job was to subdue and restrain the other. They'd go so far as to chase each other around the house and play hide-and-seek until one of them was captured. Their game of captivity was always carried out with an air of playful sexuality so that by the time one of them was caught, he or she succumbed willingly to sensual servitude.

Restraining your partner can be a turn-on, but the best part of the game of bondage is pleasing your mate once the shackles are in place. Before diving into your partner's hot spots, take the time to tease and titillate him or her. Focus on the areas on your mate's body that you may never have explored before. Use your hands, lips, tongue, and teeth to caress, lick, and nibble your partner to ecstasy.

Although bondage in any other context except fun and playfulness is unacceptable, as a sexual game between two lovers it is absolutely permissible. It is just one of the many ways for you and your mate to embrace your sexuality.

Just Do It:

If you and your partner have never restrained each other during lovemaking, take baby steps before plunging into full-body bondage. Restrain only one hand or foot at a time. As he or she feels comfortable, bind the rest of your partner.

Love Me, Whip Me, Love Me

Subordination tends greatly to human happiness. Were we all upon an equality, we should have no other enjoyment than mere animal pleasure.

SAMUEL JOHNSON

IT is not uncommon for a man or woman in a relationship to have a fantasy of being sexually dominated by their mate. You may be one of these people. Wanting your mate to rip off your clothes, force you on the bed, and ravish you is not an unusual sexual desire.

As long as neither you nor your partner get hurt in the process, your fantasy can easily become a reality. The first step to making your sexual dream come true is to share it with your mate. Even if you never act it out, chances are you'll both become aroused and feel intimate by simply talking about the fantasy. If, on the other hand, you decide you want to play out your desire to dominate or be dominated, go for it.

Sylvia and Bruce's lovemaking had always been soft and tender. Being sensitive to each other's needs, they were careful not to go to extremes in pleasing one another. Their sex was caring to the point of being polite.

Sylvia loved Bruce's gentle manner, but for years had secretly wanted him to rule over her body. She had played the scene several times through her mind. Bruce would burst into the bedroom and order her to take off her clothes. Not satisfied with the speed with which she undressed, he would rip off whatever was left of what she was wearing. From that moment on, she would become the slave and he the master. His lovemaking would be firm enough to make her feel dominated, but not so rough as to scare her. Her sexual fantasy was an incredible turn-on for her.

After making love one night, Sylvia got the courage to share her fantasy with Bruce. Although he was completely shocked, he was game for acting out Sylvia's hidden desire.

Because this kind of lovemaking was so foreign to them, they decided to talk about the details of their sexual vignette before playing the parts. They chose their bedroom as the setting, picked out what outfit Sylvia would wear, and even rehearsed. The most important element of their production was their decision to say "curtain down" if either of them became uncomfortable and wanted to stop the fantasy.

Joan Elizabeth Lloyd, author of the book, *Come Play With Me: Games and Toys for Creative Lovers*, sets sound ground rules for fantasy play in an adult relationship. She says, "Both parties must understand before they begin that either has the right to stop the game at any time. As a matter of fact, each has the obligation to stop whenever he or she gets the feeling that things have gotten even a tiny bit uncomfortable. If you cannot stop when asked, or if you're not sure you are able to say stop when you want to, *don't play*."

As long as you and your mate have agreed on the ground rules for your domination fantasy, go ahead and play the game. Even if you never act it out, at least share it with your partner. He or she may be stunned by your secret desire, but once the shock wears off, you'll both be turned on.

Just Do It:

If you have a hidden sexual fantasy, domination or otherwise, share it with your mate. If you both agree to act it out, enjoy the show!

Forbidden Fantasies

Oh, the secret life of man and woman—dreaming how much better we would be than we are if we were somebody else or even ourselves, and feeling that our estate has been exploited to the fullest.

ZELDA FITZGERALD

EVERYONE has sexual fantasies. You may think about what it would be like to make love to another man or woman. You may even include your mate as a spectator in your fantasy.

Fantasies are normal. You're not a sexual deviant. The question is, what are you going to do with your sexual fantasies? Are you going to keep them to yourself, or are you going to share them with your intimate partner?

If you've kept your "secret garden" to yourself, you've kept the lid on one of the most erotic, pleasure-producing tools in your sex life. What could be more exciting than imagining doing something that you would never do in a million years? Sharing a sexual fantasy with your partner lets him or her in on the secret and sends you both into forbidden, but exciting territory.

During a rather routine night of lovemaking, Miranda decided to share her favorite sexual fantasy with her husband, Jerry. Not sure how he would react, she broached the subject carefully. Thrilled that Miranda was actually thinking about sex rather than what was on her "to do" list, he was anxious to hear all the details.

As Jerry caressed and stroked Miranda, she revealed her "massage" fantasy. She described herself lying on a table being rubbed, pressed, and kneaded by an older, attractive man. With each circular motion of his hands, the man moved closer to the sides of her breasts. As she lay there, open and vulnerable to the masseuse's touch, she pictured Jerry sitting in a chair in the corner of the room watching. Not only was he watching, he was telling the masseuse what to do to her.

Miranda and Jerry's lovemaking was more sensual and heated that night than it had been their entire marriage. Jerry was so turned on by his wife's sexual fantasy that he mustered the courage to share his own.

He told Miranda he was in a client's office. After he and his client were finished with business, the client left the room and his administrative assistant appeared in the doorway, wearing a French maid costume. She sauntered over to Jerry and sat in his lap, with her long legs straddling either side of him. "Would you like something to drink?" she said as she pulled one breast out from under her black corset. Jerry bent his head over her breast and tasted, while in reality, he feasted on Miranda's.

As a result of their sexual confessions to each other, Miranda and Jerry felt more intimate than ever before. Their lovemaking, which had become perfunctory over the years, was revitalized.

Your fantasy is your own sexual fairy tale. It isn't real, but the hidden feelings of passion and desire are. Let yourself go and think the unthinkable. Give into your wildest sexual imaginings. Risk sharing them with your mate and your gamble will pay off in a big way.

Just Do It:

Pick one sexual fantasy and share it with your mate the next time you and your partner make love. If you don't have any sexual fantasies, invent one.

Anything Goes

Love ceases to be a pleasure, when it ceases to be a secret.

APHRA BEHN

B ETWEEN two consenting adults in a long-term committed relationship, anything goes. As long as permission is granted between you and your mate, the sexual sky is the limit. And why not? One of the cardinal rules of being in a lifelong relationship with someone is to commit not only to each other, but to a sense of adventure and exploration.

Whatever resources you and your mate use to expand your sexual repertoire is completely up to the two of you. In fact, living with your own deliciously sexual secrets, confidences meant for only you and your mate, is what can keep the sexual fires burning for decades. The idea that no one has a clue what you do behind closed doors, between the sheets, or on the kitchen counter makes living with your partner forever stimulating.

Paula and her husband, Fred, kept one of their sexual secrets locked in a fireproof box in their attic. Inside their hidden treasure was a series of homemade sex videos they had produced, starring the two of them. Whenever they had an interruption-free night, they'd either shoot a new movie or enjoy hours of reruns.

Instead of home videos, Dan and Kimberly's private stash contained flavored body paints. Whenever they were up for something out of the ordinary, they'd pull out their paint brushes and plastic tablecloth.

One couple I know has a CD collection. Not your ordinary assemblage of classical or jazz music, this collection consists of sexual fantasy CDs. Whenever they want to invigorate their sex life, they alternate putting on the headphones. While one listens, the other touches.

Doreen knew early on her relationship with Jake that he, at times, loved to wear women's underwear and lingerie. The soft, silky feel of the fabric was a turn-on for him. Not threatened in the least by his feminine fetish, Doreen occasionally surprised Jake with a pair of silk panties hidden in his briefcase with instructions for him to put them on once he got to work. Doreen was as sexually stimulated imagining Jake in his panties as Jake was wearing them.

Denise loved to be dominated by her husband, Les. Just thinking about being blindfolded and lovingly tied to the bedposts with velvet cords while Les tickled, stroked, and manipulated her to orgasm drove her wild.

All of these men and women understand that to live with someone for the rest of their lives takes a "no-holds-barred" attitude. As long as they explore their sexuality with respect for their mate's bodies and feelings, there isn't anything they can't do.

The same goes for you and your mate. The resources for a fresh, exciting sex life are inexhaustible. For you to make love in the same way, at the same time, and in the same place is inexcusable. The only thing in your way is the lack of permission. Grant it and anything goes.

Just Do It:

Sit down with your mate and make a list of twelve different things to do differently in your sex life, one for each month. Put your sex calendar to use and you'll give new meaning to the celebratory wish, "Happy New Year!"

CHAPTER SEVEN

Show Me the Money

ONEY, whether it comes in the form of stocks, bonds, or cold, hard cash, will always be a part of your life. Once you've accepted that money is the medium of exchange in our society, you have several choices. You can fear it, worry about it, abuse it, or preferably understand your relationship to it and embrace it.

From the time you were a child and asked the meaning behind a penny or a dollar bill, you've had a relationship with money. Over the years you've developed your personal perceptions about our world's currency and your ideas cannot help but impact your relationship with your mate. Almost everything you do with your partner, from traveling to turning on the air-conditioning, is connected to your relationship with money.

It stands to reason that when a man and woman meet and realize they want to spend the rest of their lives together, they would want to learn as much about each other's relationship to money as they could. Being such a driving force in their future, you would think they wouldn't hesitate to discuss their financial habits, fears, and perceptions.

In reality, money is the last thing a couple talks about before they get married. Instead, madly in love and hungry for a future together, they are oblivious to the impact money will have on their partnership. They don't realize they will interact with the almighty dollar more times during a day than they will interact with each other.

How you view money is more important than how much you make. No amount of money will make you comfortable if you aren't first comfortable with *it*. Because you bring yourself to any relationship, your financial fears and perceptions are part of the package. That's why your intimate relationship with money must be shared with your partner.

Talk to each other about money messages you received as a child. Share your biggest financial fear with your mate. Explain your financial goals. Describe your spending and saving habits. To have a healthy, productive, and prosperous life with your partner, you can't possibly keep financial secrets. If you haven't done it yet, expose your financial side to your mate.

Account for Your Relationship

Marriage: It pays dividends, but only when you pay interest.

ANONYMOUS

CARA and Lyle couldn't understand it. They had a similar lifestyle to their friends Maya and Sid—a two-income family with children in grade school—yet Maya and Sid were always going away together on either weeklong vacations or bed-and-breakfast weekend getaways. Cara and Lyle hadn't gone away together since their first anniversary eight years ago.

The difference between Lyle and Cara and their friends was a simple one. Their friends committed to making a financial investment in their relationship. Lyle and Cara didn't.

When Cara asked Maya how she and Sid managed to travel together every year for a week, Cara learned that they had formulated a game plan to be able to sneak away. Maya told Cara that she had opened a savings account exclusively for their relationship. Everything that was deposited into and withdrawn from the account was to be used for the enjoyment and growth of their relationship.

Maya explained that every time she and Sid received an unexpected check for anything, such as a refund from an overpayment on a bill, interest from their checking account, or the extra money they'd occasionally find in their coat pockets, they'd deposit it into their relationship fund. Although their deposits were often small, they eventually added up to enough for Maya and Sid to get away alone as a couple.

The money they would save in their relationship reservoir usually covered the cost of their accommodations. For the times when they had to fly where they were going they used a different strategy. Maya and Sid applied for a credit card that awarded them free air miles according to how much they spent. The only self-imposed restriction on the credit card they had was to charge only as much as they knew they could pay off each month. They decided to put as many of their fixed expenses—the cost of gasoline, food, utilities, and medical bills—onto their credit card every month. By the end of every year, they'd earn enough air miles for two free domestic flights or one free international flight.

You and your mate invest in everything from new clothes to your child's education. If you want your relationship to survive, you should begin investing in it as well. The dividends are quite nice.

Just Do It:

Within the next week, go to a bank and open an account to be used for only your relationship. It should cost you nothing. Begin depositing any unexpected income into your new "relationship account." After one year, you should have enough money for you and your mate to get away together.

A Goal Worth Setting

I have always thought that one man of tolerable abilities may work great changes, and accomplish great affairs among mankind, if he first forms a good plan, and, cutting off all amusements or other employments that would divert his attention, make the execution of that same plan his sole study and business.

BENJAMIN FRANKLIN

CHIEF operating officers of international corporations, owners of small companies, and even in-home entrepreneurs wouldn't think of running their business without an operating budget. As unromantic as this may sound, your financial relationship with your mate is no different than a business partnership. When it comes to money matters, you and your partner have to take a managerial view in order to survive the long haul.

Sharon Krnc, Vice President of investments at First Union Securities and a well-known investment advisor in northeast Ohio, says, "Having a financial goal or goals is a key ingredient to setting up a budget. Most people I know spend their entire adult life working for a living; i.e., earning money so they can provide for their families the basics of food, clothing, shelter, education, and some of the discretionary diversions that make life more enjoyable—like sailing in the Caribbean or seeing a Broadway show. An amazing fact that I have discovered during my career as an investment consultant, is that while people spend many thousands of hours, days, and years earning a living, they rarely spend sufficient time in learning to become adept in personal budgeting and setting financial goals."

The only way for you and your mate to set financial goals and create a personal budget based on those goals, whether your goal is to build a house, get an advanced degree, or travel around the world, is for you both to know what is important to you. What are your priorities? What is it you want to accomplish before you leave the planet?

Once you've decided within your own heart and mind what you want out of life, you have to devise a calculated plan of how you're going to get what you want. If you think you don't know enough about managing money to financially plan your life, you have two choices. You can learn as much as possible about financial planning so as to become your own investment consultant, or you can hire a financial expert to advise you.

My husband and I chose the latter option and haven't regretted our decision. Although our investment consultant has advised us on how to invest our money, she wouldn't have been able to make a dime for us if we hadn't known what we wanted to do with our money. Once she learned our financial goals were geared toward our children's education, travel, and retirement, she knew which investment plan to implement.

As soon as we had a clear understanding of our financial objectives, creating a personal budget felt like a natural next step. Before my husband and I make any major purchases that could affect our personal budget, we always think about what impact our purchase would have on our fiscal goals. If we think that buying whatever it is we want to buy would drain our education fund or retirement fund, we either decide not to make the purchase, or we revise our objectives.

It's great to have options and choices when making financial decisions, but if you don't have financial goals to start with, trying to decide how to spend your money is like playing Eenie, Meenie, Miney, Moe while wearing a blindfold.

Your relationship with your mate is meant to be nothing short of romantic, fun, and intimate. If, however, it can't "operate," it *will* eventually go out of business. If you haven't done it already, set financial goals now—before your relationship goes bankrupt.

Just Do It:

If you and your mate have already set financial goals, make an appointment with each other within the next week to review them and possibly revise them. If you've never set financial goals, make an appointment with each other to discuss what is important to each of you. By the time your meeting is over, you'll know where you want your hard-earned money to go. I can guarantee you it won't be down the drain.

Money Memories

The childhood shows the man,
As morning shows the day.

JOHN MILTON

G REGORY felt suffocated. He couldn't understand why he was having such trouble breathing since he had outgrown his childhood asthma thirty years ago. All he knew was that he and his wife, Leela, were arguing more, and he had begun to use his inhaler again.

Leela and Gregory's confrontations usually revolved around money. What would start as a conversation about overspending traditionally flared into an argument with Gregory feeling like a carefully monitored little boy. All he wanted was to feel like a hardworking, middle-aged man who deserved to buy a woofer and a tweeter for his stereo system if he felt like it.

Gregory saw his wife's money habits as tight, constraining, and life-limiting. He couldn't fathom how she could live with so many financial restrictions. Gregory couldn't understand because he and Leela had never talked to each other about their personal relationship to money.

What Gregory didn't know was that Leela was raised by parents who drummed a clear and simple message into her head: Money doesn't grow on trees so you better use it sparingly. To say that her parents were frugal would be an understatement.

Leela had distinct memories of her father driving on the freeway during a family vacation and always stopping on the side of the road to rest the car for ten minutes every hour, explaining to his two children that resting the car prevented unnecessary wear and tear on it.

While most of society was into the swing of a disposable lifestyle, using paper plates, cups, napkins, and silverware, Leela's parents prided themselves on never throwing anything away. Family picnics were always made up of reusable plastic dinnerware and linen napkins. "No sense in spending money on something you'll just throw away when you own things that can be reused," Leela's mother would say.

Leela's childhood memories around money helped form her values and approach to spending and saving. Gregory's memories helped form his monetary values as well, but he was taught to spend money and enjoy life as well as save for the future. Unfortunately, Leela and Gregory entered into a lifelong, committed relationship without ever having shared each other's financial upbringing.

Suze Orman, money expert and author of *The 9 Steps to Financial Freedom*, tells us, "Messages about money are passed down from generation to generation, worn and chipped like the family dishes. Your own memories about money will tell you a lot, if you take that step back and see what those memories taught you about who you were—and whether those memories are still telling you who you are today."

Because your perceptions and habits around money are formed early in your life and are an integral part of who you are, denying your mate such revealing information is the same as embarking on a lifelong journey without the proper navigational equipment. Without sharing each other's relationship to money, you and your mate will be thrown off course in no time.

Whether you and your partner have been together one day or fifty years, sharing your money memories with each other will enlighten your relationship and open the door to understanding. Regardless of how different your financial views may be, it's never too late to get back on course.

Just Do It:

If you've never heard your mate's childhood money memories, ask him or her to share them. Even if you and your mate have already shared your childhood memories about money, do it again. In order to understand your partner's perceptions about finances, you have to hear his or her story more than once.

The Spirit of Money

Probably the greatest harm done by vast wealth is the harm we of moderate means do ourselves when we let the vices of envy and hatred enter deep into our own natures.

THEODORE ROOSEVELT

I T'S been called evil, a temptress, and the source of greed, jealousy, and hate. By itself, money is none of these things. It is simply energy. How that energy is directed is how money becomes defined.

I wholeheartedly agree with William Bloom's perception of money. As author of *Money, Heart, and Mind: Financial Well-Being for People and Planet*, he says, "I also have this sense of the true spirit of money. It is far more than a unit of account and a store of value. As an agent, a medium and a language that passes between human beings, it is a creative facilitator of human relationship and human community, a facilitator of ingenuity, productivity, and wealth. It is a creative medium that serves human relationship."

How, if at all, has money served your relationship with your mate? As a language, how has money been communicated between you and your partner? Has it been passed back and forth freely and openly or has it been hoarded and used manipulatively?

Debbie was a scorekeeper and had been ever since she was a child. To her, money was something she counted, recorded, and remembered. As a little girl, birthdays and Christmas were holidays spent noticing how many presents she was given compared to her older sister. As a teenager, Debbie was caught rummaging through wastebaskets in hopes of finding gift receipts to confirm her suspicions of her parents paying more for her sister's clothes than for hers.

As much as Debbie's parents worked to discourage her from financial scorekeeping, she carried this childhood habit into her relationship with her husband, Cary. Instead of accepting whatever her husband gave her, she always compared one gift to another. Rather than embracing the flow of money into her life in whatever form it took, she was a slave to her expectations. Her rigid perception of money and what she thought it was supposed to provide for her put a wedge between she and her husband.

As William Bloom says, "Money needs to breathe more freely . . . It is a medium of material communication between human beings. It has helped create fantastic material wealth and complexity, but its spirit is emotionally confused and neurotic. It needs to flow and to move."

The energy of money can't buy you and your mate happiness. It can ride on the coattails of the happiness you already have. If allowed to flow between you in a generous and soulful way, money will energize your relationship. It's not the money that matters, but what you do with it that counts.

Think About It:

Starting today, think differently about money. Instead of tangible paper and coins that appear to be the key to your security, look at money as intangible energy that allows you to love and live more fully. Channeled in the right direction, money is a transformative force.

Money Mentor

Ignorance is not innocence but sin.

ROBERT BROWNING

THE EEO, Equal Employment Opportunity, is now one of the building blocks of our society's foundation and is an important principle upon which our nation thrives. Equal Financial Opportunity is an important building block for your relationship with your mate, one that will help you prosper and thrive individually and as a couple.

Equal Financial Opportunity in a relationship simply means that both you and your mate have the same chance to become investment educated, money management savvy, and well versed in your day-to-day finances. No matter who is delegated to handle the checkbook, bank statements, or investments, both you and your mate need to seize the opportunity to learn as much as possible about the ins and outs of living with money.

If you are the one who directs the financial show in your household, you have a duty to become a money mentor to your mate. It is up to you to teach your partner how to run the "family business" in the case of your absence. Make sure your mate knows where you keep files on every savings account, checking account, IRA, mutual fund, as well as anything else in your portfolio.

Even if your mate is clueless as to what your financial paperwork means, respect your partner enough to expose him or her to its whereabouts and to the phone number of your financial advisor. By hoarding this information out of fear or a need to feed your ego, you may not live to regret it, but your partner will.

Morissa became one of the ever-growing statistics among women—she had outlived her husband. After forty-nine years of being married to the same man, she felt as if she'd had been thrown off a precipice into a bottomless pit of sorrow and ignorance. Aside from being wracked by pangs of grief, she was surrounded by the stark reality of financial inexperience.

Her husband, Carlisle, had never told her much about their money matters. At the time of his death, all she knew was that their house was mortgaged. To what bank, she didn't know. It took several months and the help of her children to put together the financial puzzle her husband had left behind.

Money mentorship lies not only in the hands of the person in control of the finances, but also in the hands of the one who is supposed to learn. If you are the mate who is in fiscal darkness, be willing to be taught the basics of money management. Whether you think you're good with money or not, you'll be forced to deal with it sooner or later. When the time comes, be prepared.

Just Do It:

If you are the financier in the family, teach your mate how to manage your money in your absence. If you are the student of finance, pay attention and learn.

Reap What You Sow

I would as soon leave my son a curse as the almighty dollar.
ANDREW CARNEGIE

IT goes against the grain. It's contrary to conventional wisdom. The idea that once you're an independent, self-sufficient adult you should spend your money and enjoy your life so that you eventually die broke is an unorthodox concept.

Society trains you to believe that your goal is to save, save, save until at the time of your death you're worth as much as possible. Personal assets symbolize the much sought-after golden ring. Once you've accumulated as much wealth as you can, you die and pass your hefty nest egg to your heirs—the government, being one of them.

I've enthusiastically joined the ranks of thinkers such as the authors of *Die Broke*, Stephen M. Pollan and Mark Levine. They suggest, "Rather than looking to acquire assets in some futile quest for immorality, in the new world you should focus instead on getting the maximum use out of your assets and income. There are financial tools available that can ensure you won't outlive your money while guaranteeing you'll leave nothing behind. Free from the burden of building an estate, you can use your money to help your family and improve your own life."

Morris and Adele owned a shoe store until they sold it when they were in their sixties. Having built a diversified financial portfolio, they had enough money to enjoy the lifestyle they had worked for. Although they no longer wanted to own a business, they loved working with the public and continued to sell shoes part-time.

Their newfound freedom and profits from sound investments gave them the chance to enjoy their money and watch their children enjoy the fruits of their labor. They decided they didn't want to wait until they were lying in a casket to give their children and grandchildren their inheritance. They wanted to watch their loved ones receive their legacy while they were still alive.

Morris and Adele's son had been in school working toward his doctorate, and hadn't been able to afford to take his wife and three children on a traditional week's vacation. Adele and Morris were ecstatic to be able to surprise them and take them to Disney World for five days.

The fifteen thousand dollars that Morris and Adele gave to their daughter helped finance her dream of owning a small neighborhood bookstore. Their financial boost to their daughter's dream gave them an incredible amount of joy as they watched her bloom into a thriving entrepreneur.

Morris and Adele's game plan was to stretch their dollars over their life span in a way to allow them to travel together and with family, enjoy the amenities of life, make memories as a couple, and share their prosperity with their loved ones right up to the very last minute. The only thing they planned on passing down to their children was enough money to cover the cost of their funerals and any debts they may have incurred from living a full, rich life.

As extreme as their strategy for living may sound, it is what I believe to be a much preferred option to the standard version of work, work, work... save, save, save... die, die, die. I opt for the work, save, give, and enjoy method myself.

Think About It:

Think about how much time you've spent working to earn money. How much of that time has been spent enjoying the fruits of your labor? Do you and your mate really want to pass along your harvest having never gotten the chance to derive pleasure from it as a couple? It's time to reap what you sow.

Savvy Spending

Thank God we're living in a country where the sky's the limit, the stores are open later and you can shop in bed thanks to television.

JOAN RIVERS

BOTH Gordon and Robin liked to shop. It didn't matter whether it was for new shoes, another book, or more perennials for their garden, they found time to "hit the mall" with regularity. They enjoyed the fun of the search and the thrill of the purchase.

What they didn't enjoy was the sinking feeling they got when they realized they had racked up too many purchases on their credit card and could only afford to pay the minimum payment each month.

To curb their spending, Robin and Gordon agreed to give themselves an allowance. They decided that $150 a month for each of them would be a fair distribution for fun money. Although they were proud that they had ended the month within five dollars of their limit, they were stymied when they didn't have enough in their checking account to cover the month's bills.

Gordon and Robin's problem wasn't that they hadn't stayed within their allowance, but that they had allocated too much money for the allowance to begin with. Having never taken the time to track how much they spent each month, they arbitrarily assigned $150 for each of them.

Robin and Gordon's monthly deficit kept recurring for one simple reason:

They were operating without a budget. Because they had no frame of reference from which to understand their money, they simply couldn't manage their money.

Debra Wishik Englander, author of *How to Be Your Own Financial Planner*, tells us, "Writing down all your expenses on paper is an easy way to keep track of what you're spending. By keeping a written record of your expenses and your earnings, you'll learn more about your spending and your savings habits. Armed with this new knowledge, you can then make positive changes in your finances. You can choose to save more or spend less on discretionary purchases."

For Gordon and Robin, living within a budget didn't mean they couldn't allocate a monthly allowance for their spontaneous shopping sprees. It just meant that they could determine what kind of allowance they could afford.

Never seeming to have enough money doesn't come from not having enough money, but rather from not knowing how much you have to spend in the first place. A budget makes you accountable to your own account.

Just Do It:

If you and your mate have never created a budget as a way to record your expenses as well as your income, now is the time to do it. As tedious and annoying as it may seem, making sure that what you spend is less than what you earn is worth every minute of going over the details.

A Valued Risk

*Risk! Risk anything! Care no more for the opinion of others,
for those voices. Do the hardest thing on earth for you. Act
for yourself. Face the truth.*

KATHERINE MANSFIELD

MONEY management can be a risky business. If, however, you play life safely and never invest in things like stocks, real estate, or a new business venture, you'll minimize the risk. You'll also minimize your net worth and your fun.

I am a firm believer that some things in life are worth the risk. The key to whether or not something is worth investing your hard-earned money in is whether or not there is an important personal value attached to it.

You and your partner will make hundreds of decisions in your lifetime together, financial as well as others. To move forward in life and stay on the same path together requires a commitment from both of you to remain true to your mutually agreed upon value system. Conflicts over spending money arise in relationships when one mate values something differently from the other mate. That is why making sure you and your mate have congruent values before you get married is so crucial.

My husband, Dick, and I knew before we got married that travel and taking vacations was a priority. Married eighteen years, we've both cherished the love, laughter, and memories we've created whenever we've traveled with each other or with our children and extended family.

Our belief in the importance of vacationing was put to the test in our first year of marriage. I was six months pregnant with our son, Dick's business was about to fold, and we had no money. As a wedding present, one of my husband's colleagues gave us a week's stay in her vacation home in Hilton Head, South Carolina. During our last day there, Dick noticed that one of the hotels on the island was offering tours of their time-share units. Being curious myself, I agreed to go along on the tour.

This particular time-share was owned by Marriott and was located right on the beach. As we walked through the unit, we periodically scraped our jaws up off the floor. We fell in love with the spacious two-bedroom, sleep-six condo that overlooked breathtaking, rainforestlike landscaping surrounding two pools. A view of the ocean could be seen from two large picture windows. As I stood on the veranda and soaked in the sights and sounds of pure luxury, I fantasized about someday bringing our yet-to-be family to a place so wonderful.

Thanking the time-share salesman for his tour, I walked away sighing and wistfully saying, "Someday . . ." when I suddenly felt my husband's hands on my shoulders. He spun me around, looked me dead in the eye, and said, "I want to buy that time-share unit."

Incredulously I looked at him and said, "Are you nuts? We can't afford that."

To which he replied, "We can put it on our credit card." I couldn't believe what I was hearing. We had a baby on the way, a business on the way out, and he wanted to put $6400 on a credit card!

While I was still in shock, Dick sat me down and reminded me how much we valued vacation time together and that our dream was to be able to take yearly vacations with our children someday. The difference between my husband and I was that *my* "someday" was years later and *his* was that very instant. He convinced me, however, that there was absolutely no reason to wait, that every year we delayed our decision would be one more year of missed memories with our children and each other.

The more he talked, the more I felt grateful that he was so well-rooted in our value system and that he respected our relationship enough to discuss wanting to take a risk rather than taking it without my support. He had a clear vision of what we believed was important—what we thought mattered in life.

It is with great joy and pride that I can say that this summer will be the twelfth straight year we have taken our family, and often friends, to our vacation home in Hilton Head, South Carolina. At the time we invested in our future, it was a daunting risk—one I am forever grateful we took.

Just Do It:

If it hasn't already happened, it will. A risk is going to be presented to you and demand you to either turn it down or take it. If the risk carries with it something of value to you and your mate—something that gives meaning to your lives—it's worth taking.

Love What You Do

Man's unhappiness, as I construe, comes of his greatness; it is because there is an infinite in him, which with all his cunning he cannot quite bury under the Finite.

THOMAS CARLYLE

I N many couple's lives, so much focus is put on earning money that what a man or woman does to make a salary gets very little attention. People are so busy scrambling to earn enough to cover their expenses to keep up with their lifestyles that whether or not they like what they're doing becomes secondary.

Not liking what you do for a living can put a huge amount of stress on your relationship with your mate, for your relationship is only as happy as the two people in it. If what you're doing to earn your wages is not your heart's desire, no amount of money will make you happy. Money can pacify your mind, but not your soul—and your soul won't let you rest until it wins out.

My husband has worked in the same industry most of his adult life. As a psychologist and management consultant he is waist-deep in corporate structure. Although he enjoys the monetary rewards of his much sought-after expertise, his soul has been sending him distress signals for years. Begging to be rescued from a lucrative yet familiar field, his soul has whispered his heart's desire and he has finally decided to listen.

Born to be a psychologist, my husband loves to spend one-on-one time with people, listening to their feelings, their thoughts, and their dreams. A cheerleader dressed in business apparel, he enjoys nothing more than motivating people to follow their hearts. His passion for seeing people succeed has led him to start his own executive coaching business.

Although he continues to be steeped in corporate America, my husband realizes that the best thing for him and for our relationship is for him to do what he loves, if only for a few hours a week. His dream is to eventually retire from his day job and devote more time to his coaching career. In the meantime, working part-time at his soul's desire makes him happier as an individual and us happier as a couple.

Living with a mate who earns an income but is miserable with how he or she does it is like living with a time bomb waiting to explode. If the bomb doesn't get diffused, be prepared for your relationship to take a big hit.

Just Do It:

If you hate or are just bored with what you do to earn a living, take one baby step this week to change direction. Whether you talk to someone who is in a field you've always wanted to be in or you read about your desired profession, do something to get you thinking about doing what you would love to do. Take at least one small step every week until your steps add up to a giant leap and you find yourself and your relationship in a happier place.

Live to Give

Generosity is nothing else than a craze to possess. All which I abandon, all which I give, I enjoy in a higher manner through the fact that I give it away.

JEAN-PAUL SARTRE

ALTHOUGH the following statement may seem like a contradiction, I believe it represents pure truth: The ability to give is the greatest gift you will ever receive. You were born with this ability and it will never be taken from you, but how you give back to the universe or whether you give at all is completely up to you.

How the act of giving affects your life as a couple is nothing short of remarkable. When you and your mate are open to opportunities for giving, whether it be individually or as a couple, you automatically attract abundance into your lives. As long as you give for the joy of giving, without fear of losing something or expecting something in return, more love, money, health, joy, peace, and happiness than you can imagine will be yours.

My husband and I have given both in fear and in joy and the difference between the two is incomparable. It's amazing. When we look at our checkbook and reason that by giving a certain amount of money we'll be giving beyond our means but do it anyway, our desire to give outweighs our fear of lack. We are filled with wonder when somehow we end up with more money by either getting an unexpected bonus check, tax refund, or financial gift in one form or another.

If, however, we give calculatingly, concerned that by giving we'll lose instead of gain, our giving goes flat. It's void of joy and therefore we receive exactly what we give—little or nothing.

Whether you give to a charity, a school, a church, or a homeless person doesn't matter. What matters is that you and your mate allow yourselves to be open channels for the spirit of giving. Trust your instincts. Listen to your heart and you will always be shown in which direction to give.

I awoke this morning as I awake each morning by thanking God for my life and requesting one thing: that I be given the chance to give today. It is a selfish request in that I know that by giving I will receive. I settle for no less than pure joy. I live to give.

Just Do It:

If you and your mate aren't used to giving your money away, learn to do it. Because true giving means giving joyfully, you have to start listening to your heart. It will tell you without a doubt to whom or what you should give. Sit back and enjoy your inherent gift to give, then accept the abundance that is sure to follow.

Expect to Be What You Already Are

Wealth is an inborn attitude of mind like poverty. The pauper who has made his pile may flaunt his spoils, but cannot wear them plausibly.

JEAN COCTEAU

IT'S a popular belief that the rich get richer and the poor get poorer. I'm convinced that in many instances the poor stay poor because they live their lives thinking about and expecting scarcity. They are surrounded by lack and therefore believe that lack is their destiny. They live down to their expectations.

The same principle applies to you and your mate. You and your partner have a simple choice to make. You can decide to believe you are prosperous, thereby creating prosperity or you can believe you are poor, thereby creating scarcity.

You both were born with a functioning brain, an active imagination, and the ability to communicate. You came into this world with eyes to see, hands to create, and a spirit to guide. You were a bundle of prosperity the moment you inhaled your first breath. No one, not your parents, your teachers, nor your employers have robbed you of your inheritance called prosperity.

If you think prosperity doesn't belong to you, it is only because *you* have turned away from it. Your mate is no more prosperous than you are and vice versa. You both have within you all you will ever need to live a life full of giv-ing and receiving. You lack nothing and you never will. Whether you believe that is completely up to you.

In his book *You Can Have It All*, Arnold M. Patent says, "Everything is provided for us. The reason we are without anything is because we believe we cannot have it at that moment, or more accurately stated, we really do not *want* it. Remember, having, believing, and wanting are synonymous. That is the law of cause and effect. If we do not have anything we think we *want*, it is only because we do not *really* want it."

If you and your mate are in an unattractive financial position, you have some soul and mind searching to do. What is your true belief system for your present moment and your future? Are you seeing your situation as a dead-end one with fear and scarcity as your roadblocks or are you open to multiplying the abundance you've had all along?

You *are* prosperous. It is your destiny. It's up to you to follow it.

Think About It:

Within the next week, you and your mate need to talk to each other about whether each of you is a prosperity thinker or a scarcity thinker. Trace back to the beginning of your mind-sets. How long have you been thinking this way? If you're a prosperity thinker, think on. If you're a scarcity thinker, think again, and differently.

Wish Upon a Contract

The palest ink is better than the best memory.

CHINESE PROVERB

WE assume that romance, dedication, and undying love are all that is needed to keep a couple together for a lifetime. But as much as we may recoil from this fact, legal contracts and agreements are also part of the ties that bind.

There was a time when the phrase "prenuptial agreement" made the hairs on the back of my neck stand at razor-sharp attention. My reaction to hearing that a couple had drawn up a premarital financial contract to prevent post-marital burns was the same reaction I'd get from hearing nails scrape across a chalkboard. "What about faith and trust in a relationship," I would think. "If a man and woman love each other, shouldn't they share and share alike?"

Now gloriously happy in my second marriage of sixteen years, I don't think that way anymore. Having a family of our own, consisting of one son from my husband's previous marriage and two children between us, I finally understand the benefits of a prenuptial agreement. Although we don't have one, I can now see its value.

With the help of an investment consultant, we've acquired enough assets to force us to look at how we might someday like to distribute what we've accrued to our children. Having grown up in a family business, some of which was bequeathed to me, I am very protective of my inheritance. As much as I love my stepson, I feel it's important to pass a portion of my parents' legacy on to my two children. By the same token, if my husband were to die before me, he wants to ensure that his son receives his share of the other assets.

Although my husband and I never signed a prenuptial agreement, we discussed our feelings and thoughts about how we would someday distribute our resources. Once our funds grew large enough, we used estate planning as a vehicle for communicating our wishes.

In a world where blended families are as common as dual-income families, it's important to put in writing to whom you want your money and assets to go, whether they are distributed while you're alive or after you're gone. Without a written contract, whether it be pre- or postnuptial, your lifelong desires may turn into cold, hard decisions made by your local and/or federal government. Talking about your wishes with your mate is a first step, but without the second and vital step of putting them in writing, you might as well wish upon a star.

Just Do It:

Don't count on a verbal agreement between you and your partner to ensure that your wishes come true. The state acts on written agreements, not hearsay. Before the sun sets on this day, talk with your mate about how you would like your funds distributed after you're gone. Before the sun sets on too many more days, make your wishes legal—put them in writing.

On the Contrary

Light is meaningful only in relation to darkness, and truth presupposes error. It is these mingled opposites which people our life, which make it pungent, intoxicating. We only exist in terms of this conflict, in the zone where black and white clash.

LOUIS ARAGON

ONE of the most universal complaints I've heard from couples over the years is that one mate is a spender and one is a saver. Lamenting about their money management differences, these couples miss the favorable reality of their situation—that in all likelihood, their financial styles balance each other out.

Think about it. What would life be like if you and your mate were both spenders? If this is the case for you, my condolences. Each of you would have difficulty reigning in the other because you'd be too busy signing checks, using your charge card, or visiting the automatic teller machine to notice your partner was doing the same thing. In short, your middle name would be Debt.

If, on the other hand, you were both savers, true, you'd be without debt, but you'd also be without a life. Tucking money away for a rainy day is admirable, but as far as I know, the afterlife is without a weather pattern.

Because opposites attract, my guess is that between you and your mate, one of you is of the savings species and the other is of the spending variety. If so, know that it is meant to be that way. One of the reasons you were attracted to your partner was that you realized, if only on a subconscious level, that your mate had qualities in him or her that you didn't have and may never have. The closest way to ever attaining these attributes was for you to live the rest of your life with someone who owned such characteristics. Possibly without realizing it, you were drawn to the idea of balance.

As nature continuously models for us, balance is the foundation of harmony. For food to grow, there must be a balance between sun and rain. For animals to live proportionately, there must be a balance between the predators and the prey. Without balance, the world would be chaotic and eventually self-destruct.

What is true for nature is true for your relationship. Instead of creating turmoil over the fact that you and your mate have different money management styles, use those styles to your advantage. If you spend when all your mate would have you do is save, or your mate spends when all you would do is save, be grateful you and your partner bring each other back to center. The middle ground is a wonderful place to be.

Think About It:

Before you get into World War III over the fact that your mate doesn't handle money the way you do, consider the fact that he or she is around to neutralize the way you handle money. Think about what it would be like if your partner had your exact money habits. Now think about how nice it is to have balance.

Surviving a
Financial Storm

> After you have exhausted what there is in business, poli-
> tics, conviviality, and so on—have found that none of these
> finally satisfy or permanently wear—what remains? Nature
> remains.
>
> WALT WHITMAN

I F a list of all the things human beings worry about was made, the one
thing that would glaringly stand out more than any other would be
money. Whether it's worry over not having enough, what to do with what
you have, or how to make more, money and your relationship to it have the
potential to cause tremendous stress, strain, and tension during your lifetime.

Grappling with your relationship with money is hard enough as a single,
uncoupled adult. Take your dysfunctional relationship with the almighty
dollar and plug it into your relationship with your mate and you have the
makings for major problems.

I know a couple who like almost everyone, worries about money. The difference between them and the average husband and wife is that they have a
strategy for staving off financial worries before their fretting chips away at
the foundation of their relationship.

Not long ago, Julian was told his company would be bought out and that
he'd have the choice to either relocate or lose his job. Not wanting to relocate,

he chose to leave the company. He had six months to plan his future before his last day on the job.

"That period could have been the most stressful time in our marriage," said Julian's wife, Reva. "Although we had a steady income for six months and Julian was actively searching for a position with another firm, we had to live with the possibility that Julian wouldn't have a new job once his old job ended."

Whenever they began to feel anxious about the future, Reva and Julian would hop in their car and drive to the park. "Walking the bike paths in our metropark helped us cope more than any amount of career counseling or financial planning," said Julian. "Moving amongst the massive trees and delicate flower trails made us realize that somehow we would be taken care of. The awesome, resilient power of nature reminded us that we, too, could survive the storms of life."

As it turned out, Julian received a job offer with a local firm before his last day at his company. Reva and Julian credit the perfect employment timing to their jaunts to the park. They turned what could have been an excruciatingly worrisome time into a faith-filled, spiritual experience. They adopted the philosophy that if divine order was good enough for nature, it was good enough for them.

Think About It:

The next time you're tempted to become engulfed in the shroud of financial worries, think about nature. Reflect on the tiniest most helpless plant or creature and its ability to survive the elements. Surviving a financial storm is no less possible for you than surviving a thunderstorm is for a weed.

Handle It

Money doesn't talk, it swears.

BOB DYLAN

MONEY is power. Because it carries so much potency, the use or misuse of it can easily destroy anything in its path—including your relationship. That's why managing it is a delicate process.

Who "handles" the finances in a relationship can make the difference between a well-run ship that's on course and a craft that is tossed aimlessly from one wave to another. Although there are relationships in which both partners share financial duties, most couples agree to have one or the other pay bills, reconcile bank accounts, and oversee the monthly budget.

From the start, Preston knew he shouldn't have been the one to preside over the finances. The day after the wedding, his wife, Chelsea, handed him the checkbook, assuming he knew what to do with it. Preston had handled his own money during college, but was forced to open several different checking accounts after becoming overdrawn in one right after the other.

Afraid to tell his wife that money management was not his strong suit, he took the checkbook from her and hoped he would not mess up their finances too badly. Within three months, Preston and Chelsea's bank account had been overdrawn four times and had never been balanced. Finally, after weekly heated arguments and a disconnected phone, Chelsea demanded the checkbook back. Gratefully Preston relinquished his job as financier.

So much pain and anguish can be avoided if couples make a conscious decision about who is best suited to manage the day-to-day finances. Egos aside, you and your mate need to have an honest conversation about money management and common sense. Who between the two of you is the most likely candidate to balance the checking account, pay the bills, and oversee the debits and credits of your daily life?

Just because one person signs most of the checks does not mean the other has no say in financial goals or budgeting ideas. It simply means that one of you is better at running the nuts and bolts of an efficient household than the other.

If the financial aspect of your relationship feels unsteady, take a long hard look at who's at the wheel. It might be time to switch drivers.

Think About It:

Before deciding whether you or your mate is best suited to manage the daily finances of your relationship, talk about which one of you likes handling the checkbook responsibilities, who abhors doing it, and finally, who would be the best at it. Go with who would be the best at it.

CHAPTER EIGHT

To Your Health

YOUR physical, mental, emotional, and spiritual health acts as a cradle to your relationship with your mate. Your good health is a vital support system for your coupleness. You wouldn't think of putting a newborn baby into a dilapidated cradle or basinet for fear that it might collapse. Your relationship should be equally protected by surrounding it with good physical, mental, emotional, and spiritual health.

Your life together as a couple is a living, breathing entity and will benefit from good health, suffer from poor health, or fall somewhere in between. Because your relationship is only as healthy as the two people in it, it stands to reason that you and your mate have the power to affect its well-being.

The next time your partnership ails, whether it's suffering from poor communication, a lack of sex, or financial disaster, you need look no further than you and your partner to find the source of ill health. The next time your relationship begins to falter, do a self-check of your own physical, mental, emotional, and spiritual well-being. Pay attention to your body. Are you experiencing pain or fatigue? Are you mentally sharp or are you distracted, depressed, or stressed? Are you in emotional pain and feeling worried, angry, or resentful? Look at the state of your spiritual health. Do you give yourself time to reflect and pray? Do you have a relationship with God? These questions invite you to know yourself intimately on every level. Without self-knowledge, your relationship's chance of long-term survival is slim at best.

It's easy to look to outside influences as the source of your relationship's malady. It's easy to blame your career for causing stress rather than looking to the power within you to handle the responsibilities of your job. It's simple to point a finger at your mate for making you do too much around the house rather than taking responsibility for setting limits by saying *no*. It's easy to accuse society for setting a hectic pace instead of developing the self-discipline to create time and space to quiet your mind in prayer and meditation.

Don't take the easy way out and look outside of yourself for reasons for ill health or imbalance. It is an ongoing temptation that only distracts you from the true reason for unhappiness in a relationship—*you*. Here's to *your* health. Here's to your relationship! Here's to your taking responsibility for your health within your relationship.

Give Your Mate an Airful

Of all the ebriosity, who does not prefer to be intoxicated by the air he breathes?

HENRY DAVID THOREAU

I F someone told you that one single breath could strengthen your relationship with your mate, would you believe it? It's true. Health professionals will tell you that one of the best ways to stave off tension and anxiety is to breathe. As inconsequential as this involuntary act may seem, if done properly, its effects are far-reaching.

Under anxious circumstances, your knee-jerk reaction is to hold your breath. As soon as you stop breathing, you automatically tense up your muscles and block the flow of oxygen to your brain, making it less likely for you to think clearly. It's amazing how long you can unconsciously train yourself to hold your breath. Although it's a wonderful quality to have if you're snorkeling underwater, lung control is not going to help you in your relationship.

Three deep breaths from your diaphragm, inhaling through your nose and exhaling through your mouth, will give you more instantaneous results to calm anger, reduce anxiety, and alleviate frustration than any medication I know. Combined with closing your eyes, deep breathing prepares you to meet most, if not all, of life's challenges.

Kirk was the first to admit it—he was reactionary. It didn't take much for him to respond emotionally to a situation. Whenever he did, his wife, Claudia, recoiled. The more he'd go off on his warpath, the less she wanted to interact with him. For Kirk, learning to breathe in the midst of frustration or anger is what saved his marriage to Claudia.

Now whenever Kirk feels like he's about to blow his top, he stops talking, closes his eyes, and takes three deep breaths. Inhaling slowly buys him time enough to collect his emotions and remove himself from the situation until he gathers his senses.

You have a wonderful resource at the tip of your nose that will not only nourish your body, mind, and spirit, but also your relationship. That resource is air. It is limitless, abundant, and yours for the taking.

Just Do It:

The next time you find yourself about to explode, stop. Close your eyes and take three deep breaths. If you need to, remove yourself from the situation and repeat your breathing again. Breathe until you feel calm and can think clearly again. Proceed with your relationship.

Reaching Your Limit

I was angry with my friend:
I told my wrath, my wrath did end.
I was angry with my foe:
I told it not, my wrath did grow.

WILLIAM BLAKE

WE all have limits. You and I have the inalienable right to say *no*. We were born with this right and at no given time has it ever been or ever will be taken away. Your job while you're on this earth, and particularly in your relationship with your mate, is to use that right.

Even in the most intimate relationship, such as one with a spouse, there must be boundaries; lines that should not be crossed. Without limits, without the freedom to say *no*, you will surely lose yourself in what I call limitless love. Under the guise of loving your mate, it is possible to neglect loving yourself, thereby laying the groundwork for an unhealthy, unbalanced relationship.

Taking advantage of someone is not something most of us consciously set out to do. If, however, another person provides a steady opportunity to take from him or her, we'll usually oblige his or her unspoken but clear request to become a doormat.

A marriage where one mate figuratively wipes his or her feet on the other is a relationship with a huge problem. The fatal mistake, however, lies not

244

with the person doing the wiping, but with the person allowing it to happen. As unhealthy as it is to take advantage of your partner, it is more unhealthy to be the one who gives until there is nothing left to give.

Carla loved to entertain. Whether it was a casual evening of card playing or a formal black-tie gala, she enjoyed nothing more than opening her home to guests. Carla's husband, Barry, met Carla at one of her parties and knew from the beginning of their relationship that being a hostess was her passion. He didn't, however, expect to feel like a proprietor of a party center within the first few months of marriage.

Carla devoted each weekend and some weeknights to entertaining family and friends. If she wasn't having people to dinner, she was hosting a basket or Tupperware party. With every social gathering, she solicited Barry's help to run errands, clean the house, or rearrange furniture.

For the first few weeks Barry obliged and even enjoyed opening his home to people, but after the seventh week of spending his only day off fetching ice and other party goods, he couldn't stand it anymore. He knew that if he didn't set limits for what he was and was not willing to do, his increasing resentment would damage his relationship with his wife.

In a calm but firm manner, Barry explained to Carla that he was feeling resentful about spending much of his free time helping her plan parties. He told her he would be willing to share his home with guests, but would only be able to help by giving her two hours of his time between 9:00 and 11:00 A.M. on Saturdays. By setting clear, specific limits, Barry did the best thing for himself and for his relationship with his wife.

Dr. Henry Cloud and Dr. John Townsend, authors of *Boundaries: When to Say YES, When to Say NO, To Take Control of Your Life*, tell us, "Remember that a boundary deals with yourself, not the other person. You are not demanding that your spouse do something—even respect your boundaries. You are setting boundaries to say what you will do or will not do. Only these kinds of boundaries are enforceable, for you *do* have control over yourself. Do not confuse boundaries with a new way to control your spouse. It is the opposite. You are giving up control and beginning to love."

For the health and longevity of your relationship, you must love yourself and your partner enough to learn to say "no." Resentment toward your mate comes from not knowing your own limits. Gift yourself and your relationship with the knowledge of what is and is not acceptable to you. Sit back, relax, and enjoy the benefits of boundaries.

Just Do It:

If you feel that your partner is taking advantage of you, realize you are responsible for allowing it to happen. Rather than resenting your mate, set clear and specific limits for yourself. Say no.

A New Low

I am in that temper that if I were underwater I would scarcely kick to come to the top.

JOHN KEATS

IF you're an American male or female adult, chances are you will suffer from some form of depression at one point or another in your lifetime. The spectrum of depression ranges from a mild case of the blues to psychotic depression requiring immediate psychiatric care. You and your mate will, at some point, fall somewhere between the ends of this spectrum.

Eugene couldn't pinpoint exactly when his depression descended. All he remembers is that he began having a hard time getting himself dressed for work. A heaviness would fall over him while taking his morning shower. The smallest tasks, from shaving to putting on a pair of socks, became huge mountains that felt insurmountable. His drive to work seemed like a drive to an electric chair.

Eugene's wife, Dawn, had always been an upbeat, happy person, but even she was feeling the effects of her husband's low mood. Where their family of four used to have lively dinner table conversations, she'd catch Eugene staring off into space during supper. When awakened from his reverie, he would apologize but finish his dinner quietly. Eugene's change in personality was taking its toll on his wife and on their relationship.

It wasn't until Dawn noticed a change in the sound of her husband's voice that she decided they needed to talk about the obvious. He was depressed.

Once very animated, his voice had lost its intonation. He had begun speaking in a monotone.

One of the things that helped Eugene face his problem of depression was his willingness to face his family history. His mother had struggled with depression her entire adult life.

Doctors Laura Rosen and Xavier Amador, authors of *When Someone You Love Is Depressed*, tell us that genetic, biochemical, and psychological factors contribute to depression. They say, "All life changes, positive and negative, bring stress. For a person who has a biochemical susceptibility to become depressed, a major life event can precipitate a depression."

In Eugene's case, he had been working for a company that had recently been bought out by a huge conglomerate. Major changes were made in the company that affected his work environment and the way in which he was paid. No longer feeling like a vibrant, valued member of a corporate team, he felt pushed aside and unappreciated. Although he had been a loyal employee for more than twenty years, Eugene felt helpless to change the situation. His feeling of helplessness coupled with his genetic predisposition for depression is what convinced him he needed help.

If you suffer from depression or have a mate who suffers from depression, know that you are not alone. You are in the company of millions of other people and need not suffer from the isolating feeling of depression or the isolating feeling of living with someone who is depressed. There is help for you and for your relationship with your mate.

Just Do It:

If you or your mate suffers from depression, have a conversation with each other about how you're feeling. The first step to making positive changes is admitting there is a problem. Once you've decided to address the situation, approach it from two sides—emotional and physical. Your general physician can give you basic information about your health and direct you toward another professional, either a psychologist or psychiatrist who can lead you closer to a solution.

A Gut Feeling

Every human being has, like Socrates, an attendant spirit, and wise are they who obey its signals. If it does not always tell us what to do, it always cautions us what not to do.

LYDIA M. CHILD

YOU and I both have intuition resting inside of us. It is a gift, nestled within our soul and ready to guide us whenever called upon. One of the healthiest things you can do for yourself and your relationship is to listen to it. Unfortunately, many people turn a deaf ear to their own intuition. They get a gut feeling, a nudge, a knowing, and instead of following the gift of clear guidance, they doubt their internal compass and follow outside advice.

One of the best ways to stave off resentment in your relationship is to learn to trust your gut feelings. If you're unclear about a situation, certainly ask your mate for his or her ideas. Examine your options and when the choices are spread before you, use your gut to make the final decision.

When I was given the chance to follow my intuition a few years ago, I seized it with gusto. My husband and I were flying to Las Vegas to meet another couple for a weekend of nonstop entertainment. It was a freezing, blizzardlike November day in Cleveland as we sat on the runway for two hours watching the wings of our plane be de-iced. As we finally began to taxi toward our takeoff position, the plane's brakes came to a screeching halt. The captain of the plane announced that we had to go back to the gate because of a mechanical problem. After a half-hour inspection, the captain of the aircraft announced that although the mechanics had verified that the computer system that controlled the balancing mechanism in the plane was faulty, they had a backup system and would be cleared to take off momentarily.

Upon hearing the captain's words, every bone in my body told me to get off of the plane. It was as if I had an alarm system hardwired into my gut and it had gone off. As my husband rebuckled his seat belt, I looked him in the eye and said, "I'm getting off this plane." In response to his incredulous statement of "What? We're about ready to take off," I stood up, grabbed my carry-on bag and said, "I'm getting off the plane. Are you coming with me or not?" Not waiting for a reply, I beelined it to the front of the plane to a flight attendant who looked at me with consternation and said, "Excuse me, ma'am, you need to be seated for takeoff," to which I replied, "I want to get off of the plane. Please open the door." Exasperated, she radioed the ground crew to open the luggage compartment and retrieve our luggage. As I learned later, we hadn't been the only passengers the ground crew had been asked to accommodate.

Although my husband was momentarily infuriated with me, and the plane we left eventually landed safely, I had to do what my intuition told me was right for me. Had I listened to my husband and stayed on the plane, I would have been a nervous wreck the entire flight, angry at him, and angry at myself for having listened to him instead of my intuition. In short, it wouldn't have been healthy for our relationship.

I believe when you follow your gut feelings, you are always guided to the best outcome. When you ignore your intuition, you usually live to regret it. In my father's case, he didn't.

Thirteen years ago, my father had a heart attack and was told that his only option for recovery was to undergo a procedure called an angioplasty that would open up his clogged artery. I stood by my dad's bedside as the doctor described the procedure. I could see that my father was clearly uncomfortable with the prospect of having a catheter attached to a balloonlike mechanism snaked through the artery running from his groin to his heart. No amount of explaining or diagram drawing erased my father's furrowed, worried-looking brow.

The morning of his scheduled angioplasty, a friend stopped by to see him. In response to his friend's asking him how he was feeling, my father said, "I don't know. I don't feel right. Something's not right." After my dad's visitor left, his internal gut-based alarm sounded. He got himself dressed, packed his suitcase, and marched up to the nurse's station to announce that he was checking out of the hospital. Under much pressure from the nurses and medical staff at the hospital, my father ended up listening to outside forces instead of the force within him. My father had the angioplasty and died on the operating table.

My father taught me an invaluable lesson: Never doubt your intuition. To be true to your relationship with your mate, you must be true to yourself. Your "self" speaks to you and wants nothing more than for you to listen. When you do that, it frees you to walk a path of peace and joy—a basis for a glorious relationship.

Just Do It:

The next time your gut tells you to do or not to do something, listen to it. Paying attention to the wisdom within you will empower you and your relationship.

Beat the System

When you suffer an attack of nerves you're being attacked by the nervous system. What chance has a man got against a system?

RUSSELL HOBAN

IT is not a revelation to discover that the stress of everyday living can erode the human body, mind, and spirit. Pressures, time constraints, and life's little annoyances can ruin your health. Because you are half of the equation that adds up to your marriage, your health directly affects the well-being of your relationship.

Vernon never worked well under pressure. Unfortunately he was employed by a company that was driven by the bottom line. As a salesman, Vernon was constantly under pressure to meet a monthly sales quota. Convinced that he was dispensable relative to his performance, Vernon was a walking bundle of nerves.

Once he was home, his stressed-out nature lay dormant, merely waiting for the minutiae of life to set him off into an emotional frenzy. As soon as his power drill quit working or the television show he wanted to watch was pre-empted, he'd have a stress-related temper tantrum.

Vernon wasn't handling life well at all and his relationship with his wife, Dominique, suffered for it. His tension-filled demeanor had a direct affect on how he and Dominique communicated. Vernon was on edge most of the time so when he was asked a question, his response was always impatient and biting. Swamped in worrisome thoughts about his job performance, he was incapable of focusing long enough to listen to his wife whenever they had a conversation. Stress consumed their marriage.

Dr. Lyle H. Miller and Dr. Alma Dell Smith, authors of *Stress and Marriage*, describe the ramifications of stress in a lifelong relationship. They say, "Every human relationship has its stress points, and marriage is no exception. The problem is not that there are stress points, it's that stress points, neglected, turn into fracture lines, and fracture lines weaken relationships, making them ever more vulnerable to stress. Neglected fracture lines become the fault lines that devastate marriages."

Think about all the things you have to manage: your money, your household, your time. Managing these things creates the one thing that needs managing more than anything else—stress.

If you let it, life can wreak havoc on your nervous system. Get help and beat the system!

Just Do It:

If stress is eating away at you and your relationship, call a nearby hospital that will be able to provide you with information about a stress management program. If the hospital doesn't have one, the staff should be able to point you in the right direction.

Detach with Love

There is nothing heavier than compassion. Not even one's own pain weighs so heavy as the pain one feels with someone, for someone, a pain intensified by the imagination and prolonged by a hundred echoes.

MILAN KUNDERA

S HIRLEY couldn't sleep. Her mind raced and her stomach churned. As she stood staring out the window at a neighborhood streetlight, she popped another antacid. Shirley had been waking up at 2:00 A.M. for the last two weeks, ever since her husband, Abe, got the news.

For months, Abe had been waiting to hear whether or not the promotion he was up for was going to be his. Now, after thirteen long weeks, he was told that the decision about the position for vice president of marketing would be delayed for three more weeks.

Abe, a man with a usually calm and quiet nature, appeared edgy and nervous lately. Shirley knew how much he wanted the promotion. She loved her husband so much that she found herself wishing and fretting about his situation more each day. His possible promotion was the first thing she thought of when she woke up, the last thing she thought of when she fell asleep, and now, the only thing she thought of as she stared out her window at 2:00 A.M.

Shirley was exhibiting more than empathy and concern for her husband and his situation. She was enmeshed in it, and dangerously so. In caring about her husband to the point of taking on his emotions, she put their relationship at risk. Her objectivity was gone. Instead of being compassionately supportive, she became ensnared in the problem, thereby stirring up what was an already sensitive situation. Her worrying about whether or not Abe would be the new vice president made him feel more nervous and created a huge amount of tension in their relationship. What Shirley needed to do was to love and care for her husband, but to do it with detachment.

Understanding your mate's problems and dilemmas is the cornerstone of a loving, empathic relationship. A listener with a caring and attentive ear is what your partner wants. What your mate doesn't want or need is for you to jump into the emotional waters with him or her. Be present for your partner in a way that shows love and understanding. Then take an emotional step back, let go of the situation, and detach for the sake of your own health and the health of your relationship. Being a caring but somewhat objective observer is what compassion is all about.

Just Do It:

The next time you feel the impulse to take on your mate's emotions, stop. *The last thing your partner needs is a clone of him or herself. Detach from your mate's emotions, but do it with love and compassion.*

Madness to the Max

Insanity is often the logic of an accurate mind overtasked.
OLIVER WENDELL HOLMES, SR.

Y OU'VE heard of them; you may have even taken advantage of them— mental health days. Whether you use your personal days, your sick days, or your vacation days, sometimes you just have to excuse yourself as a professional or a homemaker and give yourself the gift of an empty calender or schedule.

The stress that precipitates your taking a mental health day for yourself is often the same stress that wears on your relationship. Pressures at work build up, conflict at home reaches a fever pitch, or the things on your to-do list feel like they're eating you alive.

Just as you save a day specifically for you and you alone, you need to set aside an occasional day as a mental health day for your relationship with your mate. Once you've worked out the logistics to free up time for each other, it's up to both of you to decide what would be the best thing to refresh and rejuvenate your coupleness.

One couple I know, Evan and Paula, drop everything they're doing and make a beeline for their pop-up camper whenever their relationship begs for a mental health day. To them, their eighteen-foot recreational vehicle is the best medicine for an ailing stress-ridden relationship. Surrounded by fresh air and woods, they pump peace and quiet into their partnership as if pumping gas into their car.

"Distractions are reduced to a minimum," says Paula. "No phones ring, no children call our names, and best of all, there's no television to compete with."

Evan explains, "With nothing to concentrate on, other than the beauty of a sunrise and sunset, we can focus on each other."

When you're stressed to the max, I advocate getting off the merry-go-round of everyday life and taking care of yourself. Once you've done that and feel refreshed and ready to carry on, don't forge ahead without looking back to see how your relationship is faring. It, too, may have suffered the slings and arrows of outrageous stress. If so, it deserves a mental health day.

Just Do It:

If what surrounds you and your mate is sheer madness, proclaim for yourself and your relationship a dose of sanity by taking a day off from the real world. The mental health of your relationship depends on it!

Move!

Our growing softness, our increasing lack of physical fit-ness, is a menace to our society.

JOHN F. KENNEDY

FITNESS gurus agree on one thing: to stay healthy, you've got to *move*. It's common knowledge that a sedentary lifestyle will catch up with you, often leading to heart disease, illness, or depression.

Physical exercise not only contributes to your health, it pumps new blood into your relationship. Everyone has heard of the "couch potato" syndrome. You know the one I mean—where a man sits in front of a football game drinking beer and eating potato chips or a woman becomes glued to three hours of prime-time soap operas.

As "The Love Judge" on *The Morning Exchange,* Cleveland's and the nation's longest-running morning television talk show, I have answered questions weekly from viewers who want help with their relationships. One question that gets asked more than any other has to do with how to get a mate away from the TV and its accomplice, the remote control. The television station gets letters, calls, and e-mails mostly from women all over the city saying they're tired of their mates "lumping out."

If you're one of those people who has a tendency to turn into a slug the minute you walk through the front door after work, looking to collapse and be technologically entertained, you're not going to like what I have to say.

Believe it or not, exercise gives you more energy. When you feel so tired you can barely walk from point A to point B, one of the best things you can do for yourself is to exercise. Take a walk, do some calisthenics, or ride your bike. When you're finished, you'll have gotten an incredible energy boost.

Whether you exercise alone or with your mate, moving your body for an extended period of time will rejuvenate your relationship. It has to. Because you will have done something for yourself, you'll have more energy to invest in your relationship by doing things like talking with your mate, giving him or her a massage, or planning a date night.

Your relationship is only as healthy as the two people in it. Take responsibility for your half.

Just Do It:

Exercise at least three times a week, preferably more. It doesn't matter what you do as long as you move your body. The new surge of energy you'll get will spill over onto your relationship and make you feel more alive for yourself and your partner.

The Dance Of Denial

Overemphatic negatives always suggest that what is being denied may be what is being asserted.

JONATHAN RABAN

Y OU haven't felt well for a while, but you tell yourself you're too busy to go to the doctor. You convince yourself that you don't have time to be sick. A positive attitude does contribute to healing, but only if denial isn't its silent partner. If you ignore physical symptoms that beg for attention, you inflict pain on yourself and your relationship.

Marty had been experiencing discomfort in his stomach for months. Heavily into self-diagnosis, he was sure he had a bad case of indigestion. His wife, Jenny, urged him to see a doctor, but Marty said he didn't want to pay someone to tell him what he already knew. He continued to pop antacids and endure the pain. As the months passed, Jenny became angrier and angrier. "Fine," she thought. "If he wants to kill himself, he can go right ahead, but doesn't he care enough about our relationship to want to stay healthy and live a long life?"

Because Marty risked his health, he sent his wife a clear message that he was willing to put their marriage at risk. It wasn't until he vomited blood, passed out, and was rushed to an emergency room that he found out he had been suffering from a perforated ulcer.

Whether you're protecting your ego or your pride, being a "brick" can rock the foundation of your relationship. I remember the night my dad had a heart attack. He hadn't been feeling well all evening and thought he was coming down with the flu. Suddenly, he felt pressure on his chest and pain that radiated up to his neck and down his arm. I remember my mother telling him that she wanted to drive him to the hospital. Stubbornly, he insisted that his symptoms would pass. When my father's lips turned blue, my mother ignored his protests and called an ambulance.

Granted, admitting you are sick enough to need medical attention is scary, but if you don't address your symptoms properly, you'll create a huge amount of tension in your relationship that will only exacerbate whatever physical problem you already have. Finally, your mate will resent you for putting him or her, as well as your relationshijp, through the proverbial wringer.

Just Do It:

Whatever self-satisfaction you get from being tough is not worth the stress to which you'll subject your relationship. Show the true meaning of strength and stand up to denial. Do what it takes to diagnose your health problem and begin to heal.

To Nurse or Not to Nurse

Compassion is the antitoxin of the soul. Where there is compassion even the most poisonous impulses remain relatively harmless.

ERIC HOFFER

YOU and your mate are going to get sick. Whether you get a common cold, a migraine headache, or pneumonia, your immune system is going to go on hiatus at some point in your relationship. When it does, the healthy one of the two of you will assume the role of nursemaid.

I'm not particularly proud of this fact, but I'm being honest by telling you that I have never been what you'd call a fabulous caretaker. Even with my children, I'm good at inserting the thermometers and fetching glasses of water, but beyond that, Florence Nightingale I'm not.

So when it comes to my husband, I often fall short of giving him the attention he needs when he gets sick. Considering he can put a thermometer in his own mouth and get his own glass of water, I'm basically around to say, "So, get over it already." The fact that my husband moans when he gets sick doesn't help matters much.

When I'm not feeling good, I like to be left alone. During the very painful forty-two hour labor that I had with the birth of our son, I remember wishing that the nurses, doctors, as well as my husband, would all go out for coffee and leave me alone.

Where I've made my mistake in our relationship is to assume that because I prefer to face pain and discomfort privately, that my husband does also. *Wrong!* My husband wants the cold compress placed on his head. He wants the vapor rub lovingly smeared on his chest. He wants to be periodically awakened to the sound of my voice saying, "Just checking on you. Are you doing okay?"

When most couples get married, they don't ask each other the very important question, "How do you like to be taken care of when you're sick?" Newlyweds usually don't think twice about the unavoidable prospect of illness in their relationship. Learning your mate's caretaking expectation before he or she ever gets sick will do a lot to prevent disappointment on the part of the person who is ill and frustration on the part of the person who is playing nurse.

Think About It:

Whether your mate is the kind of person who wants lots of attention while he or she is sick or would rather be left alone, try to put yourself in his or her shoes and respect whatever form of caretaking your partner desires. Think about how it would feel to want attention and not get it, or to want to be left alone and constantly be bothered. One of the best things you can do for your relationship is to be a flexible nursemaid. Find out what your mate needs, then be it.

Flirting with Fatigue

And if tonight my soul may find her peace
in sleep, and sink in good oblivion,
and in the morning wake like a new-opened flower
then I have been dipped again in God, and new created.

D. H. LAWRENCE

YOU wouldn't think that something as basic as sleep could affect your relationship with your mate, but it does. Think how you feel during the day when you've had less than your daily requirement of shut-eye. Whether your job is to court clients, care for children, or drive a truck, your performance suffers from sleep deprivation.

It only makes sense that if fatigue threatens the stability of your work, it will also play havoc with your relationship. Listening, expressing yourself clearly, and truly being in the present moment with your partner takes major energy. Energy that comes from taking care of yourself—from getting enough sleep.

Try having a conversation about anything with your mate when you've had less slumber than usual. Irritability, impatience, and aggravation do their ceremonial dance in preparation for an explosive encounter.

When I think back on my husband's and my cycle of arguments, I see a pattern. There was a time early in our marriage when we used to have Saturday afternoon arguments, and now I know why. Because we both worked outside of the home, Saturday was our only day to "get things done." I was borderline fanatical about managing our time on Saturdays so that our errands would get done with efficiency. So driven was I that the first words out of my mouth upon awakening were, "Here's what we've got to do." I was a newly wedded walking to-do list.

My husband, patient man that he is, would go along with my program until around 2:00 P.M. That was always the bewitching hour when annoyance would rear its ugly head. Just when I thought we were on a roll and moving down our errand list quite nicely, he'd put on the brakes by saying he needed a nap. The thought of stopping the steamroller momentum on the only day of the week that we had to "get things done" was unthinkable to me. My husband would take his nap, but not until after we were through with our Saturday afternoon argument.

Although it took me a few years, I finally figured out that my husband wasn't taking a nap because he wanted to shirk his errand-running responsibilities. He was taking a nap because he needed sleep after a long week and a full morning. Without rest, his mind and body weren't going to function properly, and neither was our relationship.

Whether your or your partner's rest comes from having a nap in the middle of the day or from a couple of extra hours sleep in the morning, the extended repose is an investment in your relationship. Remember, your marriage takes energy. Energy comes from rest.

Just Do It:

Flirting with fatigue is dangerous. When driving, it's deadly. In a marriage, it's no different. Sleep is your relationship's fuel tank. Let it become empty and you invite unnecessary dis-ease. Keep your relationship healthy—sleep.

Tell It to Yourself

He who undervalues himself is justly undervalued by others.

WILLIAM HAZLITT

CONTRARY to popular opinion, you're not crazy if you talk to yourself. Unless, of course, you're saying things like, "I'm so stupid. What a jerk I am," or "I'm such an idiot." Self-talk, as long as it's positive, is a wonderful way to build your self-esteem and strengthen your relationship with your mate.

While most of Brett's friends' wives were critical of their husbands, Brett had what he felt was a much bigger problem. He had a wife who was extremely critical of herself. Joanie had a repertoire of self-reproaching statements she used regularly to berate herself about almost everything, ranging from how she cooked to how she looked. Nothing she did seemed good enough in her eyes and she wasn't shy about voicing her opinion about herself, especially when Brett was in the room.

Joanie began to realize that if she didn't change the negative self-talk, she was going to lose her husband of eight years. Chronic self-chastisement was not attractive to Brett and was pushing him away.

Desperate to stop putting herself down, Joanie decided to change how she was behaving. With the help of a regime of positive-thinking audio cassette programs as well as several visits to a therapist, Joanie discovered she could change her self-perception after all. Over time she learned that although she couldn't minimize her mistakes, she could minimize her negative reaction to them. Whenever she'd make a mistake at anything, she'd force herself to say, "Oops, I guess I'll learn from that," instead of "I really blew it. I'm so stupid." On the days when she couldn't find anything good to say about herself, she'd concentrate on not saying anything, even if a string of negative expletives ran through her mind. Eventually, what felt like contrived self-affirmations turned into almost involuntary positive thoughts that made patting herself on the back very easy.

It took several months for Joanie to reprogram the negative messages she had lived with over the years, but her determination to do so turned her marriage completely around. As her self-esteem sky-rocketed, so did her relationship with her husband.

Talking to yourself positively is much harder as an adult, especially if you've spent many years berating yourself. My husband, my children, and I have made a daily ritual out of self-affirmations. Every night at dinner we each say what we are grateful for and what we are proud of. Our pride has to come from something each of us has done instead of what someone else has done. After we each say what we are proud of, everyone at the table applauds.

This exercise may sound corny, but it has put us all in the habit of speaking positively about ourselves. Being in a relationship is a serious business. The number-one rule of entering into one is to do so feeling good about yourself.

Just Do It:

Once every day brag to your partner about yourself. The more you love yourself, the more your mate will love you.

Secret Confessions

> Men with secrets tend to be drawn to each other, not
> because they want to share what they know but because
> they need the company of the like-minded, the fellow
> afflicted.
>
> DON DELILLO

I F it's your mate's birthday and you've planned a surprise party, keeping a
secret is fun and exciting. If you've got good news to share with your partner, but want to wait for the perfect time to tell him or her, hiding information may be your best plan of action.

If, however, you're carrying around secrets that you've deliberately kept
from your mate because you're afraid to tell him or her, the expression,
"You're only as sick as your secrets" applies to you and your relationship.

The truth, whether it's been hidden for days, weeks, or years has a way of
showing itself sooner or later. Your relationship can withstand the unveiling
of a newly hidden truth much better than it can withstand a truth that's been
covered up for months or years.

A few weeks ago, when a friend was visiting, I could tell something
weighed heavily on her mind. As soon as I asked if she was okay, she began
to cry and said, "My husband is going to kill me." Apparently, her husband's
sister owed him $900 and when she paid him the money, he gave it to my
friend to deposit into their bank account. Instead of taking it directly to the

bank, my friend carried the money around for two days while she did errands. When she reached for it in her purse two days later, it was gone.

Although I empathized with her fear and helplessness, I encouraged her to tell her husband the truth. "If I tell him the truth, I'm afraid he'll be so mad at me that he'll leave me," said my friend. I told her that if that were to happen, and I highly doubted it would, her husband would have more of a reason to leave her for keeping her mistake a secret than making the mistake at all.

Truth can be excruciatingly painful in a couple's relationship no matter when it's revealed, but truth that has been harbored and hidden for long periods of time has triple the negative impact on a couple's relationship than truth that is disclosed immediately.

When she came to visit me two weeks later, she told me she had followed my advice. As scary as it was for her to unload her secret, she did it. Her husband was shocked and upset, but had no intention of leaving her. As it turned out, my friend had left the money in an envelope that she had mailed with an electric bill. An honest man at the electric company called her the next day to let her know her $900 was safe and sound.

Have enough faith in your relationship that it will withstand the truth and you won't have to carry a backpack full of secrets. The key to unloading a secret is to do it before it gets a chance to be called a secret. At the heart of every ailing relationship is at least one secret. Confess yours and you'll quickly heal.

Just Do It:

If you're keeping a secret from your mate, no matter how small you may think it is, share it with your mate. You're only as sick as your secret. There is no better time than now to get healthy.

Stir Your Emotional Pot

Individuality is founded in feelings; and the recesses of feeling, the darker, blinder strata of character, are the only places in the world in which we catch real fact in the making, and directly perceive how events happen, and how work is actually done.

WILLIAM JAMES

EXPRESS them. Vent them. Display them. I don't care how you do it, but for the sake of your relationship, release your feelings.

The only way you can convince me that you don't have feelings and emotions is if you're dead. True, you can be in a position where you think you no longer feel. You may have become so masterful at hiding, suppressing, and stuffing feelings that you've talked yourself into believing you're void of them. You're not. They're still there, but you may not be expressing them.

Although the following is a rather crude analogy, it illustrates my point. A relationship in which one or both partners hold in their feelings is like a badly infected pimple. Your feelings are like the fluid that sits encapsulated, pressure sensitive and waiting to be released. Once the pimple is squeezed, the infectious matter escapes and healing occurs.

When feelings aren't released, they eventually turn inward and fester. They create an infection of the heart in the form of resentment, hurt, and pain. Sadly, left unattended long enough, these inverted feelings become wounds— wounds that often can't be healed.

270

Because you were born with feelings, grew up with feelings, and will die with feelings, you need to face the music and learn how to express them. A good first step to describing how you feel is to begin saying the words, "I feel." Even if an interminable silence seems to follow those two words, say them anyway.

Naming a feeling is an art, and one well worth crafting. In order to have a healthy relationship with your mate, you must be able to offer your true self to him or her. Because you can't offer what you don't know, naming your feelings is the best way to learn about the real you.

In his book *Love & Survival: The Scientific Basis for the Healing Power of Intimacy*, Dr. Dean Ornish explains how your feelings are the passageway to the real you. "There is great power in authenticity. If you say, 'Gee, everything is fine' when it isn't, then there is a disconnect between what you are really feeling and what you are expressing. At some level, when you are inauthentic with yourself and with others, it is a betrayal of your own integrity and your own body, your own immune system, your own cardiovascular system. At some level, your body knows that."

When a feeling comes to the surface, look at it—face it. Instead of judging it by telling yourself you shouldn't feel a certain way, embrace the feeling and accept that it's there because it's a part of who you are. And who you are is all you have to offer your mate. Deny your feelings and you deny your relationship of authenticity.

Just Do It:

Today is the first day of your emotional workout regimen. Three times a day stop what you're doing at any given moment and talk to yourself by saying, "I feel _____." Fill in the blank with whatever feeling comes from your heart. If a feeling doesn't come to the surface right away, don't give up. This exercise will help you stir your emotional pot and keep your relationship cooking.

spiritually speaking

THE expression "Two's company, three's a crowd" does not apply when it comes to inviting the Holy Spirit into your relationship. You can't feel cramped, smothered, or claustrophobic when you make room for your creator.

In this chapter, I use the words God, Spirit, and Him interchangeably when referring to spirituality. Regardless of which word I use, my message remains the same: Your relationship with your creator has a direct affect on your relationship with your mate.

Spirituality is not about religion. Religion is simply *how* you choose to be spiritual. You and your mate can be an interfaith couple who allow each other the freedom to practice your religious preferences, but still may not make space for spirituality in your relationship.

Spirituality is about your relationship with God. It's about your conversations with Him and His with you. It's about listening to His guidance and following it. It's about living from your soul—from who you really are, not from what others think you should be.

Spirit wants more than anything to work through you and your relationship, but unless you share yourself as a spiritual being with your partner, God can't pull up an extra chair at your quiet dinner for two, join you on your getaway weekend, or be present at your most intimate moments.

Don't let the idea of inviting Spirit into your relationship intimidate you. You don't have to be entering the priesthood or be "enlightened" for spirituality to do its work in your coupleness. Every time you tell your partner the truth, every time you forgive him or her, every time you pray for or with your mate, or every time you are grateful for his or her life, God accepts your invitation and responds in kind.

You can live a lifetime with your mate without inviting Spirit into your relationship. You and your mate can raise children, take vacations, save for retirement, and when it's all said and done, boast about having stayed together for fifty years. Go ahead. Give it a try. When you look back, however, you may find yourself saying, "But there was something missing . . . something that could have helped our relationship to be deeper, richer, more meaningful. That something was God.

Breaking Spiritual Ground

The soul can split the sky in two,
And let the face of God shine through.

EDNA ST. VINCENT MILLAY

WHEN you foster a sense of spirituality between you and your mate, it adds a dimension deeper than you could achieve doing anything else for your relationship. There isn't anyone or anything that can convince me otherwise.

I want to make it very clear that when I speak of spirituality, I do not mean religion. What I'm referring to doesn't have to do with whether or not you attend a church or temple or whether or not you call yourself Christian, Buddhist, or Jewish. What I believe to make a monumental difference in your relationship with your mate is whether or not you have a relationship with God, Spirit, Source, or whatever it is you wish to call the being that bestowed the gift of life upon you.

Your relationship with God is your pipeline to your relationship with everyone and everything else on this planet, especially your mate. How you relate to your partner will have a lot to do with how you relate to God.

If you never acknowledge a supreme being in your life, it doesn't mean that you won't be able to have a functional relationship with the people around you. You may very well live your life one day at a time and never know the difference. If, however, you approach your life with the attitude that it is a gift from God, and your partner as a part of that gift, you will draw to you the love, wisdom, and grace necessary to enjoy a full, rich, and meaningful marriage.

When your conversations with God precede your conversations with your mate, you bring to your relationship an open heart and mind. By making your connection to God primary, you open yourself to let Spirit guide you in your dealings with every person in every situation, including your lifelong partner.

As your relationship with God deepens, talk to your mate about it. By sharing with your partner the impact that Spirit has on you, you construct a bridge between your two souls. That bridge can be built whether your relationship with God is active or nonexistent, as long as you include your mate in on the "project."

As you begin to see your life here on earth as a spiritual experience as well as a human experience, share your insights and perceptions with your mate. Life has just as much to do with what can't be seen as with what can be seen. Let your mate in on the invisible.

Just Do It:

Talk to your partner about your relationship with God, or lack of it. Exploring your spiritual nature with your mate is a sacred process. To deny your coupleness of this experience is the same as living with an invaluable treasure buried beneath your feet without ever picking up a shovel and breaking ground.

A Magic Carpet Ride

The most beautiful emotion we can experience is the mystical. He to who this emotion is a stranger, who can no longer wonder and stand rapt in awe, is as good as dead. To know that what is impenetrable to us really exists, manifesting itself as the highest wisdom and the most radiant beauty, which our dull faculties can comprehend only in their most primitive forms—this knowledge, this feeling, is at the center of true religiousness.

ALBERT EINSTEIN

LIVING your life not only as a human being, but as a spiritual being means you will see life and your surroundings differently. Rather than noticing what is simply in front of you, you will sense that there is so much more to life than what you can physically touch, hear, see, smell, or taste. You'll begin to understand that those things that cannot be explained, and are often categorized as coincidences, are not coincidences at all, but are there to remind you that you are first and foremost a spiritual being with a spiritual side to your life.

As you and your mate begin to acknowledge each other's spiritual nature, your life together will take on a much deeper, richer dimension. You'll feel something about your existence changing and at times it will be hard to put your feelings into words.

As foreign as it might feel to talk about this new sense of your life, it's important to share your unfamiliar feelings and experiences with your partner. You will no doubt feel vulnerable as you expose your spiritual side to your mate, for it is truly a leap of faith to do so. When you do, your relationship will become more fulfilling than you could possibly imagine.

There isn't a day that goes by that I don't recognize there is so much more to life than what I can see in front of me. Sometimes things happen to confirm that fact. When they do happen, my husband is always the first person I tell.

It was the tenth Father's Day since my father had died. I awoke that morning and instantly thought of my dad. I spent the next several minutes lying in bed remembering him, missing him, and talking to him. Once I got out of bed, the morning progressed as usual as my husband, my kids, and I ate breakfast and drove off to church. Although our family celebrated the father of our house, my husband, I carried my dad with me throughout the day.

Once we arrived home, I checked our phone messages on the answering machine. As I listened to the one message that had been left, I stood frozen in time, overcome with a combination of shock and complete joy.

The message was from our next-door neighbor who said that while her husband was working in their garden, he came across a gold Cross pen that had an inscription on it. She said they thought it might belong to me because the inscription on the pen read, "To Dad, Love Kathy."

I immediately ran next door to look at the pen. As I stared at it, I couldn't believe my eyes. It was a pen I had given my father twenty years before on Father's Day. I hadn't seen it since our house fire, which had occurred the year before. Another neighbor happened to be present as I explained how long ago it had been since I had seen the pen and how incredible it was that it should be found on Father's Day, especially when I had been thinking so much about my dad. The neighbor quickly dismissed the discovery as sheer coincidence and began talking about how many flats of petunias she had to plant by the end of the day.

Realizing my neighbor wasn't able to share the joy that this "find" had brought me, I ran back home with my newfound treasure to share my excitement with my husband. For a split second I wondered whether or not he would join the ranks of people like our earthbound neighbor and dismiss

what I was sure was a spiritual experience as being just a fluke. My momentary doubt disappeared as soon as I told him the story. My husband wrappe
his arms around me, held me close, and whispered in my ear, "This doesn
surprise me. What a wonderful Father's Day gift for you."

"Coincidences" that occur in my life occur in yours, too, but you have t
pay attention in order to notice them. When they happen, you have a choic
You can rationalize them away and go on with your day, or you can look a
them differently than you would with your earthbound eyes. Once you rec
ognize that there are some things that can't be explained, you'll be able to le
go of the need to rationalize and stay open to Spirit.

If you're listening to the story of your mate's spiritual experience or sensa
tions, he or she is counting on you to accept what is being said. Just becaus
you can't explain why it happened doesn't mean it didn't happen. Allow you
mate's spirit to unfold, then jump on the magic carpet and go along for th
ride!

Just Do It:

The next time something happens that you think is a coincidence,
think again. Instead of rationalizing your experience away, share it
with your mate. Stay open to the possibility that there's more to
what happened than you might think. Trust Spirit enough to share
your new awareness with your partner, and Spirit will work wonders
in your relationship.

To Tell the Truth

Plato is dear to me, but dearer still is truth.

ARISTOTLE

THE honest to God's truth." You hear that expression whenever someone is explaining what they believe to be real and true; as if to say, "What I'm telling you is so true that I've even been honest with God about it."

Truth comes from Spirit because it is made from love not fear. If truth is at the core of your relationship with your mate, Spirit makes it a packaged deal. If, on the other hand, deception is at the center of your relationship, Spirit is nowhere to be found.

Be honest with your partner. You don't have to be brutally honest, mind you, but you do have to be truthful. Believe me, even those little white lies that you think are harmless will build up. No matter how afraid you are to tell your mate the truth, it won't compare to the fear and panic you'll feel after you realize you've not only been untruthful about one thing, but many things.

Celeste sometimes thinks about her fifteen-year marriage to her husband, Victor, and is amazed at how close they came to breaking up, all because she started the relationship dishonestly. Before she met Victor, Celeste dated and had become heavily involved with Steve, a man who unbeknownst to her, was a friend of Victor's. Three weeks after she stopped seeing Steve, she met Victor. Every time she and Victor went out together, she wanted to tell him about her relationship with Steve, but was afraid that if he knew the truth he might not want to see her anymore. There had been nothing wrong with her having a former relationship with a friend of Victor's, but the longer she hid it from him, the more the deception grew.

Months went by and Celeste felt worse and worse about what she was hiding. The thought that Steve might mention their short dating relationship to Victor made her even more anxious.

Eight months after they had met, Victor proposed to Celeste. As he presented her with the engagement ring, Celeste was elated and devastated at the same time. She knew she couldn't accept his proposal until she told him the truth, so she revealed her relationship with Steve to Victor. Victor was understanding about her having dated his friend, but was flabbergasted and hurt that she had waited eight months to tell him the truth.

As hard as it was, Victor did the only thing he felt he could do at the time. He asked for the ring back along with time to think about what had just happened. With tears streaming down her cheeks, Celeste handed back the ring, sure that their relationship was over.

Two days later, Victor called Celeste and asked her to meet him in the park. He told her that after much thought, he understood her fear about telling him the truth, but that he didn't want a relationship based on fear and deception. They talked about how important truthfulness is in a relationship. They decided to continue dating, but to give themselves time to process the whole ordeal. It didn't take long for them to realize they had learned a valuable lesson. They were married six months later.

For spirituality to become a part of your relationship, you have to be prepared to live and breathe the truth. The honest to God's truth is what your relationship deserves. Tell it.

Just Do It:

You have a split second to decide whether you will tell your mate the honest to God's truth or your version of it. Next time you're given the choice, listen to Spirit and the truth shall set you free.

Raise Your Soul

You must learn to be still in the midst of activity and to be vibrantly alive in respose.

INDIRA GANDHI

BECAUSE your spirituality has such a dramatic effect on your relationship with your mate, you want to do everything you can to nurture your soul's development. Although you can exercise your soul by taking religious studies, listening to spiritual teachers, or attending church services, the best way to "raise your soul" is to be still.

Whether you're in the midst of a crisis or a celebration, it is when you slow down long enough to be silent that wisdom, insight, and guidance befalls. The ideal way to get quiet is to place yourself in an environment that feels safe enough for you to stop talking, close your eyes, and breathe deeply. Because life doesn't always present ideal situations, it's important to learn how to go within for peace regardless of the mayhem that surrounds you.

I sometimes find myself turning within in search of peace whenever I'm on an airplane and am experiencing a turbulent flight. I remember one flight in particular when the tossing and turning of the aircraft was frightening me as well as a screaming toddler a few rows behind me. I buckled down into my soul, focused on my little friend's and my fear and repeated the words Jesus used to calm a storm at sea, "Peace. Be still." Although chaos ensued as call lights summoned flight attendants, passengers reached for their little brown

281

bags, and luggage shifted in the overhead bins, I was determined to reach the silence within.

As Marianne Williamson tells us in her book, *Illuminata: Thoughts, Prayers, Rites of Passage*, "The more we allow our internal world to be illumined, the more our external world will take on meaning . . . To go within is not to turn our backs on the world; it is to prepare ourselves to serve it most effectively." The best way to serve your relationship is to first serve your soul.

Your soul needs less attention than you would think. Going within doesn't mean you have to lay down a blanket, light incense, and sit cross-legged in meditation for hours. All you need to meet with your soul is the desire to do so. Peace can happen in an instant. A moment of clarity is all it takes to restore your serenity.

When you come to your mate with a refreshed soul, you bestow a most wonderful gift upon your relationship. Your coupleness is only half as centered as you are.

Just Do It:

Once this week visit your soul in the midst of chaos. Wherever you are, stop what you're doing, close your eyes, and breathe deeply. Repeat these words to your soul, "Peace. Be still." Visit your soul twice next week. Get comfortable enough living in moments of silence so that you can do it in a second's notice. Share the effects of your "soul chats" with your mate.

The Materialistic Marriage Machine

The people recognize themselves in their commodities;
they find their soul in their automobiles, hi-fi set, split-level
home, kitchen equipment.

HERBERT MARCUSE

A S strange as this question may sound, think carefully about your answer. Who are you married to, your culture or your partner? You may not realize it, but your culture seduces you every day of your life and the media is the method. Print, radio, television, the Internet, and major motion pictures work to convince you that bigger is better and that the more you acquire, the more you'll feel you've "arrived."

No sooner are the "I dos" said than most couples are off and running to the races. Whether it's a race up the corporate ladder, a race to finish building a bigger and better house, or a race to purchase the eighth week of a time share, they're busy creating what I call the materialistic marriage, and believe me, this union is anything but spiritual.

When you and your mate decided you wanted to spend the rest of your lives together, you were not concentrating on whether your home should have a three-, four-, or five-car garage. You thought only of how good you felt when you were together and how you wanted to keep that feeling going for a lifetime. It was who you were to each other that mattered, not what you owned.

Whether you realized it or not, in the beginning, your relationship was generated from spiritual energy. At some point, you looked into each other's eyes and connected on a soul level. You knew deep down that this was who you wanted to *be* with forever. The key word here is *be*.

When you and your mate are so busy *going* wherever it is you think you have to go or *getting* whatever it is you think you have to own, you can't possibly *be* with each other.

If I had a dollar for every couple I've heard abut who "has everything" but is miserable, I'd have enough money to open an IRA account. I'm not saying that you can't have dreams and goals for a more fulfilling career or a vacation home on a lake. Just make sure that in your race to get these things that you don't leave your relationship in the dust.

There was a time in our marriage when my husband and I got sucked into the materialistic marriage machine. We were so enamored with building a big house full of all the latest amenities that we never stopped to think that what we were building was so far away from my husband's office and our children's school that we were going to spend more time in the car and less time together.

It took us three years to finally figure out that talking to each other on a cellular phone was not how we wanted to be married. So, we "downsized" into a smaller home that was a block away from our children's school and ten minutes from my husband's office.

We felt so proud of ourselves for reprioritizing our lives. Actually, smug is a better word to describe our attitude toward our newly acquired humble abode. But it was while watching that humble abode burn from an electrical fire that the real meaning of humility descended upon us. As we walked away from our charred residence that day, owning nothing but the clothes on our backs, we were reminded that our spirits were intact, and more important, so was our relationship.

Just Do It:

Pick one evening this week and have an honest discussion with your mate about the materialistic marriage machine. Talk about whether you feel you have constructed one in your relationship. Whether you want to downsize your wardrobe, make holiday gift-giving simpler, or own one less car, talk about how to disassemble it.

Dying to Live

All men think all men mortal, but themselves.

EDWARD YOUNG

WE take the people in our lives for granted until we either lose them or are struck with the fear of losing them. This sad fact is no truer than in our relationship with our mate. Day by day we settle in, get comfortable with our lifelong marital status, and act as if our partner will be around forever.

In his book *Tuesdays with Morrie*, Mitch Albom interviews his long-lost college professor who has only four months to live after being diagnosed with ALS (Lou Gehrig's disease). On his fourth Tuesday with his teacher, Mitch listens to Morrie talk about death.

"How can you ever be prepared to die?" asks Mitch.

"Do what the Buddhists do," says Morrie. "Every day, have a little bird on your shoulder that asks, 'Is today the day? Am I ready? Am I doing all I need to do? Am I being the person I want to be?' "

Morrie looks at Mitch, a middle-aged workaholic, and says, "The things you spend so much time on—all this work you do—might not seem as important. You might have to make room for some more spiritual things . . . Mitch, even I don't know what 'spiritual development' really means. But I do know we're deficient in some way. The loving relationships we have, the universe around us, we take these things for granted."

Morrie believes that if you really listen to that bird on your shoulder, *if you accept that you can die at any time*—you might not spend that extra hour at the office, spend so much time worrying about finances, or hold onto feelings you've been afraid to share.

It never ceases to amaze me that as mortal as we are, we humans don't hesitate to wear the mask of immortality. Intellectually, we know we are going to die, but as if to laugh in death's face, we take life and the people in it for granted, waste precious time, and live with a "someday I'll do what I want to do" mentality.

Sheila and Dean's fifteen-year marriage was healthy in that they didn't argue every day, they went on a date every week, and they exchanged birthday presents every year. Their "comfortable" relationship was virtually stress-free. The problem with their marriage was not only was it stressless, it was lifeless.

It wasn't until Sheila heard the words reverberating in her head, "I'm sorry, but your husband suffered a massive heart attack and was dead on arrival" that she wished she had been a different spouse to Dean. Why hadn't she told him that morning how striking he looked in his new tie? Why hadn't she sat and talked with him after last night's dinner instead of cleaning the linen closet? Why hadn't she agreed to take the hot-air balloon ride with him last summer?

Face it. You're going to die and so is your mate. As Morrie told Mitch, "The truth is, once you learn how to die, you learn how to live."

Just Do It:

Pretend that you've just learned you have only one year to live. Write down five ways you would treat your mate differently if this were the case. Treat your mate this way for the rest of your life.

soulmaking

Nothing can cure the soul but the senses, just as nothing can cure the senses but the soul.

OSCAR WILDE

ALTHOUGH lovemaking is usually thought of as a body-oriented activity, it is meant to be a spiritual experience as well.

Remember, much of spirituality has to do with the unseen rather than the seen. Lovemaking can be a soul-bearing experience. You can enjoy the fabulous sensory experience of making love and still be open to the gift of spiritual energy that passes between you and your mate. As partners, naked in each other's arms, you and your mate put yourselves in an open, vulnerable position. By agreeing to share each other in this way you commit to a level of trust and intimacy that no heart-to-heart talk or warm embrace could reproduce.

In my opinion, sexual pleasure is to lovemaking as a bonus check is to a salary. Yes, the bonus is exhilarating, but the regular salary is what is sustaining. The "meat" of lovemaking is the energy of love that is produced during it. When you focus on loving your partner with all of your heart and soul, as well as your body, your physical pleasure will do nothing but increase.

Thomas Moore, in his book *Soul Mates: Honoring the Mysteries of Love and Relationship*, tells us that sexual intimacy is but one of the many paths leading to your soul. He says, "One way sex weaves people into soul is through repetition, the mere sleeping and dreaming, and the years of breathing skin to skin. These are part of sex, and they are what give the soul its invisible threads of intimacy."

Admittedly, when making love to my husband, I do not always concentrate on our soul connection. When I do, however, our lovemaking is deeper, richer, and more meaningful. It is when I focus on how much I love him during lovemaking and how I cherish his life as a gift from God that our souls touch.

Moore maintains that the soul of sex has transforming power. He asserts, "The soul of sex has the power to evoke relationship, to sustain it, and to make it worthwhile. As with all things of soul, we are asked to stand out of the way and be affected by its power to quicken life and to transform us from practical survivors into erotic poets of our own lives."

Get out of your soul's way and your lovemaking will become the spiritual experience it was meant to be.

Just Do It:

The next time you make love with your mate, focus on transmitting loving energy to your partner. By all means, enjoy the sensory feelings you get from sexual intimacy, but take direction from your soul and you'll invite Spirit into your lovemaking.

The Spirit of Giving

While you have a thing it can be taken from you . . . but when you give it, you have given it. No robber can take it from you. It is yours then forever when you have given it. It will be yours always. That is to give.

JAMES JOYCE

T HE Spirit of giving. We hear about it throughout the year, especially around the holidays. This holiday "buzz phrase" is what I believe to be the cornerstone of spirituality in a lifelong relationship.

What is the Spirit of giving anyway, and how do you get into it if you think you don't have it to begin with? I believe we are all born with it. As we grow, our human nature interferes and wants us to believe that giving only leaves us with less of the pie for ourselves. That's why it was so difficult to share that first toy or split that Popsicle in half with another child.

Incorporating the spirit of giving into your relationship takes a leap of faith. As human beings we are so fixated on immediate gratification that unless we receive soon after we give, we get fidgety and feel cheated.

This is where we have to trust Spirit. The true meaning of giving is giving for giving's sake, without expecting anything in return. The irony of it all is that when we give in this way, we get our equal share in return and even more.

If you take this principle and plug it into relationships, you create a foundation for a partnership without standoffs and scorekeeping. You lay the groundwork for a marriage that is guided by Spirit and not ego.

For couples who find themselves in a relationship that is lackluster, stagnant, and what I call common, it's the Spirit of giving that finally pulls the relationship up by its bootstraps. After going through the usual standoff of "I'm not putting any more energy into our relationship if he's not going to . . ." and "I'm not putting any more energy into our relationship if she's not going to . . . ," it's the person who's willing to make the first move to give to the other who reaps the benefit of the Spirit of giving.

As I teach this idea of the Spirit of giving in workshops, there is inevitably one person in each class who announces that he or she is not going to budge to give one more inch to his or her mate. Charlene made it very clear that she was sick and tired of "giving, giving, giving" to her husband, Grant, and never getting anything in return. As I explained to her that the true Spirit of giving is to do so without expecting anything in return, her eyes rolled so far behind her eyelids that I thought we'd never again see her pupils.

After much coaxing, she agreed to take on her week's personally designed homework assignment. I told her that once during the week she had to give to her husband, but had to do it for the sake of giving and not receiving. Whether she gave him a back rub, an "I love you" phone call, or a new watch, didn't matter. Her assignment was to simply concentrate on the Spirit of giving.

Charlene came back to class the following week a believer. She said that after some thought, she decided to give to her husband by making his lunch every day that week. This was something she had done when they were first married, but had stopped doing because of her scorekeeping mentality.

She told us that the first two lunches were made begrudgingly, but by the fourth and fifth lunch, she was enjoying the act of giving and forgot about her payoff. "It was like I was a kid again," said Charlene. "I found myself picking up little goodies like bubble gum and candy bars to stick in Grant's lunch. I even tucked in some naughty notes just for fun."

Charlene said she was basking in the wonderful feeling that giving for giving's sake provides when a dozen red long-stemmed roses were delivered Friday afternoon with a note from her husband that read, "Thank you for five of the best meals I've ever eaten. With love, Grant."

Remember. You were born with the Spirit of giving. It's your choice to tap into it or not. The Spirit that lives in both you and your mate has the power to transform your relationship at any given moment. It's a gift that has been bestowed upon you. Allow it to work in your life.

Just Do It:

Put the Spirit of giving to the test. Whether you give your partner your time, your creativity, or your money, give with absolutely no expectations of getting anything in return.

Three Powerful Words

How shall I lose the sin, yet keep the sense,
And love th'offender, yet detest th'offense?

ALEXANDER POPE

YOU'RE going to make mistakes and so is your partner. If after living a lifetime together, you could remember and enumerate how many times you wished you hadn't said or done what you said or did, you'd probably have a list long enough to hang from ceiling to floor.

Living with someone whom you've hurt is hard enough, but living with someone who isn't willing to forgive you is even harder. If you've ever made a mistake, you know what it feels like to want to be forgiven. That feeling of wanting to be forgiven is exactly what can empower you to forgive your mate.

It takes spiritual power to be able to forgive someone. You have it inside of you because you were born with it. Have you ever noticed how easily children forgive? I can't tell you how many times I've said something in anger or thoughtlessness to one of my children and then asked for forgiveness. Without hesitation, my children have forgiven me. As I've watched them accept my apology, I've stood in awe of their ability to forgive so freely. Children are truly our best teachers.

Even if your partner has done something atrocious to you such as abuse you physically, emotionally, or mentally, I believe for your own sake you need to eventually forgive him or her. Forgiving someone doesn't mean you have to accept their behavior into your life. It does mean you have to release the power they have over you when you don't forgive. By hanging onto the pain and resentment, you do nothing but hurt yourself by giving the other person power over you.

Forgiveness is a spiritual process and needs to be an integral part of your relationship with your mate if you want to be healthy. Granted, it takes time to process your feelings around the hurt and pain that's been inflicted. To think that you can shut off your painful feelings as if you're shutting off a garden hose is unrealistic.

Forgiveness begins with owning your feelings and expressing them as your own. As you share with your partner what bothers you, do it from the heart. If you open your heart in this way, your mate will be more likely to open his or her heart enough to apologize. When this happens, you will have reached a vital crossroads in your relationship. The ball will be in your court and it has forgiveness written all over it.

Although you may find it difficult at first to forgive instantaneously the way children do, keep your heart open and forgiveness will reawaken from its long, uninterrupted slumber.

Just Do It:

Practice saying the words "I forgive you." Believe me, you'll have plenty of opportunities. The next time your mate apologizes to you, open your heart and accept it. The spiritual power of the three words, "I forgive you" will make miracles happen in your relationship.

Body and Soul

We are truly indefatigable in providing for the needs of the body, but we starve the soul.

ELLEN WOOD

ALTHOUGH it may have been your mate's physical appearance that initially attracted you to him or her, it was your partner's spirit that made you decide to spend the rest of your life with his or her body.

We would all do well to remember the spiritual connection that once occurred between our mates and ourselves. Without this reminder we risk being sucked into what I call body bewitchment.

Your body *is* important. It is the vehicle for accomplishing what you are supposed to accomplish during your life, and throughout your life you'll do everything from maintaining it, to healing it, to adorning it. But be careful lest you become chained to your own body and its image.

Your body and the senses that go along with it exist for you to enjoy and share with your mate. It is, however, the perceptions and neuroses attached to your body that can get in the way of your relationship.

Our society's fixation with weight loss and body image has created almost unattainable goals for people. There are men and women every day who pass up opportunities for physical intimacy with their mates because they think they're too overweight or out of shape for their partner to want to "be" with them.

After forty-four years of marriage, my mother confided in me that the reason she had stopped going out in social situations with my father was because of the size of her stomach. After years of fad diets and abdominal exercises, which she believed were unsuccessful, she slowly became more and more reclusive. Not wanting to live the rest of his life getting ready for bed at 8:00 P.M. my father would invite me to the jazz concerts and symphonies to which he had hoped my mother would go. Although my dad and I made some wonderful memories, they were really memories that were meant for my parents.

My mother's body image haunted her up to her very last days. After being diagnosed with lung cancer that had metastasized to her brain, she underwent radiation treatments to her skull. The loss of her hair tormented her much more than the disease that ravished her body. During one of our conversations, the anguish of her hair loss seemed to be devouring her. I gently suggested to her that as painful as it was to lose her hair, I hoped that she would somehow take solace in the fact that she was so much more than her body. I remember so clearly her responding, "But no one ever told me that when I was growing up." How right she was. Very few children are raised with the idea that they are spirits first and bodies second.

Your mate is first and foremost a spiritual being. Although your partner will gain or lose weight, hair, or suffer more dramatic physical changes, his or her spirit will remain constant. Love your partner from the inside out and your love will remain constant as well.

Think About It:

Take five minutes of your time to think about how you love your mate. Ask your partner whether he or she feels loved by you from the inside out or the outside in. Does he or she feel loved for body and soul?

Spirit of Gratitude

A man's indebtedness . . . is not virtue; his repayment is. Virtue begins when he dedicates himself actively to the job of gratitude.

RUTH BENEDICT

S OME people seem to have an uncanny ability to get through the most awful times. These are the people who, when diagnosed with a terminal disease say, "I'm scared, but I'm so grateful to have made it this far." These are the people who have gone financially bankrupt and say, "At least I have my health."

I'm often reminded of a couple I know who had a late-in-life baby. Lydia and Archie had tried for years to have a child and when they finally did, they were in their fifties. Their struggle to have an only child made losing him to a lawn-mowing accident at the age of seventeen that much more devastating. But it was Lydia and Archie who, at their son's funeral, stood up and told all who were there how grateful they were to have had him for seventeen years.

I have been blessed to have been surrounded by several of these kinds of people in my life. What makes these people, often couples, different from others is that they come from a place of gratitude.

If you break down the word "gratitude," it's a combination of two words: grateful and attitude. A grateful attitude is not something you get from this world. You can't apply for it. You can't go to school and earn a degree in it. You can't go to a bank and get a loan for it.

A grateful attitude comes directly from Spirit. Like the Spirit of giving, you are born with the Spirit of gratitude. It's inside of you, ready and waiting to be accessed at any time. Tap into it and it will transform your life on earth.

Gratitude alone can save a marriage. I've seen it happen. Whenever I teach a six-week workshop to men and women, I ask them to pack their resentments, complaints, and negativity into a figurative suitcase and stick it up on a top shelf in their closet. For six weeks of their lives I ask them to relate to their mates from a Spirit of gratitude, and if after six weeks they want to reach up to that top shelf, drag down that suitcase, and live from it again, they're welcome to do so.

It's never happened. Not one person has ever said to me after six weeks of living life gratefully, "I'm sorry, Kathy. I'd much rather fill my heart with resentments than gratitude."

These men and women in the workshops learn new information to help them communicate better, incorporate romance into their relationship, love themselves more, and do it with a different perspective—with a grateful spirit.

Just Do It:

Make a list of ten things you are grateful for in your mate and in your relationship. Hang this list someplace where you can see it every day. Read it. Feel it. Live it.

Soul Expression

Developing the muscles of the soul demands no competitive spirit, no killer instinct, although it may erect pain barriers that the spiritual athlete must crash through.

GERMAINE GREER

SPIRITUALITY is an evolutionary thing. No two people's souls develop in the same way at the same time. When you and your mate first met, whether you shared the same religious background or had completely different religious upbringings, you each had developed your own unique relationship with God.

How you relate to Spirit today depends on many things. It depends on how you "saw" Him as a child, whether or not you stayed in touch with Him as you grew into adulthood, and what you do now to maintain your connection to Spirit.

My guess is that if you and your partner sat down and talked to each other about your relationship with God, you would share completely different experiences. If you have never done this, I want you to do it—regularly.

Believe it or not, some couples live with each other for decades without knowing anything about their mate's relationship to God or whether he or she even believes in Him. This absolutely astonishes me considering the fact that how people relate to their creator affects every single aspect of their lives, especially the relationship they have with their mate.

When you and your partner sit down and share your soul's journey with each other, don't panic when you find that one is further along the path than the other. Neither of you is "better" or loved more by God because you have a more active relationship with Him than the other. Remember, spirituality is a process, not a race.

Your spiritual growth is meant to be a binding force in your relationship. Even a lack of spiritual foundation is positive in that it allows you to have a starting point from which to begin growing spiritually when the time is right.

It was after Madeline and Warren had been married seventeen years that she confided in me that she thought her husband was shallow. "There's no depth there," complained Madeline. "He goes to church with me, but I know he's just going through the motions. I don't think he even prays."

"Have you ever asked him about his personal relationship with God?" I asked Madeline. "Well, no," she replied. "I can tell by the look on his face, though, that he's just not into it."

After encouraging her to broach the subject of spirituality with her husband, Madeline finally agreed to approach Warren on the topic. She reported back to me a week later that what she had interpreted as indifference, had actually been confusion. As it turned out, Warren had had a lot of questions over the years about God and spirituality, questions he had never shared with his wife.

Warren and Madeline walked away from their conversation with a deeper understanding and respect for each other and for their soul's development. Although their spiritual journey was different, it was nice to know they were both on the same path.

Just Do It:

Set aside thirty minutes this week for you and your mate to talk to each other about your relationship with God. Tell each other how you relate to Spirit and how Spirit relates to you. Express your convictions and your doubts. The more you share your soul's evolvement with each other, the more your relationship will evolve.

A Marital Allergy

Myths which are believed in tend to become true.

GEORGE ORWELL

THE seven-year itch is that time in a relationship when one or both people supposedly get antsy and want to look elsewhere for love, affection, and companionship. I would like nothing more than to wipe this relationship myth off the face of the earth. Who came up with it anyway? Does this concept exist just because someone made a movie with Marilyn Monroe called *The Seven Year Itch* and the idea stuck? And why seven years? Why not five or ten? Actually, to assign a year at all to this marital blister is to set couples up for a self-fulfilling prophecy—dissention in the ranks of matrimony.

If you're in your fifth or sixth year of marriage, you may suddenly develop a "look behind your shoulder" mentality as you buckle down and prepare for the seven-year itch. If you've had struggles in or around your seventh year together, you automatically attribute it to, what else of course . . . the seven-year itch.

If you've managed to make it through "the big one," congratulations. If you're coming up on the dreaded number seven, do yourself a favor and don't buy into its overplayed prediction.

Regardless of how the outside world tries to convince you, you and your mate have the power to create for yourselves a marriage that can withstand the seven-year itch and a whole lot more. If you anticipate obstacles in your relationship as you approach your seventh year of marriage, trust me, that's exactly what you'll get.

The spiritual nature of your marriage has everything to do with how *you* see your relationship and nothing to do with how the *world* sees it. Your job as partner is to create a positive vision for your marriage. If you walk around waiting for conflict and tension to infiltrate your relationship, that's what you'll unknowingly invite into your marriage.

Just as you are a spiritual entity, so too, is your relationship. It has a life of its own based on what energy you give it. Be careful how you think and speak of your marriage. Think about it long enough as a dead-end relationship fraught with seemingly insurmountable obstacles and you won't be able to overcome what you've unwittingly created. As tempting as it is to believe the myth of the seven-year itch, don't.

Just Do It:

No matter what year your itch falls on, fight the urge to scratch. What you expect can come to pass. Use this power positively. Spend ten minutes writing your vision for your relationship. Talk to your mate about making it a reality.

"Thank You, in Advance"

Therefore I say unto you, What things soever ye desire, when ye pray, believe that ye receive them, and ye shall have them.

JESUS

I pray my mate through the day," said Ellie. "My husband struggles with depression and on those difficult days, especially during winter when just to get his shoes and socks on is a huge effort, I hold him in prayer."

I was touched by what Ellie told me that afternoon at a Marriage Encounter retreat. The idea of praying my husband through the day sounded like a powerful concept and one I decided to try.

I was born into a family where prayer and spirituality weren't practiced. My parents were wonderful spiritual beings who, sadly, decided to see themselves one way—human. There was this person, however, my parents had the good judgment to bring into my life who exposed me to a world I would have never known otherwise—a world of prayer.

Rose was a live-in housekeeper my parents hired to stay home with me and my brother while they ran a family business. Rose wasn't much of a talker, but she sure could pray up a storm. I remember going into her room each night before bedtime. As I would lie across her bed and watch television, she'd sit quietly in her rocking chair and pray with her prayer book in one hand and her rosary in the other. I never quite understood the connection between the two, but because I loved her so much I decided that if Rose talked to God every night, there had to be something to this prayer bit.

There are many ways to pray. Over the years, my prayers have evolved. I used the begging variety of "Please God, I'll do anything as long as such and such happens." I'd pray this way not only for myself, but for everyone on my prayer list. Then I adjusted my prayers so as to hand a little more control over to God by praying. "I'll go with whatever you want, God, but I'd really appreciate it if such and such would happen."

After forty-three years I've finally figured out that I can't control the outcome of any situation and that the only way for me to pray is to thank God in advance for the strength to handle whatever it is that happens. So now when I pray my husband through the day, I no longer ask for a specific result, but instead I give thanks that he will handle whatever result comes his way.

My husband, Dick, knows when I'm praying for him because I tell him. He has said that even though the circumstances of his life might not change on the days that I pray for him, how he handles those circumstances does change.

There is no denying the power of prayer. Use it in your relationship and it will heal and uplift beyond your wildest imaginings.

Just Do It:

If you're intimidated by prayer, don't worry. There's no right or wrong way to pray. As French novelist and political writer George Bernanos has said, "The wish to pray is a prayer in itself."

Recognize the Unseen

But those rare souls whose spirits get magically into the hearts of men, leave behind them something more real and warmly personal than bodily presence, an ineffable and eternal thing.

JAMES THURBER

S O who is this person you've committed to spending the rest of your life with? Don't start describing him by explaining what he does for a living. Restrain yourself from pigeonholing her as the mother of your child or the best cook ever. Those are all byproducts of your mate, but none of these classifications describes who your mate really is.

Until you look at your lifelong partner as a spiritual being as well as a human being, you won't be able to enjoy the truly grand gift your mate is to you. This man or woman you've chosen to live out your days with is a living, breathing miracle. This person has a unique nature that he or she may not even recognize.

There is nothing in this world like being seen by others as more than a human being. To be recognized as a divine spirit is the highest form of love one can receive.

It only makes sense that if you were born from Spirit that you are *of* Spirit. To honor that sacred part of your mate is the most powerful thing you can do for your relationship.

I absolutely love my husband's spirit and I tell him so on a regular basis. Now I know he is a human being who eats, sleeps, and gets a common cold like everyone else, but I see him as so much more than a five foot, seven-inch man with hazel eyes and broad shoulders. His packaging is wonderful, of course, but it's the part of him that I can't physically touch that I love the most. Although I can't hold his spirit in my hands, I can feel it and see it by looking into his eyes. That's why someone's eyes are so often described as the gateway to his or her soul. You can tell by looking into them whether a person's spirit is broken or intact.

Your mate's spirit is where his or her dreams, visions, and drives reside. To love your partner as a spiritual being is to love him for who he is in the present moment as well as who he or she is waiting to become.

Embracing your mate's spirit is the ultimate declaration of your faith in your relationship. When you love your partner as a spiritual being, you love that part of him or her that can't be measured by time, space, or distance. Your mate never has to produce proof or evidence of his or her spirit because your belief in it is all it needs to show itself.

Think About It:

For the next week, concentrate on your partner as a spiritual being as well as a human being. The depth you will discover in your mate you will also discover in your relationship.

Conclusion

A LTHOUGH you've reached the conclusion of this book, you are not finished, nor will you ever be finished with the ongoing process of being in a healthy relationship. Notice I said *healthy* relationship. You can *be* in a relationship easily, but being in a healthy one takes more than just the ability to survive.

By merely existing in a relationship, you invite loneliness, isolation, boredom, and depression into your life with your mate. Contract any or all of these ills and your relationship becomes diseased—what I call "common." Before you know it you are diagnosed: *married*.

If you have followed one or more of the "Just Do It" instructions at the end of the readings in this book, congratulations. You have taken a definitive step toward creating a healthy, loving, intimate, and mutually fulfilling relationship with your mate, which in our society is the "uncommon" relationship.

By having an uncommon relationship with your mate, you are in the minority. Not an easy place to be. On a daily basis you will be tempted, cajoled, and seduced to cross over into common territory—the land of the marital coma. Stand your ground. Fortunately by now, you know too much, have accumulated too many strategies, and have tasted what a healthy marriage provides to let anything get in the way on your journey toward a solid relationship.

Having an uncommon relationship doesn't mean you have to sequester yourselves from the outside world. On the contrary, the knowledge you have gained and the tools you have acquired will give you a stronger foothold in the world of distractions. Not only will you maneuver your way through the pitfalls of marriage, you will become a beacon of light for everyone who knows you.

I am convinced that most if not all of what weakens your coupleness can be prevented. May this book be your everlasting guide to your relationship's clean bill of health!

Further Reading

Albom, Mitch. *Tuesdays with Morrie*. New York: Doubleday, 1997.

Bloom, William. *Money, Heart, and Mind: Financial Well-Being for People and Planet*. New York: Kodansha International, 1996.

Cameron, Julia. *The Artist's Way: A Spiritual Path to Higher Creativity*. New York: Jeremy P. Tarcher/Penguin Putnam Inc., 1992.

——*The Right to Write*. New York: Jeremy P. Tarcher/Penguin Putnam Inc., 1998.

Chapman, Gary. *Five Love Languages: How to Express Heartfelt Commitment to Your Mate*. Chicago, Illinois: Northfield Publishing, 1992.

Cloud, Henry, and Townsend, John. *Boundaries: When to Say YES, When to Say NO, To Take Control of Your Life*. Grand Rapids, Michigan: Zondervan Publishing House, 1992.

Comfort, Alex. *The Joy of Sex*. New York: Simon & Schuster, 1972.

Corn, Laura. *101 Nights of GRRREAT Sex*. Oklahoma City, Oklahoma: Park Avenue Publishers, Inc., 1995.

Englander, Debra Wishik. *How to Be Your Own Financial Planner*. Rockland, California: Prima Publications, 1996.

Exley, Helen. *Our Love Story: A Record Book*. London, England: Oriental Press, 1995.

Fowler, Beth. *Could You Love Me Like My Dog?* New York: Fireside/Simon & Schuster, 1996.

Gattuso, Joan. *A Course in Love.* New York: HarperCollins Publishers, Inc., 1996.

Goleman, Daniel P. *Emotional Intelligence.* New York: Bantam Books/Bantam Doubleday Dell Publishing Group, 1995.

Goodheart, Annette. *Laughter Therapy: How to Laugh About Everything in Your Life That Isn't Really Funny.* Santa Barbara, California: Less Stress Press, 1994.

Gray, John. *Men Are from Mars, Women Are from Venus.* New York: HarperCollins Publishers, Inc., 1992.

Godek, Gregory J. P. *1001 Ways to Be Romantic.* Boston, Massachusetts: Casablanca Press, Inc., 1994.

Hendricks, William, and Cote, Jim. *On the Road Again: Travel, Love, and Marriage.* Grand Rapids, Michigan: F. H. Revell Publishers, 1998.

Keesling, Barbara. *Sexual Healing: How Good Loving Is Good for You—and Your Relationship.* Alameda, California: Hunter House, Publishers, Inc., 1996.

Kreidman, Ellen. *Is There Sex after Kids?* New York: St. Martins Press, 1996.

———*Light Her Fire.* New York: Dell Publishing/Bantam Doubleday Dell Publishing Group, 1991.

———*Light His Fire.* New York: Dell Publishing/Bantam Doubleday Dell Publishing Group, 1989.

Lloyd, Joan Elizabeth. *Come Play with Me: Games and Toys for Creative Lovers.* New York: Warner Books, 1994.

Markman, Howard, and Stanley, Scott, and Blumberg, Susan L., *Fighting for Your Marriage: Positive Steps for Preventing Divorce and Preserving a Lasting Love.* San Francisco, California: Jossey-Bass Publishers, Inc., 1994.

Miller, Lyle H., and Smith, Alma Dell. *Stress and Marriage.* New York: Pocket Books/Simon & Schuster, Inc., 1996.

Moore, Thomas. *Soul Mates: Honoring the Mysteries of Love and Relationship.* New York: HarperCollins Publishers, Inc., 1994.

Orman, Suze. *The 9 Steps to Financial Freedom: Practical and Spiritual Steps So You Can Stop Worrying.* New York: Crown Publishers, Inc., 1997.

Ornish, Dean. *Love & Survival: The Scientific Basis for the Healing Power of Intimacy.* New York: HarperCollins Publishers, Inc., 1997.

Pasick, Robert. *Awakening from the Deep Sleep: A Powerful Guide for Courageous Men.* New York: HarperCollins Publishers, Inc., 1992.

Patent, Arnold M. *You Can Have It All.* New York: Celebration Publishing, 1984.

Peck, Scott. *The Love You Deserve: 10 Keys to Perfect Love.* Solana Beach, California: Lifepath Publishing, 1998.

Pollan, Stephen M., and Levine, Mark. *Die Broke.* New York: HarperCollins Publishers, Inc., 1997.

Robinson, Jo, and Staeheli, Jean Coppock. *Unplug the Christmas Machine.* New York: William Morrow and Company, Inc., 1991.

Rosen, Laura, and Amador, Xavier. *When Someone You Love Is Depressed.* New York: Fireside/Simon & Schuster, Inc., 1997.

Sheehy, Gail. *Understanding Men's Passages.* New York: Ballantine Books, 1999.

St. James, Elaine. *Simplify Your Life: 100 Ways to Slow Down and Enjoy the Things that Really Matter.* New York: Hyperion, 1997.

Williamson, Marianne. *Illuminata: Thoughts, Prayers, Rites of Passage.* New York: Random House, 1994.

Winks, Cathy, and Semans, Anne. *The New Good Vibrations Guide to Sex.* Cleis Press, 1997.

Index

About the Author

Kathy Dawson conducts workshops, coaches couples, and has appeared on national and local talk shows. She has written a relationship column for the Cleveland *Plain Dealer* and has been a weekly guest on Cleveland's live television show *The Morning Exchange*. She lives in Cleveland Heights with her husband, Dick, her son, David, her daughter, Katie, and their three cats.

A portion of the author's proceeds from *Diagnosis: Married* will be donated to an organization in Cleveland, Ohio, called Center for Prevention of Domestic Violence. The center's mission is to educate, to empower, and to end domestic violence by providing two confidentially located shelters, which house up to forty-six residents (women and children).

Kathy Dawson would like to hear from you. If you're interested in receiving information about The Marriage Movement workshops, relationship coaching, or would like to invite Kathy Dawson to speak to your organization, contact:

THE MARRIAGE MOVEMENT
216-932-5016
e-mail: kd@marriagemovement.com
website: www.marriagemovement.com